The Road
to
EUROVISION
&
BEYOND

by

Nicky Stevens
(Brotherhood of Man)

© Nicky Stevens 2014

ISBN 9781906631505

Published by Arbentin Books Ltd.
5 St Margarets Avenue, Christchurch, Dorset BH23 1JD
on behalf of Nicky Stevens

Printed in the UK by 4edge Limited, Essex.

A CIP catalogue of this book is available from the British Library.

Every attempt has been made by the Publisher to secure the appropriate permissions for the illustrations reproduced in this book. If there has been an oversight, please contact the Publisher in writing.

Contents

About the Author

Nicky Stevens is a classically trained singer and musician, born in Carmarthen, South Wales. From an early age she worked as a professional cabaret artist at home and abroad supporting famous stars such as Norman Wisdom and Neil Sedaka.

It was in 1972 that she met three people who changed her life. They were Martin Lee, Lee Sheriden and Sandra Stevens. Together they formed the Eurovision song contest winners Brotherhood of Man, who won the contest in 1976 with Save Your Kisses for Me. The song became No 1 in 33 different countries. Following on with two more No 1 hits, Angelo and Figaro and a string of top twenty hits and five hit albums, Nicky and the band have earned 26 platinum, gold and silver discs each plus numerous awards.

Nicky and the group performed at the Queens Silver Jubilee Command Performance in 1977 and have topped the bill in almost every Theatre/Concert Hall in the UK including The London Palladium and The Royal Albert Hall. They have literally performed all around the world in TV, concerts and cabaret.

Nicky today

Nicky aged 3

Dedication

I dedicate this book to my loving parents Ossie and Blodwen Thomas.

I thank them for giving me life, the greatest gift of all. Through them I was born with a talent to sing. Their faith, love and support were supreme, they gave me strength and encouragement to face all that life has challenged me with.

Not a day goes by where I do not miss my lovely Mam and Dad but I remain comforted in the knowledge that they are still around me in spirit, watching over me. Their love is still there, I feel it within and it is as strong now as it always was. I am so glad that I was able to make them proud.

Foreword

A Source of Encouragement

'I recall the days when Carmarthen born songster Nicky Stevens performed at local concerts and social clubs. She appeared then under her local name of Helen Thomas.

She had a marvellous voice. She bubbled with enthusiasm. She lived for singing. Outside of her home and parents it was all she cared about and always there was this tremendous desire to make a name for herself on the pop scene. Longing is one thing, getting the breaks is another.

However, Nicky, by sheer determination and an utter refusal to accept she was just one of a few thousand stardom searchers, has made the grade.

She joined the singing foursome The Brotherhood of Man who rightly gained the distinction of representing Britain in last week's Eurovision Song Contest.

You know all the rest; the group topped the voting poll. Now there will be no searching for work. It will be there for the asking.

Yet joyous though Nicky was at her success at the weekend, I'll wager that not all those tears she shed were those of happiness.

She will remember that her father was a constant source of encouragement in the early years of her career.

He was a frequent visitor to the "TIMES OFFICE". He brought pictures of Nicky. He told us of her local talent show success and where she would be appearing next.

"MY girl has got what it takes," he would say. "She'll make it to the top one day."

Oswald Thomas died under tragic circumstances two years ago. He would be a proud man today.'

Roger Phillips, *Carmarthen Times* 1976

Prologue

"Ladies and gentlemen, the winner of this year's Eurovision Song Contest is...." My fingers were in my ears and my eyes squeezed tightly shut. Everything was clenched that could possibly be clenched and I could barely breathe. I simply could not believe this was happening, even though the score board said otherwise and everyone was screaming in delight around me, I still had to wait for the announcer to actually say the words "Brotherhood of Man"! That was it, I let out an almighty yell, threw my hankie up in the air and the celebrations began.

There was no stopping me then and the tears were uncontrollably rolling down my cheeks. The whole situation felt absolutely unreal and so unbelievably fantastic. The entire population of the United Kingdom had been behind us throughout the lead up to this moment and we had come through for them and made them proud, it was just a dream come true.

The words of my late Grandmother were echoing in my ears as we accepted our accolade. "Our Helen will get somewhere one day," she used to say knowingly to anyone who would listen. It's strange but from a young age I also had an inner gut feeling that I was going to make it. I didn't know how, why or when but somehow I knew I was destined for something big. "I will be somebody one day!" I would announce confidently to everyone.

Amongst the madness and mayhem of the moments following our unprecedented win, I momentarily paused to gather my thoughts as this was such a bitter sweet moment for me. I was ecstatic yet my heart felt heavy with grief and I would have given anything for my dear beloved Dad who had been taken from us so cruelly two years earlier, to have been right there beside me that night sharing in my joy and success. I know he would have been the proudest man in the world.

I missed him so dreadfully and although I had been through the process that everyone goes through when they lose a loved one, I felt a great deal of additional sadness that he missed out on everything that had happened since in my career. He always had such faith in me and was so supportive, especially in the early days of my singing career when he would take me to the clubs and, under the pretence that I should "rest" before my gig he would drive there and I would drive back! Crafty sod, it was only so he could have a drink or two!

Never a day went by when I didn't think of him and never a night did I put my head on the pillow without crying myself to sleep. He was the first thing I would think of when I awoke in the morning and very often that is still the case even now. He is always there with me, an important part of who I am. I consider myself to be a very spiritual person and on many an occasion I will talk out loud to him. For instance if I have a problem I will say, "Dad, come on what would you have done?" and the answer just comes. These days of course, I have both of my parents to ask.

As we partied later that evening into the night and during the whirlwind years that followed, I often found myself thinking of both Dad and my Grandmother, hoping that somehow they knew what I had achieved. Whether it was my Father's faith in me, my Grandmother's conviction or just my own determined self belief I don't know, but during that memorable evening at the Nederlands, Congrescentrum, in The Hague, Netherlands in1976, we were all proved right......

Part One

Many A Winding Turn

Chapter 1: The Journey Begins

I made my first dramatic entrance into this world already blessed with a fine set of lungs and screaming my head off as if to prove it, on 3 December 1949. I certainly wasn't about to go unnoticed and some will probably say I haven't changed since!

I was born in the family home in Carmarthen, an agricultural valley in South Wales in the same house that my Mother was to live in till the day she died. I was the second child and much loved only daughter of Ossie and Blodwen Thomas, and was named Helen Maria Thomas weighing in at around 6 pounds 4 ounces, small but feisty.

Apparently as a toddler I couldn't pronounce Maria and when people asked my name I would reply confidently "Helen Mia", which from that moment stuck and Mother called me Mia until the day she died. In fact I knew that if she called me Mia she was in a good mood and having a cracking day. There are still family members who use the name affectionately for me or when we are having a laugh which is lovely. Mother was only 18 when she first met my Father and at the time lived in a little village outside Carmarthen called Pontyberem. She would regularly go into town with her girl friends on a Saturday night where my Father would hang out in the town square with his mates and their motorbikes.

According to my Mam, he wasted no time, came straight over and boldly asked her if she would like to go for a ride with him on his motorbike to which she bravely agreed. From then on so the story goes, they started a courtship, became inseparable and a mere one year later when Mam was 19 and Dad just a few years older, they got married. No messing. Young love indeed.

Mam was born on January 18 1919 and was the second youngest of a large family consisting of a brother, my Uncle Reg the first born who was in the Horseguards Brigade in London and apparently had the honour of being decorated by the Queen. I still don't know what for or even what it was exactly but I have this wonderful photograph of the Queen pinning a medal on him to prove it. The family were so immensely proud of him. Oh how I loved Uncle Reg, he was my only blood Uncle and it helped that he was always very very kind with his regular supply of cash donations which were sneaked into my pocket with a nod and a wink!! Due to the nature of his work he lived in London but he'd often come down and visit, and in turn we would go there to stay with him which I loved. I remember posing proudly for a photograph in one of my favourite smock dresses next to a Beefeater. Auntie Gladys was the next sibling, then Auntie Lol, then my dear Mam, and Auntie Ann was the baby of the family.

In those days it was very rare for a woman to be career minded unlike now of course where almost the opposite is true. Basically an average woman's life was mapped out in front of her and fairly predictable. You went to school, you grew up, perhaps got a little job, hopefully found a partner, got married, settled down and had children. That was it and that's certainly how it was for most women, plain and simple. From what I can remember Mam always worked. At one point she was a waitress in a quaint little cafe called the Dolmar in the centre of town. In those days cafes were more like old fashioned tea rooms complete with waitress service at the table. She worked there for quite a while and wore a lovely black uniform with a white lace pinafore and a little white moon-shaped cloth cap, straight out of an Agatha Christie novel and something we would probably term vintage now.

Dad was born April 30 1914, and early on became a working musician. In the post war era he was always out playing in big bands and one night even supported Joe Loss and his orchestra.

I remember asking my Mam once what they used to get up to in those early days of courtship, eager to know a bit more about them, what naughty things they got up to, what they liked to drink and what bars they frequented.

"Oh no," she'd reply somewhat indignantly, "we didn't go for a drink, we'd go for a cup of tea."

That was so typically Mam!! No gossip to be had there then!

She would happily go along to the dances though in her best frock and thoroughly enjoy dancing with Dad when the other supporting band would be on, smiling and losing herself in the music and the moment.

Dad also had several other jobs on the go at the time. In fact during the war he worked in the Steel Works in South Wales and his job there was deemed too important for him to join the army. Instead he became a member of the Home Guard, the original Dad's Army! The earliest job I remember him having was as a taxi driver working for a company who organised funerals. They'd have the hearse, taxis, the whole flippin' lot!

One of my abiding and vivid memories as a child was me waiting for Dad to come home and him coming in through the front door turning around and putting his taxi cap on a nail above the door. Much later on in life a medium who was giving me a reading described this memory to me exactly, right down to the last detail, which I thought was very interesting and in fact quite remarkable as it was something nobody else had known and I had never shared. I mean why would I?

I was incredibly lucky to see a lot of my Father as a child. All his jobs were local even the taxi driving and Carmarthen, although it has grown somewhat now, was then a very small town where everyone knew each other. I don't even remember him working night shifts.

He was always there for us, his family, maybe because sadly he didn't have much in the way of family left and we were all he had. He was a really practical man and particularly good at DIY, turning his hand to almost anything in the house. His Mother, who was a music teacher, had passed away when he was just six years old and he was subsequently brought up by an Aunt who died before I came along. My family as I knew them were mostly on my Mother's side and Dad quite happily adopted them as his own.

Mam and Dad married in 1937 in the Tabernacle Chapel in Carmarthen, the Chapel I would attend throughout all my young life. They began their married life in a rented flat in a lovely residential area of Pontardulais very near Swansea and

Mother would often regale me with stories of when Swansea was bombed terribly during the second world war.

Apparently one night the siren went off as it often did and as usual they huddled together in a little 'lean to' down at the end of the garden. When nothing happened they eventually got so fed up that they went back to bed and promptly slept through the bombs exploding around them.

They were alright thankfully and lived to tell the tale but I think it was more luck than judgement although I was told they weren't the only ones and a lot of people got a bit blasé about the sirens after a while. My parents weren't right in the heart of Swansea, they were about 8 miles away but apparently it felt like it was all happening on their doorstep so loud was the awful noise of all the bombs dropping. Thinking about it they never mentioned how afraid they must have felt during that time. Putting myself in their position now, I can't imagine experiencing that same terror whilst sheltering in a little 'lean to' in my garden with bombs exploding all around me. It is incredible what ordinary folk had to endure during the Second World War.

A few years after they wed, their first born, my big brother Elvyn, was born in 1942, and my parents eventually moved to the house in Carmarthen that was to be my childhood home and indeed their lifelong home. Life continued fairly predictably and I was born seven years after Elvyn.

We were a Welsh speaking family and as a child Welsh was my first language and English my second. I can still speak a little Welsh now but nowhere near the fluency of when I was younger. And yes, for those of you wondering I can pronounce the name of the long village in North Wales which is one of the longest place names in the world. I am asked that question wherever I go!

Our house which was situated in a little mews leading off the main road, had two rooms downstairs, the staircase would separate with a few steps leading to the left where there was one bedroom and another to the right where there was a small single bedroom and a double bedroom. We had an outside toilet which was a good few footsteps from the house, not particularly pleasant on a cold winter's evening but we knew no different.

My very first memory in life was sitting in my high chair and my Mam putting currants and sultanas on the tray for me to eat. I can only have been a baby but I can remember watching her polishing the table with Mansion tinned polish. I don't think there was such a luxury as spray polishes or wipes then!

The fashion at the time was to have wood panelling on the walls to about half way up with a little ledge. Now Mam's brother in law's father stained this ledge for us with a comb effect varnish, highly trendy at the time and subsequently provided an ideal spot for my Dad's half smoked fags which as a teenager I would promptly nick for myself and then hang out my bedroom window smoking. Dad never asked once where all his half smoked fags disappeared too and this little charade went on for years!!

We also had a big fireplace where we would boil the kettle. There was no central heating of course, or even a bathroom, so we would use the butlers sink in the kitchen to wash ourselves. I certainly couldn't cope with that now! No matter, because we were always immaculately clean. Bath time was once a week in a huge tin bath in front of the fire with endless buckets of hot water on the go to accommodate us all. Mother would try and empty the water and refresh it as best she could but on the whole we all had to share the same water Mam and Dad included, and my older brother would always flatly refuse to go in the water after me because he reckoned I would pee in the bath. Of course he was right! I was a right little cow and I'd do anything to annoy him, it was brilliant!!

We would use a soap and flannel though and despite everything, I'm not sure how but we were always clean and never smelt!!! When we did eventually have a bathroom built, my god....we didn't know what to do with ourselves, "we were well posh now"!

Mam would invariably always be doing some kind of housework. Monday mornings would see the huge tin bath again being filled with umpteen buckets of hot water which had been boiling on the stove. Out would come the bar of puritan soap and Mam would scrub away at Dads shirt collars using an old fashioned wash board. Some years later, when we got a washing machine my brother was to use that very same washboard in his skiffle group The Tarantulas to great effect! The bed sheets would meanwhile be soaking in the bath whilst the radio would inevitably be on.

In fact the radio was our main source of entertainment. It was a small brown square device probably deemed retro nowadays, sitting neatly on a little shelf that Father had obviously put up. As I mentioned before he was a very practical man. I will never forget the theme tune to workers playtime and the children's programme 'Listen With Mother'. Mother would also enjoy reading, and was an avid reader till the day she died, losing herself in romance, travel and mystery.

I like to think that on the whole Mam was happy with her lot. One thing I can say for sure about my Mother and what she lived by, that has always stuck in my mind, is that she did not volunteer information about herself easily.

"Be private," she would say, "keep things to yourself and don't tell people everything."

She was also very careful about her reputation and what people would think and conscious of not doing certain things for fear that people would talk.

If I was naughty or bad, immediately her first and foremost worry was about what people would say and that was always drummed into me time and time again. She never wanted an ounce of scandal to touch the family in any way and would never air the dirty washing in public which was incidentally another reason I kept quiet about being abused.

It wasn't that any one of us had a criminal record or was ever prosecuted or suchlike but because she was such a devoted chapel goer, she didn't want the family being talked about in any form of detrimental way. She still liked to have a good time though and always had loads of friends. She was a very popular and sociable woman but always in respectable circles of course, never down the pubs or clubs.

She would allow herself to enjoy a drink at Christmas time when we would invariably have a bottle of sherry in, but to be respected and respectful, well thought of and not to do anything wrong was hugely important for my Mother. She had strong morals and I like to think I've taken on some of those values from her.

I wish more kids could be brought up nowadays the way we were. I firmly believe there would be far less trouble. There was no competitiveness between children back then. You wouldn't come home from school bemoaning the fact that Johnny has got the latest iPhone and why can't I have one, or I want the latest pair of trainers I'm not having those cheap ones as I'll be the laughing stock. It just wouldn't happen, which in many ways made it easier for families then.

I'm not saying it was all perfect, far from it, just that times were so very different then.

As a baby with my mother

Sporting one of mum's dodgy haircuts

Our family c. 1960

Aged 3 with
Father Christmas

On holiday in
Porthcawl
Left to right:
me, Richard,
John,
Elizabeth

At the Tower of London in my
favourite smocking dress

Me and my younger brother Dorrien

My teachers at St Marys R.C. School

Chapter 2: Baby Steps

As I said earlier radio was our main source of entertainment. We'd also play games and generally amuse ourselves until the day we eventually got a black and white television. I can't remember exactly when it was but I must have still been very young as one Christmas I was bought a little child's chair which I would sit in and be glued to the test card all afternoon, so it must have been before my younger brother was born when I was about 9 or I wouldn't have been able to fit in it.

One of the presents we would always receive at Christmas was a bath cube set along with quite a few selection boxes full of various chocolate bars and bags of sweets. There would usually be a stencilling set, a post office set and maybe a nurse's outfit. I had one teddy called Rupert and a doll called Elizabeth and that was it, I was perfectly happy. There was nothing like what children have now, but, again we didn't know any different then, and were content to play with what we had.

As well as taxi driving Dad held down several jobs to keep a roof over our heads including a salesman and painter and decorator. However, he was as I previously mentioned a very accomplished musician and throughout his life played the organ and piano. Undoubtedly I inherited my piano playing skills from my father but I got my voice from my Mam who was a beautiful singer, but sadly she never sang professionally.

The only time she did sing was in Chapel, or for our, and indeed her own amusement in the parlour, a term we used for the lounge. The parlour was only ever used for best and when visitors came. At all other times we used to sit in the kitchen where there were a couple of armchairs. I have particularly precious memories of Daddy playing the piano in the parlour. Mam would sometimes sing along with him and we would all sit and listen to the beautiful music they made. Later I too would also be allowed in the parlour to practice my piano.

Although I had my own room, from an early age I shared it with my Grandmother who had moved in with us. She had this big old brass bed with a feather mattress that weighed a tonne and I was in a little single bed. My older brother had his own room and my Mam and Dad occupied the third bedroom. Happy days!

At the age of four, I attended St Mary's Roman Catholic school in Carmarthen even though I didn't have a Catholic bone in my body and we didn't have a Catholic in the family! Children, however, were allowed to attend as non Catholics. The teachers were excellent and the school had a tremendous reputation for being the best in Carmarthen. Uniform at the school was optional, it wasn't a big deal and you didn't have to bother with it so consequently I never did.

As my brother and cousins had attended that school, I naturally followed in their footsteps. On my first day some of the children were crying pitifully at being left without their Mums. Not me though, I just didn't understand what all the fuss was about and was quite disdainful about it. I thought it was brilliant and considered it a big day out and a great adventure!

I suppose I was very lucky that Auntie Lol, my Mother's older sister and Uncle Ken her husband lived in the same street as the school, just a few houses down. It was quite literally a three minute walk away from the school gates whereas our house was a good fifteen minute walk and we hadn't yet got our first car at that time.

Auntie Lol was always extremely generous and I would go to their house for my lunch everyday instead of having school dinners. There was always a delicious meal on the table and one of Aunties specialities was good old fashioned welsh cakes and cawl cennin which is a traditional broth. I certainly always had a hearty appetite at Aunty Lol's!

The smell of salad cream, which I love now but absolutely hated then, still reminds me of their house as it was always on the table to accompany the salad. The smell of paint also takes me back to those days as Uncle Ken had his workshop in the cellar which constantly had an array of varnishes and paintbrushes soaking in turps.

St Mary's proved to be a very strict school complete with Religious Classes for an hour each morning. Although I was allowed to opt out of these and sit somewhere else in the school if I wanted, I chose to stay and subsequently learnt all about the Catholic religion. I don't know why but I just loved gaining religious knowledge and immersed myself in it whole heartedly. I would even go to the service's and sing in Latin, although this is perhaps not as grand as it sounds as I never actually learnt Latin, I just learnt a few little songs off by heart, parrot fashion. I'd then dip my hand in the holy water and cross myself, fully embracing the whole experience!! I thoroughly enjoyed it all. There was always a picture of some Pope or other on the wall which I would be fascinated by. Oh yes, I was definitely a Catholic in the week and a Welsh Baptist at the weekend!

I socialised well and friends were plentiful in the school playground. I remember my closest friends from that time vividly. One of them Mary Turner and I remained good friends for a very long time, lasting throughout our teenage years until I left Carmarthen and we lost touch.

To my surprise and delight though Mary actually came to my Mum's funeral latterly. I hadn't seen her for years prior to that and I was genuinely touched by her kind gesture and thankfully we are now back in contact.

There was also Mary Stevens, Doreen Totterdale, Julia Thomas, and Isabel Hyndes in our little gang. Those were such carefree days and we could virtually play anywhere we wanted to. We had a curfew of course but other than that all of us would go up to the park with no fear or second thoughts at all. Something you certainly can't let your seven year old child do nowadays. We could also go out and about on our bikes quite safely. The volume of traffic just didn't exist on the roads then.

We lived in a small town where basically everybody knew each other. Parents would know the families of the children you were playing with and the social life was very much revolved around family with cousins and Aunties and Uncles, basically because there just wasn't anything else. No shops or pubs would be open on a

Sunday and Thursday was half day closing. There just weren't the places available as there are now to venture to. You would go out on the street and hardly see a car 'cos everywhere was shut!

My favourite game was the game of two balls! "Really?" I hear you cry! This involved two tennis balls that you would throw up against a wall in various routines which got progressively harder as the game went along. I could quite happily have played that game all day. Oh yes it really was all good clean innocent fun back then!

I suppose I was fortunate as I didn't encounter any bullying whatsoever in my childhood. There was one girl in St Mary's who everyone thought was really 'hard', you know how kids talk, and it was a known fact that you had to be really careful what you said to her because she might 'beat you up', but that was about the extent of it really. Maybe it's because I stood up to her on one occasion in school about something and ended up having a fight with her. I came out better as it were and the matter was sorted.

At one of my birthday parties, which I believe was when I was 7 or perhaps 8 this particular girl came along, whether she was invited or not I don't remember. I have a vague memory of her bullying everybody and the party just kind of fizzled out and went totally dead. All my little friends were just sat there doing nothing as she was dominating everything. A piddly little incident though when you think of what some poor kids have endured in their lives and still do.

There were two teachers in our school who were sisters and known as the Miss Jones's. One of them taught the infants and she was to be my very first teacher. She was extremely good at teaching but incredibly strict and woe betide you if you didn't toe the line or were naughty. I can't remember ever being naughty or doing anything specific but I must have done something to make her angry as I felt her wrath on more than one occasion.

She needed little excuse though and if she was cross with you, for whatever reason, she would use the knuckle of her forefinger and tap it on your forehead just above the bridge of your nose like a woodpecker whilst telling you off to the rhythm as it were. It wasn't a pleasant experience at all and I absolutely hated it.

Eventually my Mam did have a word with her as it used to really upset me. I do know that another girl, Mary Steven's, Mam also spoke to Miss Jones about the same matter and as a result, Miss Jones's woodpecker days were thankfully numbered.

The next class up was the Nuns. We had a lovely Nun called Sister Margaret Mary whom I absolutely adored and grew very attached to but sadly she left to go to Bedford. Oh how I cried. My favourite teacher had gone and it seemed like the end of the world! I loved her so much and bless her she did keep in touch with me for a short while and sent me some pretty religious pictures. As a little girl I naturally got bored with writing after a while and contact dwindled, but I have never forgotten lovely Sister Margaret Mary.

During the years that followed I was taught by a succession of Nuns, Sister Mary Bridget, Sister Alexis and Sister Mary Andrew up until the age of 11 when I left the

23

school. All of them were the equivalent of form tutors nowadays. The other Miss Jones, sister of Woody, was involved in the musical side of school life and I would later be part of an Operetta that she put on.

Just off the playground was a door which led to the convent and from which we were strictly banned. The nuns would enter through this door onto the school premises to teach us. Also in the adjacent grounds to the school were the Catholic church and the building where all the Priests lived. I suppose it was a bit like a Roman Catholic complex really.

After the first year was completed in the infants, we were then given the 'nib'. That is to say we were now supposed to write properly in ink by dipping our fountain pens in an old fashioned inkwell. Well for those of you who remember this, you will know it was a very difficult skill to master and for young children not to make a mess was virtually impossible. I inevitably had inkblots galore all over my work. It wasn't long before one particular Nun and I can't remember which one it was, was absolutely disgusted with my page covered in these sodding inkblots and promptly hauled me along to the Headmistress, Sister Mary Andrew who was shown the results of my "work".

With that out came the leather strap with what I can only describe as fingers on it and I was made to hold the palms of my hands out while she meted out my punishment for this dastardly crime which I thought was absolutely dreadful and a huge injustice. I mean what had I done?

Later on the strap progressed to a bamboo cane, which was still used on our hands to great effect. This punishment applied for any misdemeanour carried out, ranging from being disrespectful or cheeky and naughty in class to physical fighting in the playground. It was a mixed school and everyone suffered the same fate, the same crime and punishment scenario for all of us.

To be honest even though it was a bit harsh, I suppose it never really harmed any of us and it was something we just accepted. It was our punishment end of story. Funnily enough I could accept having that much more than the woodpecker treatment which seemed like torture. Besides I only ever had the strap once as far as I can remember and that was for the inkblots, I was very lucky compared to some. You could say I was a fast learner and not keen to repeat that experience in a hurry!

Chapter 3: Gathering Speed

Although my Father wasn't a chapel goer my mother had attended chapel regularly throughout her life ever since she was a little girl, and because that was how she was raised, she automatically raised us the same way. It was a way of life for Mam really because in the days when she was growing up, Chapel wasn't just a place to go and worship, it was also a social circle and provided many other forms of entertainment such as little concerts, community evenings and coffee mornings.

In short Chapel formed the nucleus of village life, and was the hub of the community, very different to a lot of places today. In fact right up until she died my Mam would still attend social events to do with the chapel. Sadly not so many people attend now and numbers have dwindled so much that they don't have a regular Sunday service anymore, amalgamating instead with other chapels and taking it in turns to hold services.

When I was growing up though Chapel was always full and there would be umpteen of us children in Sunday school, where we were taught lessons from the bible and various songs. I made a few good friends including Joy Davis and Sharon Jory. Joy was a good singer and later on in Chapel concerts we would often sing duets together.

It's a big thing in Wales to dress in national costume on St David's Day and every year there would always be a St David's Day concert where all of us children would dress in the traditional Welsh outfits, complete with pointed black hats and shawls.

Harvest time would find us filling shoe boxes with fruit and vegetables and Mr Myrddyn Davies the top baker in Carmarthen at the time would make a fantastic square piece of bread all rolled at the sides with the shape of the wheat sheaf in the middle. We would then go along and visit various local old people's homes including the old Carmarthen Workhouse as was, but by then had been converted into a small rest home, and we would donate the boxes of fruit before singing for them.

"We plough the fields and scatter the good seed of the land, for it is fed and watered by God's almighty hand, he sends the snow in winter, the warmth to swell the grain...." and so on, our little voices would ring out with gusto. I'm not sure if the residents enjoyed it but I hope they did!

Singing has always been a major part of my life for as long as I can remember and around about this time my Sunday School teacher would often ask me to sing a solo. Every last Sunday of the month they would be a special children's service and basically every child from those who could just walk, right up to those in their teens, would have the opportunity to get up in the pulpit and do a 'turn' for want of a better expression! That's exactly what it was though. The pulpit floor incidentally could open up into a small pool where the baptisms were performed. It was a significant area, and a good width, where you could fit a small choir and was perfect for just such an occasion.

Our lovely minister, the Reverend James Thomas would duly read out everybody's name from his special list then some of the little ones, aged about three or four would trek the long length all the way up the steps into this huge pulpit just to say in welsh "God is Love" and then painfully all the way back down again!! I remember there was a little song in Welsh that perhaps about five kids in a row would sing with a different soloist every time.

The first time I actually sang solo would have been without the organ although I don't remember that occasion at all. However I can recall vividly the first time I sang a solo with the organ and even the song itself, 'If I Was A Little Star Shining Bright'.

Mother decided this would be a nice song for me to sing as she had heard Delyth Williams' rendition in one of the previous services. Delyth was the daughter of Mrs Williams one of our Sunday School Superintendents. On the Friday night before my big performance I went over to chapel to practise with Mr Grey the organist which was to become the normal routine for any future solos.

Now anybody who knows about these big pipe organs will also know that there is a slight hum, and a bit of a drone to them. I can still hear Mr Thomas now saying, and would you believe I still have it on tape "Can gan Helen Thomas", a song by Helen Thomas.

Then that familiar sound of the organ and excited little murmurs going round the congregation of "Ooh she's going to sing with the organ".

It was brilliant and makes me quite emotional just thinking about it now. Everybody congregated outside after service as they always did to have a quick chat, and so many of them came up to me to congratulate me. It was wonderful and Mother was so so proud.

Joy Davis would often sing solo as well, and there was a boy called Jeremy who could sing fantastically but unfortunately he had a bit of a nasal problem and would sing through his nose, although perfectly in tune!

Not everyone would sing of course and as you probably know Wales is a land of poets too, so many others would recite a piece, perhaps a bible reading or a few verses and it could be quite a mixture.

The church goers and people of Carmarthen generally were and still are tremendously warm people, very kind, hugely supportive, appreciative and complimentary. Recently when I went home after my Mam died, there were still some people who were thrilled to see me and proud of me as one of their own even though I have only really kept in touch with family who live there which was very heart-warming. With Carmarthen being a small town, it was such a huge deal for the townsfolk when we won the Eurovision because everybody knows each other and it really feels like one big family. I in turn am proud to be Welsh. I will always be Welsh. Welsh is my roots. Welsh is in my very heart and blood.

Although on the whole I enjoyed Sunday School, there was many a time that if I could have got out of going then I would have done in a flash, in return for just being able to play outside. But that of course was unheard of in Mother's eyes, and she strictly adhered to the fact that Sunday was a day of worship and playing outside was not allowed. You had to show respect and go to chapel come what may, there was no question about it and you would most definitely be frowned upon if you hadn't been for a few weeks. It was a big thing especially when I became old enough to go to the evening services. You were expected to demonstrate that you weren't being disrespectful and that you were going to chapel as a faithful Christian.

My first and best friend in those very early years was Lesley Jones who lived just a few doors away from us and whose Father was a baker. We are still in touch now even though she moved away from Llanelli not long after. The friend I perhaps remember the most though was Susan Williams. Her parents managed a branch of Oliver's Shoe Shop. We were friends for a long time and would go out riding our bikes and have the most wonderful times playing in the stores behind the shop.

Our imaginations would run riot as we would make use of the empty shoe boxes to pretend we were selling shoes. There was another area right at the back over this wall which was totally overgrown with brambles and I'm talking now way above our little heads, however tall we were then! We made a pathway through and a cosy den, gathering little bits of furniture to make a house inside these brambles. It was our little secret place to go and we pretended it was our very own house. These are such fond memories for me.

As a younger child though my very favourite place in the world was the park in Morfa Lane. That park was everything and became the centre of my universe. We all used to meet there, take a candle with us, grease the slide up and then fly down it like bloody Concorde. Bloody marvellous! We'd spend all day up there and I vividly remember when it was the summer holidays and the excitement I felt about going up the park every day!

I can actually close my eyes and just put myself back in that time, remembering the joy of all us kids meeting up there. We'd play traditional games whilst making some up our own and of course it meant we were outside all of the time, running, exercising and playing with such a sense of freedom. No computers just our minds and imaginations running wild in the fresh air. I won't go as far as saying they were long hot summers but I certainly don't remember them like they are now where at the end of it all you are left wondering what happened to the summer if in fact you had one at all!!! Summers were hot and winters were definitely cold.

There was an old oak tree in Carmarthen near where I played which was a bit of an historical and mythical land mark. Legend had it that Merlin came from Carmarthen, although Cornish people believe he came from Cornwall. The story goes that Merlin prophesied that 'when the old oak would fall then Carmarthen would too' which is why the tree was kept safe for as long as possible complete with railings and cement surrounding it. Eventually though there was only a large bit of bark left.

When I went home not so long ago, I went down that very road and shock horror, it had gone! I'm pleased to report that Carmarthen is still there, it hasn't fallen, if anything it's expanding and is now a totally different place from where I grew up. Perhaps that's what Merlin meant!

We were all very close as a family growing up and many of our relations lived in Bridgend and the Rhondda Valley. Granny, that is Mother's Mam, was one of 13 children of which we only knew a few but meant there were so many cousins to play with.

At the time there was no such thing as package holidays. Many of my childhood days would be spent at various family members' homes and families would holiday with each other. That is we would stay at each others houses and that was classed as a holiday. Somewhere, somehow, somebody would always put you up.

However as a large family of Aunties, Uncles and cousins, year after year we would also all hire caravans in Porthcawl at Treco Bay at the same time. Sometimes it was just Mam, Dad, Elvyn and I. Another time Auntie Lol, Uncle Ken, Billy and Elizabeth come along, and then maybe Auntie Gladys and Uncle Henry, another one of Mum's older sisters would join us and finally to complete our happy band there'd be Auntie Ann, Mum's younger sister and her lot.

They were the only ones who didn't live in Carmarthen. She had four sons, Robert, Edward, John and Richard and lived in a little place called Goodwick just outside Fishguard in Pembrokeshire West Wales which is about 48 miles west of Carmarthen and where I spent some of my favourite times as a child. I treasure those memories now as some years later Richard was to tragically lose his life in a car accident, which left us all completely devastated.

I've got one photograph where I think the world and its friend was there regarding our family on one of those holidays. The caravans were very old fashioned; they were almost ball shaped and all nestled amongst these tremendously high sand dunes which have all since been flattened. Well, you can imagine what it was like for a child to jump off and play on these sand dunes, it was absolutely fantastic.

On a typical day, we'd get up in the morning, having slept on the dining table which had folded down into a bed. We were all squashed in like sardines. There were no toilets in the caravan, so we'd then make our way to the big concrete building known as the 'toilet block' for our communal wash and ablutions. It was a bit like what you expect at camping sites but not quite as posh or advanced.

I didn't care though as I was in my element with my cousins. There was only just two years between Robert and me so I guess you can say we were the closest. Our favourite game was that I was Queen of the Castle and he was my loyal subject. He did ask me to marry him, but at the age of 6 or 7 we were both a bit on the young side!!

What wonderful memories though, and what great fun we had with not a care in the world, enjoying ourselves in the fresh air and dipping in and out of the sea all day long. A few years on when I was a teenager, more places of entertainment began to spring up but in those early days up to the age of eleven there was nothing. You made your own fun. Later on in life, I remember having a conversation with my mother and commenting that it was never much of a holiday for her as she still had to cook and clean. Her reply was that it was a change of scenery. Bless her.

We did occasionally go further afield and would stay in rented caravans. I remember once us all going down to Cornwall and bearing in mind in those days there were no motorways, from South Wales it took us two days to get to Cornwall! There was no Severn Crossing then or Severn Bridge so we had to go up as far as Gloucester and then turn and make our way down country. I must only have been about 7, and it seemed an eternity. We even had to stay in a Bed and Breakfast en route. This was the first hotel I had ever stayed in and oh how I hated that cooked breakfast in the morning. The egg was all snotty, the grilled tomatoes were all mushy and the bacon hadn't been cooked enough. Yuk!

We travelled in two cars and for anyone familiar with classic cars, we had a black Ford Popular. I can still remember the registration OLO 653 and if I remember correctly Auntie Lol and Uncle Ken had a Hillman.

We had a wonderful holiday and I recall my father found the journey back unbearable. I must have eaten something dodgy as I did nothing but break wind for the whole journey home and my poor Father had to open all the windows. He was a great comedian though, and provided great entertainment to the rest of the family who were following behind and always knew when I'd let off as my father would drive with his head out of the window. Even now my older brother and cousins have never let me live that one down!!

Mother wasn't a drinker, and not really bothered about going to clubs or pubs. Therefore a night out would often mean a run out into the country to maybe a visit an "Auntie" or "Uncle" that lived several miles away. There was one particular couple Lorna and Bryn Richards, Auntie Lorna and Uncle Bryn who had this lovely cottage in a place called Crwbin outside Carmarthen, a little village which was really just a smattering of houses.

What used to amaze me was that nobody used to have telephones, they would arrive totally unannounced and yet it was no problem. It was accepted because you couldn't let anyone know you were coming to visit, not unless you wrote them a letter and pre warn them to be in as you were on your way in a few days!! That's how it was.

Anyway, I remember Auntie Lorna and Uncle Bryn had this wonderful Welsh Dresser, groaning with the most tremendous China. They also had an authentic Cuckoo Clock; none of these battery operated ones. I used to think that was amazing!! Everyone would sit and chat, then the table would be laid always with delicious things like ham, tomatoes, beetroot and pickle, lovely thinly sliced bread, with welsh butter and endless pots of tea and home made cakes. It was tremendous. There were two other sets of family friends Auntie Lizzie and Uncle Dan, and Auntie Winnie and Uncle Hubert whom we would regularly visit in the countryside. It was a simple yet wonderful way of life. I'd spend many a happy hour watching Mam cooking and baking and would especially love to watch her make a Victoria sponge or pastry. Even better though was when I was allowed to get stuck in and help, usually after I'd worn her down with my persistent pleading, and the joy when she let me help mix the ingredients which I entered into with great enthusiasm.

Mam made absolutely wonderful cakes. Sundays were by far the best day for food with her lovely roast dinners often followed by her homemade rice pudding with the skin on top which was to die for. We'd have it 'neat' as it were, with no jam, syrup or suchlike. My nephew Dean, still maintains to this day that "I have never tasted rice pudding as good as Nan's."

Apple tarts, sponges and Welsh cakes were also regulars on the menu. At Christmas time we would have Mam's Christmas pudding where one lucky recipient would find the threepenny bit.

Eventually I was given the special responsibility of making mint sauce to accompany our Sunday dinner which was a job I loved doing and made me feel very self important. There was no stopping me then. We used to grow mint in the garden and I would regularly go and pick the mint, chop it all finely with sugar and put it into vinegar all under Mam's instruction. Of course the traditional accompaniment to beef is horseradish but for some reason, probably because we had such an abundance of mint growing or possibly because I kept on making it, we would always have mint sauce, whatever the meat. I never did anything half heartedly and would enjoy all the praise for my efforts. I think Mam drew the line at us having it for breakfast though.

It was always Daddy's job to wash up on a Sunday after the roast. He might have helped throughout the week but, "Mother you have cooked the dinner so I'm washing up," he would announce.

He certainly never allowed me to do it because he reckoned I only gave them a "cat's lick" and was probably right. He was always prepared to help in that respect but when he was at work all day Mother for her part was more than happy to do all the housework. Those were the traditional roles in those days. The man worked to provide for the household and the woman kept the home tidy, and the one thing I could say for certain about Mother was that you would never find a speck of dust anywhere, however hard you tried. Indeed you could literally eat off the floor. She maintained her high standards even when she returned to work as a waitress when my younger brother went to school.

Looking back on myself as a girl I would describe me as very loud and a show off. What can I say, as surprising as this may seem to my friends now I just loved to show off and be the centre of attention!! It certainly wasn't because I was vain, I just wanted to make people laugh and my friends love to remind me of my efforts and how I entertained them endlessly. I suppose I took after my Dad in that respect. If Ossie Thomas was at a party everyone was guaranteed a good laugh and I wanted to be just like that.

I wasn't much into dolls, and preferred my teddy bear named Rupert who still shares my bed to this day. I would sometimes try and join in my brother's games much to his annoyance. If the boys had a cricket bat you could guarantee my friends and I would be there giving it our best shot. Once I sneaked up behind my brother when he was doing his homework in his bedroom and hit him over the head with a cricket bat. How I never killed him or caused any permanent damage I really don't know?! It is something I have always totally regretted and I am appalled as to how and why I did it. What a dreadful thing to do?

I also loved climbing and would basically climb anything that could be climbed! I wouldn't say I was a tomboy exactly but I certainly wasn't a prissy pretty little girl, all hair and frocks. I was a boy's girl and loved playing boy's games in a frock!

Due to the freedom we had in the park we were all able to play together quite happily, girls and boys alike. There was this one game called commandos where I used to out run the lot of them. It was great fun and I was brilliant at it if I say so myself. I also enjoyed rounders. Both these games brought out the competitive instinct in me and I discovered I was actually quite sporty. This stood me in good stead and much later on in Grammar School I played in the South Wales County Netball Team and entered various competitions in running etc. I thrived on that competitive team environment which I suppose in turn stood me in good stead for what was to come later on in my life.

We were a very average family of the time and were extremely fortunate that we never wanted for anything and there was always food on the table. Nobody earned bundles of money but Mother was a great 'manager of money'. All my Aunties and Uncles were similar but Mam was absolutely marvellous. I really wish I could have been like that and taken a leaf from her book.

Absolutely nothing was ever wasted which I attribute to her experiences in the war and learning how to ration. She once queued up for two hours to get a tin of pears and then rejoined the queue again from the back to get another tin. It's unthinkable nowadays but she had no choice then or she would have starved. That way of thinking stayed with Mother until the end of her days. For example if there were two lettuce leaves and half a tomato left, she wouldn't dream of binning it. Instead it would be put on a plate with another plate over it as we didn't have a fridge let alone Clingfilm in those days. It would then be kept to one side and utilised later perhaps in a sandwich with a bit of cheese.

"Waste not," was Mam's mantra.

Oh yes it was definitely partly down to Mother, god bless her, that we never wanted for anything and were certainly never hungry.

Another of my most treasured memories of that time was a typical Sunday night at home, because we would have what was left of the roast beef cold cut, and then all the vegetables and potatoes would be fried in the frying pan and served up with lovely slices of bread and welsh butter. I would put every sauce available over this including, brown, tomato and of course mint. Sunday night suppers were the highlight of my week and even now when I make vegetables I make enough so I can have that fry up the next day. It's funny what memories stay with you, and that one always has. I suppose it represents an uncomplicated time in my life.

I have so many happy memories to choose from in my childhood though it is difficult to pinpoint any particular ones that stand out. However, the worst memory without a doubt was losing my Grandmother and was my first introduction to bereavement. Looking back my Mam coped with it marvellously well although I did witness her sobbing which was upsetting for me as a little girl as I had never seen my Mam so out of control and grief stricken. She obviously had great support from my Father and of course all the family were close by and everybody was there for her.

Whatever trials and tribulations my parents might have been going through or whatever sadness they had to cope with my Father could always make Mother laugh. She had this wonderful infectious laugh which I can emulate wonderfully but cannot write down therefore you will have to imagine this big 'Wooh ha ha ha' it would start and her hand would rise up as she laughed. Dad would tell her the most ridiculous jokes to set her off.

"What do you call a Chinese man with forty children?" he'd say. She'd try and think and offer up silly answers until his punch line of "Daddy"!! The simplest, most daft jokes and she would laugh obligingly. She would love to tell people over the years about Dad's jokes, particularly after one or two sherries.

Bless her heart she was so sweet, but oh my god, if you had done something wrong look out, you'd know about it. She wouldn't take any back chat from any of us which of course isn't a bad thing although we didn't appreciate it at the time. She'd give us 'a right row' and maybe a smack.

However where Mother would shout, Dad would reason. I would say she definitely could be more volatile. Mam and I would argue, boy did we argue. Nothing major you understand, nothing that scarred my childhood or anything like that but as I like to say now, "argument is a discussion of ignorance because nobody ever gets anywhere. It's point scoring". Whereas with my Dad, reason was a discussion of knowledge. He would sit me down and say, "Right, what was in your mind when you did that? What made you decide to do that?" Whereas Mother was, "Get upstairs, you've been naughty, go to your room for an hour!!" They had totally different approaches. I never saw my Father lose his temper with me once in his life. I saw him losing it against other people, who had been disrespectful to me but as children we never heard him shout at us.

Dad was very even, laid back and quite calm most of the time. I admit freely that I take after my Mam when it comes to moods, although my bark is worse than my bite and once I have had a bit of a rant and rave, then I'm fine. I always think those who keep their emotions in are the worse ones and when they go they really go!!

Mam and Dad would argue and have words as every normal married couple but nothing out of the ordinary. They were like chalk and cheese but it worked.

Chapter 4: Wrong Turning

When I was eight years old, something happened to change my life forever. At the time one of my friends and I would often play in a particularly favourite place of ours at the time when this certain 'man' began to regularly turn up and hang around with us.

We just thought at the time that he was a nice friendly young chap. Looking back I suppose he was possibly around the age of eighteen or nineteen. He quickly gained our confidence by befriending us and of course at that time we had no concept of danger or anything untoward or sinister whatsoever. We were just innocent young girls playing our childhood games with no sexual awareness at all.

I've since come to learn that these 'people' are very crafty and have often thought how clever this guy was that over a period of time he convinced us, two little girls, to allow him to touch us in intimate places and to even say it was ok to do that. It didn't happen every day and my friend and I were always together. He would make the other one watch as if to assure us, saying, "Look I'm not hurting her. Everything is fine. She's not crying."

And of course he didn't 'hurt' us and no, we didn't suffer any physical pain. It would have been different perhaps if we had. But he was very careful not to inflict any pain on us.

It just repulses me when I think of it all now. I read so many stories about sexual predators today or hear about them on the news, now more than ever, and my stomach turns over for those innocent children. Of course as we now know, we were groomed. Very cleverly and always with the threat that if we told anybody they would think we were bad or naughty and dirty, but at the same time he made us believe that what we were doing was alright and we were just having fun.

Looking at it from a paedophile's point of view, if you ever can, he hadn't had any form of sexual intercourse with us and it was obviously beginning to get too much for him. He was now getting very frustrated and needed to move on with his sexual abuse and did so by one day suddenly dropping his trousers. As a little girl who hadn't seen anything like that in my life, I just knew instinctively that this was wrong. He then grabbed me. I was absolutely terrified.

I've tried my best to go back into how I felt at that time so I can rationalise my feelings more. I don't know what it was, but somebody was definitely looking out for me that day as I just felt this innate fear. Up until that point he had my full trust but now I instinctively knew that what was about to happen or what he was going to try and do was something absolutely horrendous. As he grabbed me roughly I just screamed and screamed at the top of my voice as if my life depended on it. That panicked him and gave us that small window of opportunity to run away as fast as we could.

We both vowed that from then on we would never be alone with him ever again and we wouldn't tell anyone what had happened because they would blame us. We never went to that particular haunt again.

With the type of family I come from the scandal of what had happened would have destroyed my Mam and I hate to think what my Father would have done. I honestly think he would have killed him if he could have got hold of him. It would have been incredibly difficult if not impossible for Dad to sit back and let the law take action. I mean he might have done, as a lot of parents do and have to of course, but I very much doubt it. My friend and I never mentioned or referred to it again. I suppose in a way I was subconsciously protecting my parents' feelings as well as my own, they just couldn't have coped with it. And of course I had to consider my friend and her family as well. I was raised to be a good Christian child and not to do anything that was out of order and we truly believed if we told our parents or anyone else they would think we were very naughty, bad and dirty even though we knew that we weren't. He'd basically put the fear of god into us.

The strange thing is I managed to wipe the whole episode out of my mind. I didn't realise quite how much until years later at the age of around eighteen or nineteen, I saw somebody that knew him and suddenly all the feelings came flooding back. I mentioned him to this person, only to be told that he was now in prison as a convicted paedophile. Although I was relieved to hear this I then of course had to deal with the guilt of wishing I had gone and told somebody as it might have stopped him. After all who else did he abuse? I have always hoped that I can be forgiven for never telling anyone at the time as it would have saved some other poor children suffering sexual abuse at his evil hands. Unfortunately, you don't think that rationally when you are a little girl.

My reason for staying quiet as I got older was to prevent other innocent people being dragged into it that might want to keep it quiet and just forget about it as I did. It would have involved hurting a lot of people and I just couldn't bring myself to do that.

I have since been told though that there were one or two people who suspected something but they just couldn't prove it or catch him out. My immediate reaction to that was, "Oh my god thank god they didn't, that would have been terrible to have been caught with him being bad and dirty." Not, "Why the hell didn't you catch him?"

It's frightening to think what a narrow escape we had on that fateful day. God alone knows what further things he was capable of and what he may have gone on to do had he not been imprisoned. He could be dead now for all I know but as far as I'm concerned he has been dead for a very long time and the memory of what he did will always be in my mind.

As kids of course you have a new best friend every day and this particular friend and I eventually lost touch. I have never seen her as an adult and I sincerely hope she is well and happy.

Over the years I have often felt the heavy burden of guilt that I allowed him to do those things. Even though I was the victim, I still feel that guilt. I still feel that I was dirty and bad and nothing will ever wipe that away from me. I feel that it was I who was in the wrong. I feel repulsed and sick when I hear stories now of child pornography and of course if a child came to me now and told me a similar story, it would be so so different but it has stuck in my mind and I can never erase it. I just can't. However much common sense and logic tells me otherwise I just can't eradicate those feelings. Such is his legacy.

Later on in life as an adult, having sexual relationships and being married, sometimes yes, it was fine but at other times these feelings would rear their ugly head telling me that what I was doing was dirty, even though I would try to rationalise them by firmly telling myself, "Hang on now Nicky you're an adult now and married, this is all ok," but then that little voice would whisper back in my ear that no, it's dirty, and rude and wrong.

Thinking about it now and bringing it out into the open is still bringing those feelings of guilt to the surface again, after all these years, however hard I have tried to bury them. The whole episode of abuse lasted about a month in total but has stayed with me a lifetime.

Mum and dad out dancing

Me playing the Queen in Snow White

The School Choir; I am in the second row far right

Chapter 5: Back on Track

On the surface, life continued much as before and music became increasingly important to me. I found I could forget everything instead focussing and losing myself in the piece I was learning. As I mentioned earlier my Granny didn't have a home of her own and lived with Auntie Lol for a while prior to coming to live with us.

I loved her dearly, and we all got along so well as one big happy family. She was such a lovely lady and even my Dad thought a lot of her too, having lost his own dear Mother at such a young age. All of us cousins were very close to Granny and I would often play the piano and sing for her. She may have been a captive audience but was certainly a very appreciative one.

When my younger brother Dorrien was born, the house was a bit over crowded bed wise and sadly she went back to live with Auntie Lol. I for one missed her greatly.

One thing Granny always used to say was

"Our Helen will get somewhere one day. If it's not playing the piano it will be with her singing".

Gosh how right she was, even though at that age I had no designs whatsoever in carving a career for myself in music. She was always so proud of me and reluctant visitors were forced to listen to my latest piano piece or the song I was learning, clapping and nodding politely whilst Granny looked on with a proud smile on her face. In later life, I have had several readings from various mediums, and she has always been identified as my 'guardian angel' which really doesn't surprise me.

She particularly enjoyed listening to me playing Handel's Largo on the piano. I remember so well her saying, "Play Largo for me".

How she loved that tune, and when she died a few years later, it was a fitting tribute to her at her funeral, when the organist played it at my suggestion. I know I am extremely fortunate to be able to say that it wasn't just Granny but indeed all of my family who encouraged me to develop my talents at a young age and every one of them had a part to play in influencing and shaping my young life. Learning music though was never a chore for me as I was passionate about playing the piano and singing; it was something I had always wanted to do.

I began showing an interest in playing the piano at around the age of five or six, playing predominantly by ear at that point and I would plonk away on the keys in the parlour. Before my seventh birthday I could already play Beethoven's Fleur de Lys, which I had taught myself.

I was well chuffed when I started having proper piano lessons with Auntie Nan at the age of seven which incorporated theory as well as practical. Auntie Nan was a very close family friend. Her husband had tragically died in a drowning accident and Aunty Lol subsequently took her in as a lodger for a while, after which they remained firm friends.

Just to explain, anybody in those days who was a close family friend we would be allowed to call Uncle or Auntie which was a respectful alternative to calling them Mr or Mrs So and So, and subsequently resulted in quite a few Auntie's and Uncle's outside of the family who weren't related at all and ended up being quite confusing. Auntie Nan taught piano to all of us in the family as well as many others including Billy and Elizabeth, older brother Elvyn and later on she was even to teach my younger brother Dorrien.

I have to say she was a wonderful wonderful teacher and an accomplished pianist, making a good living for herself from her teaching. She would duly come along and give me a lesson every Thursday regularly, and woe betide me if I hadn't practised what she had taught me, or for even daring to believe for one moment that I could get away with it. She knew alright and would then get extremely annoyed with me and brush my fingers down the keyboard. Oh god did that hurt. I tell you there wasn't many a time I didn't practise! I eventually took my piano exams, passing each with distinction and still proudly have my certificates to this day!

As a child I didn't attend any live theatre at all, not even a pantomime, but I did go to the Saturday morning film at the Lyric Cinema which was 1/6d in old money. There were always two films screened, a starter and a main course as it were and these were mainly geared towards children. The small undercover entrance housed various 10 x 8 colour stills behind glass panels. These were 'previews' of future up and coming films which didn't really give you any information at all, but I suppose gave the cinema goers an idea of what they were all about and whet their appetite. Little did I know then that I was later to perform at that same venue as part of 'Brotherhood of Man'.

The Lyric I believe is still there today and was managed for years by a lady called Liz Evans, who is the Mother of the 'Go Compare' Tenor, Wyn Evans, who himself also hails from Carmarthen. There was another cinema in the town called the Capital but for some reason I always favoured the Lyric.

I suppose as I hadn't really encountered any live music or theatre at that age there was nothing that really influenced me or inspired me at that time. Therefore although my life revolved around playing the piano, and I was taking it very seriously, I never dreamt of pursuing it. It didn't even enter my mind, I just loved learning to play music, it felt so right and seemed effortless to me.

Mam and Dad also never thought for one minute that I would follow music as a career path, believing it to be a hobby. They, along with the rest of the family were just encouraging me to be the best I could, and even better than that. Although my Father would play every week on his piano or organ, I think I was into my teens before I first saw him play publicly as he always played on licensed premises.

The piano was his instrument. His own Mother had taught him how to play as she herself was a music teacher. Auntie Lol's husband Uncle Ken also played double bass in the band with my Dad. Talk about a family affair! Dad would sing the odd song but didn't like to make a habit out of it. One of his songs was "You Were Meant for Me". There was the odd occasion when he might play as a trio but it was very rare.

Mam was quite happy to stay at home looking after us children on those occasions, as she had seen him play in the big band countless times before I was born. Perhaps we gave her a good excuse!!

One memory from that time that sticks in my mind is 'The Sunday Outfit' and the importance attached to it. I had what we would call nowadays a suit. It was a jacket and a matching skirt but my Mam's name for it was 'a costume'.

Even latterly she would say, "Ooh I've bought a nice costume," so where that term came from I don't know.

I always either had a nice costume or a coat and usually some sort of a smart hat and equally smart shoes. One of my 'costumes' was very pale apple green with a box type jacket and skirt, respectably knee length of course, with two pleats in the front and two pleats in the back.

Back then it was very fashionable to have a band of about four to five inches wide which fitted on your head like an alice band and was all feathers. I'd go off to Sunday School like a little swan!!! That whole ensemble would ONLY be worn on a Sunday. Never on another day, as that was your Sunday best, end of. Sometimes the clothes were bought from a catalogue and sometimes C & A in Swansea. Mother didn't sew or make our clothes, they were always brand new.

I like to think Dad was a handsome man. He certainly wasn't on his last course of ugly pills. He too was a smart dresser and sported two suits. One every day for work and one for weekends and best, when he was out playing the organ or if we were going anywhere tidy.

Not like now where people wear jeans and trainers with a tee shirt practically anywhere it seems. No, Dad was always in a suit and shirt with detachable collar. The shirt itself could then be worn for more than one day and he'd have an array of collars to choose from which would then fasten on to the shirt itself.

My Mother was also a beautiful dresser, always immaculate and very glamorous, and looked fabulous up to her dying day. As a young woman she had dark, shoulder length curly hair but in later years wore it much shorter and always permed. Mam would put her own hair in pin curls. A little kiss curl twirled round and then clipped to keep it in place. I never knew Mam to go without a perm. She too had a certain coat and hat with matching handbag and shoes for Chapel.

At home though she always wore a pinny or a housecoat and if she was dusting or doing any housework she would also wear a scarf Hilda Ogden style to keep her hair dust free!! She had to as we didn't have such a thing as a Hoover. It was a Ewbank or carpet sweeper and a stiff pan and brush for the stairs. There was no such thing as a fitted carpet then. You'd have a big rug and linoleum on the floor and of course that would get washed.

Any small rugs would be on the line in the garden having bloody merry hell being beaten out of them. I think Mam enjoyed beating any anger or frustration out on these rugs. Wash day was on Monday with the puritan soap, tin bath and scrubbing board.

Whenever Mam went out it was a different story. She was a beautiful lady who had the most wonderful taste in clothes and was very glamorous. I remember her dresses so well particularly the ones she wore when accompanying Dad on his special work 'do's'. She would save hard for her clothes which were complemented by a little bit of powder, a touch of rouge and a bit of lipstick which she would just dot on to colour her lips.

I would spend many happy hours trying to copy her, mucking around with all her pearls and trying on all her clothes and shoes as little girls do. What I really used to love was if she had a pair of shoes which she had had for a long time and wasn't fussed about wearing anymore. They would then become fair game for dressing up stuff which of course for me was marvellous.

Her hairdresser at the time was Nancy Gowman in Bridge Street. In fact she sent me along to Nancy for a perm when I was attending St Mary's RC. It was one of those perms where you put the rollers in and then you were wired up to the electric lights. Marvellous stuff!

There was this sort of skull thing hanging there with all these wires attached to the perm rods. Some older people will probably still remember that. There was only one type of perm then - TIGHT!! I'll never forget one particular time when she had my hair permed for a school concert. Oh god I was mortified and thought I looked dreadful but my hair was always done how Mother wanted it!!! End of!!

My hair was always naturally dead straight. I've still got this fabulous picture which was taken by a professional photographer, where my fringe goes up at a forty five degree angle because Mother had cut it. Ok maybe not quite forty five degrees but it was as straight as a winding road, bless her. We didn't have a hairdryer so after she washed our hair she'd plonk these small metal clamp things with teeth, like people use now to hold their hair up, in our hair to make waves and there they would stay until our hair was dry.

I still maintain now that the natural kink I've got in a certain part of my hair is due to these blessed clamps I had. At the time though, even though I really hated it, I just let her get on with it! Mother knew best.

As far as fashion went as a little girl, if the dress flared out when I spun around on the balls of my feet, then it was fine. As simple as that. As for my footwear, I would test shoes out to see if they were good to run in. Good or bad runners were how I measured shoes then. Nowadays I am happy if I can walk in them! My favourites were a pair of royal blue suede brogues with a flat wooden heel and a tee strap which had become fashionable. I thought they were wonderful.

I can still picture vividly my favourite dresses. One in particular I adored, and had a front panel which was all smocking. The background was cream and there were different stripes about half an inch wide going round in a circular way in yellow, blue, green and red. Oh how I loved that dress. Another had a cream background again, this time with French writing and flowers on it with a beautiful coral sash around the waist. I still maintain a love of fashion, image and style which I inherited from both parents but particularly Mam. I'd like to think I am as glamorous as she was when I eventually leave this world.

On one particularly average day I had been playing outside as usual. When I came home, Mam was sat at the dining table in the kitchen clutching a little baby's outfit and looking quite pensive.

"Who's that for?" I enquired bluntly, as any child would, but she wasn't immediately forthcoming with the answer and remained quiet. "Come on tell me."

I persisted and with that she burst into tears. I remember Granny consoling her and telling her not to upset herself so, at which point I blurted out, "Are you having a baby Mam?" To which she then reluctantly confirmed that yes that was the case.

"That's fantastic," I shouted and immediately it was a case of goodbye teddy and dolly, I've got a real live one on the way now. I still don't know to this day why she cried before telling me. She never told me if it was a planned pregnancy or not but over the years I have had my suspicions that possibly it wasn't planned.

She was now aged about 40, and I suppose that was quite old to have a baby back then and posed a significant health risk. Of course I knew nothing about any of this. I was just so excited at the prospect of a baby sister in the house and quizzed her about everything. I'd beg Mam to be allowed to go to Littlewoods and buy the baby something. She would give me money to go and buy a couple more nappies or a little romper suit. She had the most beautiful maternity coat which was what they termed in those days a 'swagger' coat, meaning it was quite flared and very roomy. It was grey with a lovely thin black lined pattern on it. I can still see her in it now and of course it disguised the baby bump quite well.

One of the stories she told me later on which I had completely forgotten was when I asked the classic question, "Mam how did the baby get in your tummy?" obviously having no idea how it actually did get in there at that tender age. She then proceeded to tell me about the seed being planted and how it would grow etc etc and I must have gone away and thought about it, came back a little while later quite perturbed only to ask how on earth you get in there to water it?!!! As you can imagine that story was told quite a few times around the family!

My next concern regarding the baby was how she would know when it was going to come out. She duly told me that a little door would pop open and the baby would come out of this aforementioned door. I can tell you I spent many an hour wondering where the hell this flipping door was!!!

I still wondered though how she would know when it was ready to come out of this mysterious door. Having told me that she would have a very bad pain, I remember on that fateful day she was on her knees washing the kitchen floor when she suddenly gasped and held her stomach to which I responded loudly and with great excitement, "Yeah the baby's on its way, the baby's on its way."

Oddly enough I read recently in the paper that this is now the recommended thing to do to bring on labour if your baby is overdue. The experts say getting on your hands and knees and washing the floor helps to position the baby correctly into the birth canal.

I was immediately told to go and get my father so dutifully ran round to where he was working at the taxis. He in turn went to fetch my Auntie Gladys who ably assisted the midwife and while my poor Mother was upstairs giving birth, my older brother and I were downstairs bashing merry hell out of each other.

"It's a boy."

No it's a girl."

"No it's a boy."

"No it's a girl......" we screamed whilst hitting each other with every comment. Of course Auntie Gladys came downstairs and told us to shut up in no uncertain terms!!

Despite desperately wanting a sister, I adored my baby brother and did everything I could to help and would regularly bath him and change his nappies. In those days it became fashionable to name your baby after the Doctor who looked after you or maybe the Nurse. My Father wanted to call my brother either Alan or Michael but my Mother insisted on naming him Dorrien Wynne after our Doctor Dorrien. This became the bane of my little brother's life in primary school, because small town as it was, he would get teased in the playground with kids taunting "Can we play with you Doctor Dorrien?"

Despite seven years between Elvyn and I, and an even bigger gap of ten years between me and Dorrien, bar a few months, we all got on reasonably well. Like all kids we had our punch ups or little scraps but nothing serious.

It's funny as well, I never remember any sibling rivalry between us or my parents favouring any of us as children which I put down partly to the age difference and partly because we were all so very different. Most of my childhood was spent with Elvyn as the gap was so big between Dorrien and me. It worked well, Elvyn looked out for me and I looked out for Dorrien. We all had our own unique characters and all got into trouble with our own misdemeanours. And for those we were all punished equally!!

Even as we have grown older this remains true. There is no resentment or jealousy between us and I like to think my brothers were and still are proud of me. My career though is just something we have all grown along with and we have known no different. At the time Eurovision came along, the only person still living at home was Dorrien.

I can safely say that my young childhood was very secure, very happy and very safe, despite the isolated abuse episode. For some reason and amazingly so, my mind has decided to consign that particular memory to the darkest depths of my consciousness for most of the time.

Chapter 6: Next Stop

By now, I was very active with my singing in school and Miss Jones our music teacher had seemingly discovered my talents. The school was to put on a full length operetta of Snow White and the Seven Dwarfs and I was to be cast in the lead role. However, there was a particular note which was so high; it was a top 'G' if I remember correctly. I was so fearful of that blessed note. Just the one note in the one song managed to put me off the role of Snow White altogether. I just didn't have the confidence to really go for it and although I could reach it under normal circumstances with no problem, during rehearsals, my lack of confidence meant I would very shakily reach it and I begged to be given the role of the Wicked Queen.

And so Mary Turner went on to play Snow White. She was very good and sang well and there was no rivalry at all between us. In fact I was quite happy, the songs were a lot easier for the Wicked Queen!! It was all so exciting, a big stage was built and we ran for three nights I think.

I don't remember what my first reviews were like but suffice to say my parents loved it!! As a matter of interest, a similar thing was to happen later on in life when I was offered the role of Aladdin.

"I'm not playing a bloke," I said indignantly.

I was adamant that I was to play the part of the Princess and said so in no uncertain terms. I got the part I wanted, and that as they say was that.

Not long after came the results of the eleven plus. I was the only one in the class that cried when my name was read out as having passed. I think I must have had a bit of the drama queen in me even in those days!! Some of my classmates including Mary Turner fell about laughing. They just couldn't understand why I would be crying when I had passed the exam. For me though it was a mixture of relief and elation. We had all passed which meant I could go to grammar school with all my friends.

The down side was we had to say goodbye to the boys as it was an all girls school! St Mary's was renowned at the time for having the highest amount of passes in the eleven plus. I was absolutely thrilled as I enjoyed school, and I thoroughly enjoyed learning so for me it was a case of Queen Elizabeth Grammar School for girls, watch out here I come!!

It was a bitter sweet time for me as my lovely Granny passed away in her early 70s when I was eleven. I was absolutely heart broken, I loved her so much and I remember being totally inconsolable.

Granny had been laid to rest in an open coffin in one of the rooms at my Auntie's house which was commonplace in Wales at the time. The Minister would then come to the house on the day of the funeral and say a prayer while all the close family were gathered together. The coffin would be put in the hearse and off you would go the Welsh way, to the Chapel or wherever you were to be buried.

My Dad tried to persuade me to see Granny in her open coffin but I was scared and did not know what to expect. I remember Dad saying to me, "Come on Helen, come and see Granny in the coffin..." which I really did not want to do. It's funny in the end he convinced me by saying that she wouldn't hurt me. I reluctantly agreed to go and must say she looked calm and seemed at peace which was somewhat comforting.

For quite a while after I wondered why he would have wanted me to see her dead but with hindsight I think he was trying to teach me something at that age. Perhaps it was not to fear death. I like to think that anyway.

I was also allowed to attend the funeral, held in a little village called The Meinciau which was quite a way out of town, but Granny was to be buried in the grave with her husband, my maternal Grandfather, Tom Davies who had died when Mam was only a teenager so sadly I had never known him.

On the day of the funeral, when we arrived at the church I suddenly froze and couldn't go inside. No one and nothing could make me so I just sat at the grave hearing the muffled strains of Handel's Largo and waiting for them to bring her. I was quite distraught and must have looked a pitiful sight.

That night Daddy came up to my bedroom where I was in bed breaking my heart. He tried his best to offer comfort and make me feel better but nothing could help me at that moment.

As a family we were all so close. We gathered together regularly, lived together, shared the housework, the baking, the cooking, and went on holiday together. That's how it was back then. The flip side of that of course is the devastation when you lose a beloved member of that family.

To this day I still tend Granny's grave at home. This is something I promised my Mother I'd continue to do when she had gone. She herself had faithfully tended it throughout her life and when I go back now and look up at this little graveyard set on a hill in Wales, I can still picture Granny's funeral procession coming round the corner, carrying her coffin with all the relatives following on. I can see it there as plain as day.

I use Granny's recipe to this day for my Christmas cake. I still have it in her handwriting on this bit of paper, which is god knows how many years old and it keeps me close to her. She was the only one of all my grandparents who I really knew although I vaguely remember my paternal grandfather who passed away when I was in my very early teens.

We didn't visit him very often and when we did I would just sit there politely. The routine was always the same. He would ask me if I wanted a sweet in Welsh, I would shyly say yes please, and he would reach up to the fireplace to the sweetie jar. We would then have a cup of tea and perhaps a piece of cake together, then we would leave and that was basically how it went, every time.

Dad was not particularly close to his Father even as a child. He was more or less brought up by his Auntie after his Mam died and from what I can hazily remember Granddad remarried again and although he and Dad remained civil I don't think they were particularly close. The only other relations on my Father's side who I vaguely knew as a young girl were Uncle Jeff and Auntie Gwyneth and their twin girls

Janice and Elaine who lived in Pontardulais. We would exchange Christmas cards and visit them now and again. I have no idea where they are now. Other than that there was never any involvement with or from my Father's side of the family, unlike my Mother's side.

Interestingly, Dad also had a sister called Betty who married an American GI after the war and went out to live in America. I imagine she would most probably be dead now but I do know she had three children who would be around the same age as me and I've often thought about trying to trace. The one relative who used to keep in touch with her, a cousin of my Father's, died long ago and in later years when I asked my Mother about Aunty Betty, she couldn't even remember where she got married so I couldn't look at parish records. I don't even know the surname of the soldier that she married, only that she went out to Arizona.

At one point I got as far as contacting Arizona Newspapers and putting an advertisement in to see if anybody would know about them but not knowing the name of the American guy she married has made it almost impossible which is such a shame. It's something to this day I always have in my mind to do. So if anybody out there knows of a lady whose maiden name is Betty Thomas who originally came from South Wales UK, married an American soldier, settled in Arizona and had three children please let me know!!! I know it's not much to go on and the details are very sketchy but if anyone recognises any links however tenuous or perhaps knew Betty I would love to hear from you!

It would be a dream come true to get in touch again with my Dad's side of the family and would mean so much to me.

Chapter 7: The Right Direction

And so the big day arrived, my first day at Queen Elizabeth Grammar School. I don't know if its the same nowadays but back then it was like death for the beginners who stuck out like a sore thumb on their first day all pristine and sparkling, in gleaming new shoes, dark navy to black tunic, white shirt, blazer, red badge, beret and satchel complete with pencil case, geometry set with compass, protractor, six inch ruler, pen, and ink.

Within two years that same poor beautiful satchel was to be covered in felt tip graffiti style with the names of big artists of the day like The Beatles, The Hollies, The Rolling Stones. We used to wear a sort of fabric belt which was also a dark navy and the side of it would be tied a bit like the knot of a tie and it would hang down at the side. At the end of each school year, pupils would be awarded posture belts which were basically exactly the same belts but in red and meant that you had kept yourself immaculately clean, extremely smart, tidy and very well groomed.

Of course there were certain girls within school who were able to keep themselves like that with no problem at all, whereas I would always have custard spots on my tunic or a bit of dirt round the collar. I suppose I was a bit of a tomboy really, and if there was a stain going I'd cop it. Ah I was hopeless and sadly never had a posture belt.

There were three classes in each year and 33 girls in each class. I soon discovered a love of French, I thought it was wonderful and loved the sound of the accent. At the end of the first year it was determined how they would segregate the 99 girls and if I remember correctly the girls in the A stream had the opportunity to learn Latin as they were considered clever enough. I also loved Biology and Algebra although not so keen on Maths or Geometry. English I always found a little bit difficult, purely because, and this is no disrespect to the teacher that we had, but I just couldn't connect with her even though plenty of people passed O and A levels under her tuition, we just didn't gel. I hated Chemistry, Geography and History were boring. French and Biology were my firm favourites, and then of course there was Music which was in a different league and always a great joy. I absolutely loved it.

At school dinner time someone would be always be appointed to rush up to the hatch and grab the tureens of food! Naturally I would always appoint myself. First of all we had to stand while the teacher would say grace before our meal and as soon as we said Amen, I was gone. I was like Concorde up there. I don't know why I was compelled to do that, the silly thing was it wouldn't have hurt to just stand in the queue. We would still have got the same food.

There would be eight of us on a circular table and we used to have this same dish every week which was like a cheese and potato pie. Now I immediately assumed I wouldn't like it see, so for four whole years I gave my portion away every Friday until the fifth year I decided to try it and oh my god it was to die for. I couldn't believe I'd given it away for four years!!! For the life of me I can't remember who the lucky recipient was but they must surely owe me a drink.

As this time was before Thatcher had become the 'milk snatcher', we had our daily allowance of milk as well, not that I ever bothered with that either. Some things were wasted on me! It's not that I didn't have a healthy relationship with food. I did and always have had. I'm lucky as I've never had any problems with diet and have always eaten whatever I liked.

I also consider myself fortunate in that schoolwork and studying always came easily to me although I must admit I could have done a lot better at school. During the first year, you'd take your exams before Christmas and then more exams at the end of the year before the school broke up for the summer holidays, and I did very well. I came 8 out of 33 for the Christmas exams with a very good school report.

But then I suppose a bit of a rebellious streak set in. There was always something about me that didn't like to conform too much. I wasn't a trouble maker as such. I was more mischievous than anything and as a result I did terribly in the end of year exam. I think I came 28 out of the same 33 because I just hadn't bothered.

That shook me as those exam results determined who was an A, B or C student and of course I went straight into C stream. That was enough to set me straight again and once we started back I made up for it and from that point onwards was always first or second in the class.

Another area I loved was sport. I loved all of it, running, high jump, netball and hockey and indeed I excelled. I would stay behind after school and play for hours. During my last couple of years at the school I was asked to play for the County with Hockey but I couldn't because the County had also asked me to play Netball and I couldn't do them both. I chose Netball and subsequently went for the South Wales trials where I was picked to play for South Wales as Shooter. We got to travel quite a lot and play different counties. There was always a match and we played loads of them, always in Wales. Of course there was the usual concerns that some schools had a really bad reputation and were a bit rough and would shove you around somewhat but we would certainly give as good as we got.

We were a good team and it wasn't often that we lost. I was believe it or not as I hate to blow my own trumpet, an excellent shooter. My judgement was brilliant for the whole eye ball co-ordination thing. Mind you not so long ago I tried it again and was nowhere near as good! I've lost it completely along the way!

I had loads of friends at this time. Like all teenagers there would be the flavour of the month. Somebody else would come along and they'd be my new best friend but on the whole there was a section of girls that I stuck with throughout all of my school days. Lesley Thomas was one of them who went on to marry Dave Edmunds and later on her second marriage was to Roger Glover the bass player of Deep Purple. Sadly this marriage didn't last either. Mary Turner was another, Sharon Jory, Joy Williams, Suzanne Richardson; the list goes on.....

We've all been in touch over the years although more so with Lesley as we would swap the odd email and I would go along to a Deep Purple Concert when they were over. Sharon, Mary and Lesley even came to my Mothers funeral and I hadn't seen them prior to that for years. It was so lovely of them to come and I really did appreciate it. Lesley lives in America now and we are still in touch by email, and we all have each others phone numbers.

Back in our teenage days Lesley's parents had a cafe in Carmarthen called the West Wales Cafe where I was to work a few years later for a short time to make ends meet whilst I was waiting for music to be written for my stage act. The family lived in the flat above the cafe and right up until her Mam died; every time I saw her she recalled fond memories of me as a teenager playing the piano in their lounge for her grandfather.

My favourite band without doubt was the Beatles. I lived breathed and died the Beatles. My first introduction to them was via my older brother Elvyn. One day we were sitting in the lounge at home and he had just bought The Beatle's very first album, 'Please Please Me". I can visualise the picture on the cover now which was obviously taken in a block of flats and they were all leaning over the balcony looking down. He said to me, "These guys are absolutely amazing. And they've written all their own songs!"

Well that was it, one listen and I was hooked. Of course I absolutely loved The Hollies and The Rolling Stones as well but to a lesser extent I also listened avidly to all the exciting new bands of the day such as The Searchers, The Swinging Blue Jeans, The Dave Clark Five. Oh and when Cilla Black, Lulu and the amazing Dusty Springfield arrived on the scene I thought they were incredible. I really looked up to these women. I bought so many records much to my Mother's horror!

"Turn that racket down!" I can still hear her shouting now! My parents had come from another era of music altogether. They just didn't understand all the Beatlemania that they were seeing on the television and girls in total hysterics!! It was completely alien to them. There was nobody specifically who influenced me as a performer. If an artist was good, then I loved them, simple as that. The trouble was they were all good, all those wonderful artists of the 60s. I can honestly say I don't actually remember any particular one that I didn't like. Suddenly there was this wonderful new era of music with different types of songs. The American scene started infiltrating with artists such as Frankie Valli and the Four Seasons. It was such a great time. I would go as far to say I think the 60s was by far the most exciting time for music.

I'm not saying that because of the age I was and the way it influenced me personally. I believe The Beatles opened the door to a whole new spectrum we just hadn't known before. I never did manage to see them live, though I knew people who did but never actually heard them amidst the screaming of the hysterical fans!! In fact the only big name I can remember going to see at that time was Paul Jones of Manfred Mann fame.

Looking back now and given a choice, if somebody said we were going to have a themed evening and what decade would I like, with no hesitation it would be the 60s. It was fabulous!

Meanwhile back in my bedroom at home, not only was it ceiling to floor but wall to wall with The Beatles, with not a square inch of wallpaper or paint to be seen. Lesley, Mary and another girl called Margaret Dark who, bless her, has since died, and myself came to a mutual agreement. Mary had bagsed Paul McCartney, Margaret had bagsed John Lennon, and Lesley wanted George which meant I was left with Ringo.

I then had to pretend that Ringo was my favourite when really I would rather have had one of the others. Sorry Ringo! We'd all get together and listen to their records.

Despite the relatively safe surroundings, Mam was very protective of me as the only girl and the fear of me falling prey to terrible boys who were always after girls!! When I was around the age of 14, I was allowed to go to the local dance on a Saturday night which was held at St Peters Church Hall in Carmarthen or the Barracks and I always used to hate it because my Father would not only come and pick me up, but would always arrive far too early when all my other friends were allowed to stay. Oh the shame!!

I had a rebellious streak which didn't sit well as Mam was so strict and so chapel and would lead to many a falling out! I wasn't allowed to wear mini skirts and would have a set of clothes in the hedge outside, so would go out of the front door in one outfit, pop into the garden and quickly change into my 'with it' clothes, put my 'square' clothes as I called them into the bin bag and into the hedge then off I'd go into town.

There were two entrances to the 'mews' where we lived and years later my Father told me that on one occasion he was walking behind me through town and I was wearing the shortest skirt imaginable. Apparently I entered the mews from one entrance and he came in through the other and when I met him at the front door I had a completely different outfit on!! He thought it was hysterical and knew exactly what I was doing. He was much more broad minded than Mam though and he never said a word to me at the time!

Out of all my friends Sharon Jory was definitely the one to watch!! She always used to have wonderful 'mod' clothes with a great sense of fashion and if she'd been away we would go to the dance on a Saturday night knowing and waiting with bated breath to see her new 'in' dance. Very craftily everybody would just slowly copy her so by the end of the night we were all doing the same! She would lead and we would follow faithfully!

I reminded her of all this when we went out on the night of my Mum's funeral for a drink, and the fact she was always the leader of fashion and dances and we were her dedicated followers!

Carmarthen was a town which was very behind the times as far as fashion was concerned. There was simply nothing there, fashion did not exist. As a 'mod' I would have to get the train to Swansea for my clothes or to get anything decent although this didn't happen very often. I just couldn't afford it. What I would do is buy any old skirt that I liked and then alter it to become a mini skirt.

Not that there was anywhere to go or much to do. On a Saturday night I remember we would walk the whole length of two streets strutting up and down just to see who was around. We would gather in a shop doorway just to chat. There was a coffee bar with a juke box which didn't sell coffee strangely, just coke! What with that and the Saturday dance that just about sums up my social life at fourteen. At least we were safe though!

Chapter 8: Life In The Slow Lane

It was around this time that I started singing lessons with Ma Griff and don't ask me why, I have no idea why she was called Ma Griff. I can't even remember if she was Mrs Griffiths, nor could I tell you how old she was but to me from my young perspective she was old.

My parents knew of her as a singing teacher and as she had a good reputation they sent me to her. The songs I would sing with her were all classical, usually in Welsh and she would teach me how to sing them properly and enunciate the words correctly. This was when my great rival of the time Margaret Morris first appeared on the scene from the nearby village of Carway. Ma Griff thought we would sing duets well together with Margaret taking the soprano part and me as a mezzo soprano taking the alto part.

I will never forget thinking what a beautiful looking girl Margaret Morris was. Not only was she pretty, with immaculate hair and beautiful clothes she also had the most amazing voice. Gosh, I was quite in awe of her and fervently wished I could be just like her.

Inevitably it wasn't long before I found myself competing against her and others at the Eisteddfods and as anyone who knows will tell you the standards of musicianship, artists, and poets in Eisteddfods is immense.

Eisteddfods are 'competitions' for want of a better description, held all over Wales in various locations ranging from schools and church halls for some of the smaller events held over a weekend and consisting of perhaps singing, poetry and piano recitals through to gigantic marquees for a week long event which also include choirs and dancing groups.

Adjudicators at these Eisteddfods are of the highest standard in their own field and know their subject inside out. I'm talking now University lecturers and Professors and such like, these are people who really know their music. It's not just a talent show with Joe Soap the local Councillor from around the corner judging. These people know their onions when it comes to music, singing and diction.

The three main Eisteddfods are Llangollen which is a huge international event and permanently set up. People come from all over the world to compete in this and it kicks off with a huge parade. My dearest friend Idris goes every year, he stays in the same hotel and he books his slot while he is there for the same time the following year along with his ticket and his same seat. The other two big ones are Urdd Eisteddfod which is held in different locations and the National Eisteddfod or Eisteddfod Genedlaethol sometimes held in North Wales and sometimes in the South. At the very end of the week they stage a big concert and mega stars are booked to perform, stars such as Luciano Pavarotti, Shirley Bassey and Russell Watson and more recently Lulu and Kiki Dee. It really is a huge and prestigious event.

And so it was that every weekend I would travel to an Eisteddfod to compete. There was a regular circle of us competing from different areas around the

Carmarthenshire, Glamorganshire area. You would see the same old faces each week and we all got to know each other. And oh boy if Margaret Morris was in the competition you quite readily resigned yourself to the fact that you didn't stand a hope in hells chance of winning!

But I didn't care whether I won a prize or not, it was like water off a ducks back to me and I would just turn up at the next one and compete again.

Sometimes all placings would have a money prize but most of the time prizes were either in some form of a silver cup or shield or a dainty little bag, made of a very pretty fabric that hung around your neck with a ribbon and had a money prize in it.

There was this young boy who always sticks in my mind from a place called Tumble in Carmarthenshire called Richard Thomas, who used to sing this wonderful song called "How Lovely Are Thy Dwellings". The songs we sang were strictly all classical, with no pop songs, and he would stand there in this suit which had short trousers clutching his lapel while he would proudly sing. He always won! As did Margaret Morris. Like I said though, it was something I just accepted. I was never deterred or put off by never winning.

Having said that I would occasionally get a placing, sometimes coming second or third but more often I wouldn't. I was surprisingly philosophical really and would think to myself there is always next time. If it was now of course I would mind very much! But back then I just accepted that there were people who were better.

After your particular section had finished and the prizes had been awarded, you could go and get the notes from the adjudicator and read the criticism of your performance which was always very helpful and whatever I learnt or was taught I did my utmost to take on board to improve my performance and make it better. One of my recurring comments was that I had too much tremolo in my voice.

At around this time my parents began making enquiries to reputable singing teachers and Mam told me they had got in touch with this particular teacher, John Hywel Williams. As luck would have it he had room for me and could take me on as a pupil. I cannot remember for the life of me how much those lessons were but I don't think we're talking extortionate amounts.

I was at that age where my voice was ready for training and I was very much looking forward to my first lesson. I suppose John was in his late 20's at the time and he had a beautiful, large house. For all my anticipation, I never sung a note during my first lesson. It was all about breathing techniques which was something completely alien to me at the time. This then moved on to scales, and different types of scales.

I would sing songs without lyrics which I can only liken to an Opera piece but instead of singing words I would sing "Aaaah" which I believe were called concone exercises. By doing this and singing the scales purposefully without any vibrato at all, he was able to iron out that tremolo in my voice for which I had been previously criticised and was also one of the first things he noticed. For readers who may not know their vibratos from their tremolos, and why would you, a vibrato is when somebody sings a note and it has a nice wavering tone whereas if someone has too much tremolo in their voice it almost makes them sound like they are hiccoughing. The training brought my voice down to an attractive vibrato as opposed to having a great big wobble which sounded like someone was shaking the living daylights out of me.

After that John then suggested I try for a singing exam. He taught me everything I needed for this exam which I passed with distinction and an impressive 98 out of 100.

Now this was a fantastic achievement as it was a very high standard of singing. It wasn't just about scales. I had to do these concone exercises. As I mentioned previously it was almost like an operatic set piece with just aahhh's and plenty of light and shade, difficult to describe but even more difficult to perform.

Of course I had certain set pieces to learn for some of the bigger Eisteddfods. One of the piano pieces I had to learn was Arabesque by Debussy, a beautiful piece of music which I practised and practised for 3 hours a day. I went to different houses, played different pianos. Bearing in mind I was at that point extremely good and achieving a high standard as a concert pianist, I came 56 out of about 90 odd competitors which shows the tremendously high standard. My god, I just knew I could not physically have played that piece any better.

For my first Eisteddfod under the tuition of John Hywel Williams he picked a song for me called Matthew Mark Luke and John that I don't think anybody had ever heard before in Eisteddfods and from that day onwards I started winning firsts, eventually beating Margaret Morris.

I was stunned and admittedly she looked surprised but as expected she was very gracious. This time when I went to get the paper from the adjudicator, what he had written about my singing was now totally different to what was written prior to my singing lessons.

It was usually the case that quite a few of the competitors would sing the same song. Sometimes in the category you were entering, for example female solo aged 12 to 15, it would be a set piece you would have to learn in which case everybody sang the same song but in other categories it would be a song of your own choosing which naturally resulted in a few people choosing the same song which you were allowed to do and was perfectly acceptable.

Competitors would always have their favourite songs as well. Margaret Morris's favourite was something about Tripping and of course Richard Thomas's How Lovely Are Thy Dwellings. Another, Denis O'Neil who was a lot older and later went on to become a very famous Welsh singer always sang Panis Angelicus in Welsh. Bara Angyllion Duw. Incidentally in recent years I did bump into Margaret Morris a couple of days after I'd appeared on the Welsh channel S4C where they had been filming me presenting a cheque for £1000 pounds to Ty Bryn Gwyn the hospice where my Mam had passed away.

I was in a shop in Llanelli and she approached me, I must say I didn't have a clue who she was at first. She told me she still sings at Eisteddfods which exist as much as ever, and she still looks as lovely and as beautiful as I remember her from those early days. She has a double barrelled name now due to her singing fame on the classical scene in Wales. I believe she has done some television work and modelling as well, which I'm not surprised about.

I used to enjoy competing in Eisteddfods; indeed they became part of my life. Sometimes I would travel there with Mam on the bus, and sometimes Dad would drop me off and pick me up later when it was all over. Occasionally even my lovely music teacher Auntie Nan would accompany me and sit with me all through the day and the night whilst I competed in the various competitions. Not only would I try the singing category but I would often compete in the piano playing as well.

Also doing the rounds of Eisteddfods was a wonderful wonderful singer, Gloria Fisher from Kidwelly who had a fabulous voice and became my partner in crime as well as a very good friend. We were two little rebels together and sadly I haven't got a clue what she is doing now. I'd love to know what became of her and have often tried looking for her. She has probably married and changed her name by now though.

Gloria had failed her eleven plus and so went to secondary school. In those days if in the first two years of secondary school your work improved, you were upgraded as it were to Grammar school. Gloria was duly upgraded and she came into the Grammar school later on, into my class, and from then on we used to sing duets together both at school and at the Eisteddfods.

There was one song which I could sing now called 'Blodyn Gwyn' meaning 'White Flower' in English. She would take soprano and I again would be the alto. There was one occasion when we were going to sing together in the Vale of Towy Music Festival which was to be the first of its kind to be held in a huge Marquis in Carmarthen Park.

I also entered the piano playing category and played a piece of music called 'The Sea'. Now as notes go it was a very simple piece of music but where the skill came in was with the light and shade given to it so that whoever was listening could close their eyes and imagine that yes this was the sea at its roughest most turbulent, and then oh yes now comes the calm. That was the true skill, the colour that you as a pianist gave to it. This time there were 96 entrants and I came first which was a spectacular result for me.

The singing part wasn't quite so successful though. One morning while assembly was in progress, Margaret Daniels our music teacher caught Gloria and me underneath the stage quickly catching up and doing our homework which of course should have been done the night before. It still makes me laugh now thinking of us scrunched up amongst all this paraphernalia, quickly trying to get this blessed homework done before assembly finished.

As punishment we were banned from singing in this concert. I did think this was a bit harsh but that was it. Luckily she couldn't stop me entering for the piano playing as this was a separate category and not under her control. We were out of the school choir too but luckily that was rectified when Margaret Daniels left and Mr Fuster the new music master joined. I went to see him one day not long after he started and told him that I used to be in the choir and wished I could rejoin.

I find it so funny now, that there I was having been thrown out of the choir for being a naughty girl, now being incredibly humble standing in front of this new teacher who didn't know me at all, as if butter wouldn't melt.

He cut to the chase and after confirming that "Yes Sir I have been naughty and thrown out of the choir and yes Sir I really want to rejoin," he said, "Alright then," and that was that.

I got on really well with him. Maybe it's because he was a man, I don't know. I do know however that he was a fabulous teacher. Unfortunately I think perhaps it was just a personality clash with me and Margaret Daniels. What followed though were truly memorable times but sadly as is the case with most teachers who shape your life, we lost touch when school finished.

Me aged 16

My school pal Mary Turner and me. We were 'Mods'

Me and my school friends
Left to right: Sharon, Lesley, Mary, me

Chapter 9: Delays Possible

Amidst all my singing I found time for boyfriends like we all did but there hadn't been anybody serious. It was all very innocent. There was one boy though who shall remain nameless to save him embarrassment, and for the purpose of this book be known as Peter, who I met at one of the dances.

I was a mod at the time complete with flares and he was a rocker complete with motorbike and he used to think it hilarious to put bicycle clips around the bottom of my flares. Well as Carmarthen was such a small town my parents quickly found out I was going out with this boy and when they found out he was four years older than me, they equally quickly forbade me from seeing him! After all I was only 14 so this was a significant age difference.

As far as I was concerned I was incredibly in love and I fancied him like mad, so, being that I wasn't allowed to see him, I worked it out that I could sneak out of the house at night without my parents knowing. In our lounge there was a little small back window and when everybody was tucked up safely in bed, I would sneak downstairs, climb out of this window and go and meet him very late at night. He had a garage where he used to keep his motorbike and all we would do is sit on his motorbike and do nothing more than a little kiss and cuddle. I think as any youngster will tell you, when you are young and in love, you can spend hours just talking. I mean god knows what we spoke about. Anyway I would return home at around three in the morning, with my parents totally oblivious to all this.

Now you have to remember our house was in a little mews. You couldn't park the car outside and had to walk from the main road into the mews. You would step out of the front door walk maybe about four steps to the little front garden which was buffered by a small one storey factory that had been there for years. The back of the house backed on to gardens that belonged to another street so there was no back door going out to those gardens. So picture if you will, I was clambering out of this little window that looked out onto other people's gardens. There was no stopping me though. Oh! I was climbing over hedges, fences, anything that got in my way like I was like a cat burglar. I felt like Red Rum, leaping over anything. I'd worked out my route with military precision.

So by now I am getting very very good at this and in the end I would shut the kitchen door and say goodnight, only to go straight out the window. I had very little sleep but I think the excitement and adrenalin kept me going!! This went on successfully for a couple of weeks but on this one particular night, my Mother was making dessert jelly and in those days we didn't have a fridge so she would put it to set on this little windowsill in the lounge.

As per usual as far as they were concerned, I had gone to bed until inevitably Mother went to the window with the aforementioned jelly to be confronted by my pyjamas at the back of the settee and the window wide open. Blissfully unaware of this development I said goodnight to my boyfriend, and started my return journey home, climbing over everybody's hedge. There was no access to these back gardens because our gardens were the other side of the house.

As I approached our house there it was.....window shut.....jelly on the windowsill. I think it was the lime jelly! Oh My God! She knew! I literally rewound, scrambled back, jumped over all the hedges again in the gardens and I knew if I shouted his name he'd hear me 'cos there were no cars around at that time of night. He did and of course I was such a drama queen.

"Oh my god," I managed to blurt out to him, "the window's shut and there's jelly on the window ledge and Mother is going to kill me and I have to run away!!"

So there I was with no plan. I just knew I had to run away, there was no other option! Anyway just as Peter was trying to calm me down we heard this clump clump of footsteps approaching us. Now bearing in mind there was not a soul about at that time of night we knew it had to be a policeman. Peter panicked

"Quick hide behind that car, lie down and then I'll pretend I'm trying to light my fag..."

As he was eighteen, this seemed plausible. The policeman duly quizzed him on his whereabouts to which he replied quick as a flash that he'd been to a party and offered a fictitious address. The policeman then asked him for his own address and of course he gave the correct one as he had done nothing wrong. He then explained he was now on his way home and had just stopped to light his cigarette in the doorway. The policeman took one long look at him before walking round to where I was cowering and shining his torch directly into my guilt ridden face.

"Come out of there," he said, "I knew you were there the whole time!"

Well I could have died.

"We were just having a laugh," I managed to gabble.

I then gave him a fictitious name and backed up the story of going to a party before trying to make a hasty exit by saying I had to get home as it was late. There I was running along the road, and Peter came out of a shop doorway.

"Take me to the garage and hide me then lock me in", I shouted.

My first thought was I could hide in the garage for a while, Peter could bring me bread and water and I'd think of a plan. I had no money of course but that was alright I'd manage somehow.

So that's what we did, Peter shut me in the garage and I lay under this blanket and fell asleep. I was awoken by a torchlight shining under the door and someone trying to open the door. Oh god I thought it's the police again, what's going on now. Whoever it was went away and I must have dropped off but was awoken yet again to the sound of somebody running towards the garage, the door opening and this time it was Peter who shouted, "You've got to come and give yourself up. The police have been to my house. Your parents know you've been out all night, give yourself up now!!!"

I felt like a hardened criminal!

I decided to go to Peter's house and in Carmarthen at that time as anybody reading this book who lived there at the time will remember was a very big, burly policeman called Goronwy. He would put the fear of god into anyone. He was a great policeman though; a great disciplinarian and a credit to the police force and everybody had the utmost respect for him. As I approached the house I thought oh shit it's Goronwy. Well you'd think I was in bloody MI5. Opposite Peter's house was a church and graveyard and there I was hiding amongst the tombstones watching what was going on.

The funniest thing was when I did eventually pluck up the courage to walk in the house they said they knew I was there amongst the graves all the time and were just waiting for me to come over!! It was hysterical looking back. Luckily Peter's parents were fine about it all. Goronwy then told me that the other policeman had checked up on my fictitious address, found I didn't live there and decided to go back to Peter who had to come clean. Goronwy then went round to my house and told my parents the whole sorry story.

I was put in a police car and whisked off home. Well by now I was terrified. This is it, I thought, I've had it now. I remember these two young police officers who were with me in the car saying in their finest Welsh accents, "Where 'ave ewe bin gal, ewe've been out all night ave ewe?" whilst tutting and shaking their heads.

I could see they were dying to laugh though.

When we got back to my house I could see Goronwy there in his long coat and I threw myself on his mercy by telling him my Mother was going to kill me and how I was dreading this. He assured me in his big wonderful Welsh voice that everything was going to be alright. The front door was slightly open and he knocked whilst calling out

"Mrs Thomas, we've got your daughter," to which she replied,

"Where is she I'll flippin' kill her!!!"

"Come on Mrs Thomas," he replied in his commanding, booming voice, "nobody is going to kill anybody; we'll have none of that."

After that my father wouldn't speak to me and my mother's response was, "Don't think you are getting away with this"

Apparently I was black all over, even my face was covered. It must have been really dirty in that garage.

Mother was adamant I was still going to school even though I'd had no sleep. So I got washed, had breakfast and went to school. Well......I could not wait to get to school could I? I was the centre of attention. I was holding court now with this story because it was so sensational!! Those that didn't know what had happened were told. I made sure everyone knew.

It was big OMG's everywhere. I now had everyone's undivided attention see!! I was in my flippin' element. Our local paper came out on a Thursday and I remember wondering if I'd made the headlines?! Sadly of course it didn't warrant a mention which brought me down to earth somewhat!!

After the initial excitement had died down, a policewoman came out to see me, wanting to know if any sexual activity had taken place. Of course it hadn't, as it was all very innocent. I can hear myself now, "No, no no no no no no no, nothing has happened, no no no !!!"

I'm not sure if they believed me but Goronwy told me they would be keeping a close eye on things from now on and making sure I didn't go anywhere near my boyfriend for the foreseeable future. Understandably I suppose they were worried about the age thing really. I was also grounded for a few weeks. My father's attitude was very different to Mam's. If I did something wrong, Mam would shout at me. Dad however had this wonderful knack of talking things through.

On this particular occasion, he sat me down.

"I want to talk to you Helen...why did you feel the need to deceive us and go out of the window? I want to know where you were coming from?"

You see he wanted to know my side of it, to understand it and then explained it from their perspective which all then made perfect sense. I think that whole episode was a significant part of my life and even though no harm came to me it brought some degree of shame on my parents. Nobody else ever knew. The rest of the family when they read this book will be finding it out for the first time and I can hear some of them chuckling now.

What evolved after that was my Father had a chat with my Peter's Father and they agreed that a couple of nights a week I could see Peter but at his house. It carried on like that for a while. Mam, eventually realising how keen I was invited him round for tea on Boxing Day. Well it was awful 'cos unbeknown to her I'd finished with him on Christmas Eve. He had bought me the most beautiful pair of boots as well and given me five pounds in cash which was such a lot then. At that age you don't have much of a conscience though do you? All I knew was that my feelings for him had naturally fizzled out after a few months. I can look back now after all these years and see that it wasn't a nice thing to do but it was time to move on!!

Chapter 10: Cruise Control

So here I was with an incredibly full life. Piano lessons, singing lessons, netball county team, school work, and still time to fit in a social life.

John Hywel Willams also had a fabulous all girl choir at the time called simply the Hywel Girls Choir, and he asked me if I would like to join and become one of his four soloists. Would I? Of course I could fit another activity into my hectic schedule! No problem! I absolutely loved the choir and especially the harmonies. Soon after I joined we went on a tour of Austria and Czechoslovakia accompanied by John himself and his wife who acted as our manager, nurse and also accompanied us on the piano when we were performing our concerts.

I remember all the parents waving us off excitedly as we boarded the coach and headed off cross channel on the ferry. John was very strict taskmaster and I remember at 4pm every afternoon we were all made to lay down for half an hour with no talking, purely for a rest or sleep. No mean feat for 47 girls with an average age of 13 and the youngest being 9!!

I remember he would always criticise my shoulder length straight hair with the long fringe at the time. Despairingly he would often say, "Helen Thomas you look like a flippin' Spaniard with that haircut". I have no idea why, maybe it was because the fringe practically covered all my eyes!! I rather liked it myself!

We performed one of the concerts in the gardens of this place in the most beautiful surroundings. I cannot for the life of me remember where or what it was but distinctly remember the way I felt at that moment. Here I was in this wonderful place, miles away from home and singing to these complete strangers! I couldn't believe it. We were very warmly received wherever we went partly because the choir was an extremely high standard and well known at the time. Many of the concerts were televised and broadcast. We were guests of honour at a reception by the British Ambassador in Prague. Concerts were held in Prague and then in Austria where we performed in St Polten, Aspang and Baden. We sang some fabulous songs, mostly in Welsh including songs from the Mikado, and we even had a jazz song in our repertoire. Whatever songs John chose for us there was never one that I disliked. They were always wonderfully challenging as a vocalist and a great joy to sing with wonderful melodies. It was a time of my life, of about a year I suppose that I enjoyed so much. It is such a great buzz when you are singing harmony with over 40 strong voices.

Even now I get a kick singing closely with other great voices, and by that of course I mean my dear friends and fellow band members from Brotherhood of Man, Martin Lee, Lee Sheriden and Sandra Stevens. I often think nowadays it must be fabulous to be in a musical and be on that West End stage singing full pelt with a massive amount of really fantastic voices.

John was an excellent teacher and even now I have not forgotten what he taught me and still apply it to whatever form of singing I am doing and put it to practise on stage. Whether it is hitting those high notes, or needing a bit of extra lung power, everything he taught me I remember and I am still using. You don't sing from the throat, when you're taking a breath to reach a high note it comes from way down deep, certainly not the throat.

The choir itself is still going to this day and still under John himself. In fact my niece Sadie has only recently stopped having singing lessons with him!! She has a lovely voice and after complaining that she could not find anyone to help her further her singing, I phoned John up on the off chance to find that yes he is still teaching people to this day.

So, by now I was approaching O level time as it was then. I was still active with the chapel activities especially if there were any concerts and now I had begun singing as a soloist in Gymanfa Ganu's, which are wonderful events that chapel's held about twice a year. I believe some of them still hold them as annual events. They're a bit like a singing fest for the congregation with a famous conductor. You would know what songs you would be singing as there would be a programme or leaflet which some chapels might have got in advance and invariably these were songs or hymns that you would know. The chapels would be overflowing for these occasions. The sound was magnificent as the conductor would be accompanied by the pipe organ. By now I was known on this circuit. I didn't get paid for it. It was purely for the prestige. And of course it goes without saying Mother was so so proud.

As I mentioned before St David's is widely celebrated in Wales and my chapel would hold a special concert. We would dress up in the Welsh National costume and various events were held as part of these celebrations. One particular time, I must have been about 15 or 16 because the Sound of Music film had just been released, I thought it would be a great idea if I took the part of Julie Andrews and gathered all the kids together as the Von Trapp children. Well the Chapel thought it was amazing and just two years before Mam died in 2006, I returned home and attended Chapel with Mother and a few elderly people who attended with us that day told me they could remember me with all the children singing Doh Ray Me and how marvellous it was. Incredible and quite humbling to think all those years and they were still attending that same chapel and still remembered me doing that. At the time no one did anything like that you see so it was quite a novelty and great fun. And to think that 'Climb Every Mountain' and 'The Hills Are Alive' was my first audition piece as a pop singer later on in life.

I made friends with a girl who wasn't at our school. Her name was Barbara and she lived with her sister who was very lenient. By now we were heavily into the mod scene and I used to tell my parents that I was going to stay with Barbara overnight. That met with their approval although if I remember correctly my Father had checked that everything was as it should be. We would then get ready and get on the train to Swansea heading for this coffee bar on Mansel Street called The Macabre.

It was called The Macabre as it was all dark inside and the tables were in the shape of coffin lids. Outside would be the most glorious array of scooters with what seemed like 50 million wing mirrors. It was a regular haunt for the mods who all used to go there, an abundance of gorgeous looking guys in parkas. Of course we had nothing like that in Carmarthen. There might be the odd guy who had all the gear but nothing on this scale. And in Swansea they also had a great shop called Nigel Howards which sold all the mod gear for men: the fabulous shirts, ties, the lot.

Well we would just go to this place and sit there all night, hoping to pull a really hot mod with a scooter, but sad to say it never came about. We were totally ignored, and never pulled, but we thought it was wonderful anyway. Coming to Swansea from Carmarthen was like coming from the Outback. We used to catch the three o'clock milk train home to Carmarthen, sneak into her sister's house, catch a few hours sleep then I'd go back home all bright and rosy for Sunday lunch complete with the famous mint sauce!

I was a mod as were all my friends, Lesley, Mary, Sharon and Joy, with all that entailed, and boy we loved all the new fashions and dances. The big dances then were The Shake, The Hippy Hippy Shake and of course The Twist which paved the way for them all. After that it seemed they were all variations on a theme. And as I said earlier, Sharon was always first to perform them!

There was a lady called Olly, who used to run a coach from Carmarthen to Tenby every Sunday morning, 2s 6d return!! We would leave Carmarthen at about 11.00 am to arrive in Tenby by midday. We would pick up the return coach at about 5 or 6pm leaving us free to enjoy the afternoon in Tenby which is a beautiful place with beautiful beaches. And of course what else did Tenby have? It had boys that we didn't know. And we wasted no time putting that right. A few of us met boys down there and there was this one boy in particular who I liked. It was so funny we would write notes to each other and write things on the back like S.W.A.L.K and I.L.Y.

Anyway one Saturday afternoon, out of the blue he decided to come up to Carmarthen on a surprise visit. Well he came and knocked on the door of my house and I nearly died. I knew my Mother wouldn't like him because one of the fashions of the time that everyone was wearing was pale blue jeans. He was sporting a pair of these with long hair and a Beatle jacket. I mean, get out of it, you couldn't have someone like that knocking on my front door with my Mother?!! She told him in no uncertain terms that I wasn't coming out! From then on every five minutes a different girlfriend knocked on my door.

"Hello Mrs Thomas can Helen come out please?"

"No she can't......grrrr" and a slammed door.

Five minutes later .... "Oh hello is Helen in...?"

"No she's not and she's not coming out......" and another slammed door.

Eventually my mother cottoned on to this see, and she went around the corner and down the lane, and lo and behold there were about ten of my girlfriends with this boy. David Attwell was his name. I'll never forget it. I can't remember how but I did eventually get out to see him. I think my Mother must have relented and said I could go and say hello as he had come all the way from Tenby and he must be serious as he's had everybody knocking at the door on his behalf, but I had to be back in an hour. I think my friends' parents were a little bit more relaxed than mine. Mam was strict but she was always fair!!

Oh and by the way, after all that he dumped me eventually. His youth club came up to visit Carmarthen youth club where I used to go and he dumped me 'cos he didn't like my outfit. Cheek! Another drama but it wasn't really love's young dream!!

Me aged 16 in the Teensters
Left to right: me, Heather and Graham

Chapter 11: Further Afield

Whilst all these mini dramas were playing out in my life, Elvyn my brother was heavily into his music and still is to this day. He was a singer and started fronting various pop groups which became very well known on the circuit in South Wales at the time: The Blackjacks, Claude Duval and the Cavaliers and then Elvyn LeRoy and the Meteorites to name a few. By now I too had a great interest in pop music. I loved anything with a great melody so of course having a singing brother gave me a little ego trip. I went to see him performing with his group at a dance and I was gobsmacked to see all these girls screaming for him. I mean here was MY brother in a group and a bit of a heartthrob. I thought it was just brilliant.

Anyone though who thinks back to their teenage days will remember what an exciting time it can be. There I was with my whole life and endless possibilities before me. The end of my school days was in sight, and there were so many different fashions that I was desperate to try out. Add to that the kudos of my brother in a group, well!! I can remember this one day so clearly now, when Elvyn offered to take me for a ride in the group van. Oh my god I thought it was wonderful. Elvyn, his wife Winnie, and I went for a drive down the Mumbles. As anyone who knows South Wales will tell you the Mumbles is a renowned coastal area and beauty spot in Swansea. We came back along the front of Swansea Bay with all of the bay in front of us whilst singing the Beatles songs. Even now whenever I hear 'All My Loving' it transports me straight back into that van. I just found it so incredibly exciting.

We then followed that with an Indian meal, for a "nosh" as we called it then, for the first time in my life and in the restaurant were a load of other well known local groups who my brother knew including The Jets and The Vikings. He at this point had formed Elvyn Leroy and the Meteorites. I was in my element as you can imagine.

Well this to me was the life, and just amazing. We had nothing like this going on in Carmarthen and I wanted more.

I was like the mental sister who used to come and stay. I was so into the groups and the current fashion. My brother and Winnie thought it was hysterical as I unpacked and named all my clothing. I had my Beatles polo neck, courtesy of the sleeve of one of their albums where they were all wearing black polo necks. I then had my Beatle tights which had patterns of actual beetles all over them. There was my Hollies shirt and then I had my Rolling Stones sweat shirt which in actual fact was just an ordinary tee shirt but because Mick Jagger had appeared at some point in Hyde Park in just this cut off tee shirt, so it was named.

Eventually I got to know all the other bands because on many a night my brother would invite them all back to his place for a coffee. Even though they weren't nationally famous, I was in awe of them sat star-struck in this lounge with all these groups. It's funny to think now, it wasn't about alcohol. I can't recall ever seeing bottles of beer anywhere. They would literally come for a coffee which was the thing. Coffee and chat, mainly about music because it was all so exciting then and they would all exchange stories about their experiences playing in the dance halls which were the big thing of the time.

When I returned home inspired by my visit I tried my hand at writing songs as this was something I really desperately wanted to do and was spurred on after hearing my brother and his friends and watching them casually strumming their guitars. Try as I would though it just wasn't a talent that I had. I could sing and play the piano and reconciled myself to the fact I couldn't do everything.

I left school with 5 O Levels under my belt: English, Maths, Music, French and Biology. It was time to consider what jobs were available to me. Some people went on to do A Levels and follow a particular career path to college or University but I didn't have a clue what I wanted to do. As far as I was concerned I'd done my O Levels and couldn't wait to get out of school into the big wide world. I just happened to see a job advertised in the local paper for a telephonist at the local telephone exchange. I seem to remember they wanted someone with O Level English and Maths and thought I may as well have a go.

There were two vacancies and a huge number of applicants and I was one of the lucky ones. I suppose, we are all guilty of taking a lot of things in life for granted particularly in the world of technology. It's only if you go behind the scenes and really take a look at what goes on and how it all works, that you can begin to appreciate the colossal amount of work involved. So it was with the exchange and I found working there fascinating. Previously I had no idea what went on to enable a simple phone call for people just to speak to each other. Back then if you wanted to dial outside the local area you just dialled zero. If you wanted a local number you didn't even need an operator and that was it as far as I was concerned. It really was an eye opener.

My first week's wages in 1966 was the grand sum of £4 and 19 shillings and 6d. On receiving this princely sum I promptly went to Swansea on the train and bought two new outfits. A lemon dress, a camel coloured skirt with raised horizontal seams and enough money left over to give Mam and Dad for my keep. We had agreed on the amount but I can't remember how much it was for the life of me although I know I had an inbuilt and strong sense of wanting and expecting to pay my way and if they hadn't asked me I would have insisted.

Not much was happening on the singing front now. I still had the odd concert at Chapel but it all seemed to be fading as my time was increasingly taken up with my new job and earning money. Plus as a sixteen year old I wanted to be out there enjoying my social life and doing other things now. My colleagues however cottoned on to the fact I could sing. They were buggers. We would be on our lunch break in the locker room and they would order me to stand in a certain spot and sing!! If I protested they would plead and it didn't take much for me to cave in!! I wasn't too keen but easily persuaded. The performer in me was beginning to emerge! I was starting to realise that hey, people are actually wanting me to sing for them outside of the Eisteddfods and Chapel?!

At my first work's Christmas party, we all finished early one afternoon to enjoy the free alcohol which had been provided. I proceeded to get terribly drunk and then desperately tried to sober up and go home. That night was also the annual Christmas do for the Telephone Exchange and I felt so rotten that I couldn't eat a thing. When I did try something I was horrendously sick, after which I felt a lot better, and ended up at the request of our head supervisor singing and accompanying myself at the piano. That was my first introduction to alcohol and not a good one!

After a relatively short time I found out that I could get a transfer to Swansea 27 miles away. I was now more than ready to get out of Carmarthen and felt there wasn't enough there to satisfy me. To satisfy what though I didn't really know at the time, all I knew was it was time to move on and I had restless feet. I asked my brother and sister in law if I could live with them and they agreed no problem at all. Looking back now this was incredibly kind of them as they had only been married a few years, trying to establish their own lives and suddenly here they were lumbered with this effervescent teenager! My parents were fine with it as I was going to live with my brother. I got a transfer to Wind St, Swansea, dead easily and it all went fairly smoothly. So now I was at a much much bigger telephone exchange, Swansea was great with shops full of wonderful clothes and shoes that Carmarthen could only dream of and I was having an absolute ball.

Elvyn and Winnie were a little bit more relaxed than my parents were about me going out and having nights out generally. I took advantage of this and one night shall we say I stayed out a little later than normal which I thought they'd be ok with. It turned out they weren't! They were absolutely brilliant though in the way they handled it. They just pointed out calmly that the time I had come in was too late and would I mind coming in a bit earlier in future, as simple as that. It was lovely, and settled with no arguments and probably had more impact than lots of shouting.

Winnie, my sister in law was great and being worldly wise would give me, an innocent sixteen year old, lots of advice on boys and suchlike, which I appreciated having left all my friends behind, although we still kept in touch though for a while at least.

I settled well into my new job and daily routine. I was part of a team of telephone operators in a huge room, all wearing headsets and sitting at switchboards each of which were linked together. We would each have a certain amount of incoming lines for example forty and when a call came in a line would light up and you would answer the call by putting a jack plug in. Your outgoing calls would be a jack plug on a lead and then behind that would be another one and that would be put into an outgoing line and you would dial out. It's difficult to explain but I hope you get the picture.

There is nothing like that in existence now of course. We would deal with all calls from Swansea and surrounding areas and we were given different rotas each week. Some weeks I would do 8 till 6 which was a hard day, and then perhaps the next day would be 10 till 4, so it was quite varied but added up to a set amount of hours each week. Of course as there were so many telephonists I would sometime look at the rota and get it wrong and then invariably be in trouble for coming in too late.

On this one day I was sat there working as usual and I heard the operator next to me talking to someone who wanted this certain number. My ears pricked up as I recognised the number. Intrigued, I signalled to her that I would take over the call and decided to listen in to the call as something made me feel suspicious. It turned out I was right and it was only my boyfriend of the moment two timing me with somebody else!! As soon as I realised, I cut her off and pressed the switch to talk to him and gave him a right bollocking! By now the word was going around to all the other operators to plug in so they could all listen. All these buzzers were going off with people calling and half the operators weren't answering them because they were too busy laughing their heads off listening to me giving him what for. They even gave me a cheer and a round of applause when I finished!!

Our supervisor came storming through when she realised the noise of the incoming calls not being answered was far greater than normal and tried to remain in control whilst furiously demanding to know what was going on!! Again Helen Thomas was in the throes of a wonderful drama as half the telephone operators in Swansea listened in to her dumping her boyfriend! Of course I was wrong in as much as you weren't allowed to do what I did and the whole incident backfired 'cos he reported me. I was hauled up in front of the Head Postmaster and subsequently let off with a severe warning!!

Inevitably I suppose the novelty of working there began to wear off. Sitting at work one day I could not understand what it was I didn't like about the job. After all it was a good job, there was room to climb up the ladder and you had a pay rise every birthday. Yet something was bugging me. I did not like the fact that I had quarter of an hour tea break, and by the time I got upstairs to my locker to get my money, that was five minutes gone. Making my way to the canteen to get my tea took another five minutes, leaving me five minutes which was just enough time to get back to my locker, deposit my bag and get back onto the floor. I had forty minutes for lunch and quarter of an hour tea break in the afternoon. It was too regimented for me. These time constrictions were something I found difficult to deal with and really did not like and I was beginning to hate it.

Winnie was working as a waitress at a night club called the Townsman in Swansea. The band at the time were looking for a girl singer and Winnie mentioned it to me, and asked if I would like to go and audition, of course she knew I could sing having seen me in many concerts. My initial reaction was "No way can I sing pop," and that was that, it wasn't for me, but Winnie and my brother managed to persuade me by providing me with a hairbrush so I could stand in front of the fireplace and practice singing along to Cilla and Dusty Springfield songs. I didn't really know any pop songs but somewhat reluctantly I went along and auditioned with two songs from the Sound of Music, The Hills Are Alive and Climb Every Mountain, which I sang very classically but to my surprise I got the job.

It was a few nights a week and I was dead chuffed because I was going to get paid five pounds a night! Mother however wasn't so keen, being a chapel goer, she didn't like the fact that I was working in a late night club where people were able to drink you see?

Father on the other hand didn't say much about it. My Mother seemed to do all the voicing of opinions when it came to that sort of thing!! I think secretly he thought it was really quite good because of course he had played in bands all his life. He was a musician and he played in clubs so to him it wasn't a problem. Mother didn't prevent me or tell me that I had to stop doing it but let it be known that she was not very impressed!

It was at this point that Ron Williams who was the band leader wanted to change my name. He didn't think Helen Thomas was right somehow and wanted to change it to something else, something more sophisticated and show biz! We are talking now about the late 60s and everybody had a 'stage name' to make them sound a little bit special.

Ron and Winnie wrote out a list of names and between the three of us we agreed on Nicky Stevens. I could have been anybody at that point! They just thought up a load of fictitious names which they thought sounded good. There was no special reason or meaning behind it. And so Nicky Stevens was created!

I was then given new songs to learn and learn them I did with great enthusiasm. The next hurdle was I didn't have a posh frock to go on stage and a girl's gotta have a posh frock, so a friend of mine kindly lent me one of hers. I suppose the whole 'gig' lasted about a month but it was enough to know that I absolutely loved it! The problem was I was singing these pop songs but as a classical singer so they sounded ridiculous! If you've heard of the programme "Pop Star to Opera Star" well this was like the opposite scenario for me. Classical singer to a pop singer, which I found extremely difficult as it wasn't natural for me after all these years.

Ron told me I had a beautiful voice but he had no choice but to let me go as I just couldn't sing pop which was such a shame. I asked him how to which he replied, "Shout, scream and do anything but use that beautiful voice like you do!!"

I was so disappointed and sad to go as I was beginning to get a real taste for this performing malarkey. Later on in life Ron was to say letting me go was the worst decision he ever made! We both laughed about it but I wonder if he would still have said that if I hadn't gone on to acquire the level of success that I did!!

Interestingly at one point Bonnie Tyler was also the singer with the Ron Williams band, although I can't recall if it was before or after me, and I got to know her, but under her real name of Gaynor, although I'm not sure if Ron invented her stage name as well!

Not long after I heard about a place called the Glen Ballroom in a town near Swansea called Llanelli. The band there needed a girl singer so I went along to audition, met Peter on the Organ, Ralph on the drums and from then onwards, never looked back. I really got stuck in, gradually improving my vocal and performance techniques bit by bit, by listening to other artists perform and listening to records, whilst trying to develop my own style.

I was there for several months but was beginning to find it increasingly difficult as at this point I was still at the telephone exchange during the day so having to get up very early for work, not easy for a seventeen year old at the best of times, and then of course getting home from the ballroom late. I was exhausted.

I persevered however and some of my Carmarthen friends came to see me and were suitably surprised. No-one had expected me to sing in this style of music and it certainly hadn't been in my itinerary of future things to do so it was quite a novelty for them and certainly for me, standing up on stage singing pop songs!

I was there for several months and like any teenager I was thoroughly enjoying the attention it afforded me. It was all so new and exciting for me. One night there was a man in the audience called Ron Watkins from Bridgend and he approached me with an offer of touring the clubs as a solo cabaret artist. Well needless to say I leapt at the opportunity! Again this was completely alien territory to me. Firstly I had to buy some stage clothes, then get music organised because of course the band at the Glen Ballroom knew all the songs and hadn't needed any dots. I too, through them had learnt a lot of the standards that were sometimes required so didn't really have to worry about it.

My criteria for selecting my new music was simply "What songs do I like?" As easy as that. I went out and bought a load of sheet music which was something like 2 shillings each in old money. Sheet music was available everywhere then and would have the picture of the artist on the front. There was no such thing as downloading from the internet back then! You bought the music and then hope and pray that the drummer would plod along with you!

The very first club I worked at was in a little village called Blaengwynfi and I went down so incredibly well and was applauded so loudly it left me absolutely flabbergasted. When I had been doing all the classical stuff particularly at the eisteddfods and cymanfu ganu there was no such thing as applause. You would finish to silence then quietly go and sit down to the sound of your own footsteps, so as you can imagine this was fantastic.

Again in my classical life I would just stand there stiff as a board without moving which is how I started my pop career! Standing still with microphone in one hand like a flippin' statue. I think it was Ron who first introduced to me to the idea that it actually might be quite a good idea to move a little on stage! I really didn't have a clue and it certainly didn't come naturally. I ended up moving around as if I was doing the three step waltz!!

For a short time I joined an outfit called the 20th Century Showband. We only ever did a couple of gigs up North and one, if I remember, in South Wales. The concept did not really work. The band consisted of a drummer, keyboard player, bass and lead guitar and a sax player, me, a girl singer by the name of Polly Brown and a male singer called Dave Lipsom. We also had two go-go dancers (now there's an old name for you!). Polly Brown, the drummer Keith Hall and keyboard player Bob Brittain went on to form the band Pickettywitch. Later on in 1976, Polly Brown and I met again when we were both in The Song For Europe in 1976 at The Royal Albert Hall. I haven't seen her since.

Ron got me an audition with EMI records and apparently the word was, although how true this was I don't know, that Lulu had left EMI so they were looking for a new girl singer to sign in her place. I duly went along to this studio at EMI and sang 'Boom Bang a Bang', which of course was Lulu's Eurovision winning entry. They had hired a pianist for me who was great as he read music and was obviously an accomplished musician. I was mic'd up and after I had finished singing the song, the mysterious panel behind the glass pane in this box were deep in discussion. Whilst we were waiting for a decision, this pianist asked me if I was hoping to secure a record deal.

"Oh ye," I replied eagerly, "I'm trying to make it," I said which was the 'in' expression used at the time. I then explained that I couldn't write songs so I was looking for the right material. He then offered to write me a song and went on to tell me that he had secured a record deal and his first record was coming out the following month.

"I'm going to change my name though. I won't be known as Reg Dwight, I will be Elton John."

I told him that was a good name! I can picture him to this day exactly as he was then with his long hair and glasses. He was really lovely but sadly I have never ever bumped into him since.

Me in 1968

The Michael John Trio 1968

20th Century Showband including future members of Picketty Witch

Chapter 12: Stepping Up A Gear

Ron Watkins eventually became my manager. He already had a few acts on his books and knew of a girl called Heather who played the organ, and Graham a drummer. He put the three of us together which became my very first band, Nicky and The Teensters! We had a Vox Continental organ if you don't mind and in those days if you had a Vox Continental organ then you were really 'it'. The notes were the opposite to normal, so the white notes were black and the black were white and then the top which was flat was bright orange. It was quite a thing to have, oh yes we were bang on trend then! Ron provided a van for us and we had a road manager called Harding who used to drive us around all the clubs, still basing ourselves mainly in and around West Wales, the Valleys and maybe as far as Cardiff. By now my image was getting better and I was much more with it! I must admit I did my fair share of watching and learning from other artists, television programmes and was constantly practising.

This was the point I decided to turn professional and leave the Exchange. I told them I was "turning pro" as the expression was then, and they were all suitably impressed. Mother was absolutely furious with me but to give both of them their due, they stuck by me! Many a time I'd come back from the North East with no money because it had all been spent and without question they'd help me out!

In due course they began to realise that hang on, maybe I was good at doing this and it wasn't just a fad. By this time they'd also seen me working as a solo cabaret artist and the whole idea was beginning to appeal to them.

Eventually Nicky and the Teensters made an EP with a recording company called Wren Records, which was just released locally in the shops. I don't know to this day how many it sold but I have to be honest it's not something I want to play and be reminded of! My Mother thought it was wonderful though and I'm sure I do have a copy somewhere. If my memory serves me well we did an upbeat version of Danny Boy with a demented saxophone player in the background. Every song ended as if a door was being slammed.

There was a wonderful group, who we got to know, on the circuit at the time called Robbie, Ray and The Jaguars. I met them through my manager who in turn knew their manager. Robbie and Ray the two brothers were songwriters and still on my quest to find some material, they wrote this most morbid song for me which was all about death. Ray is now a Pastor with a congregation of about 700 people, and we remain in touch but laugh and cringe a little about that song!

All the acts on the circuit got to know each other really well. We were all young, willing to learn and full of gusto with our careers stretching in front of us. I was the all willing all learning, all working singer and there was certainly plenty of work about. You could work every night of the week if you wanted to and there was no such thing as being out of work. The problem was in getting time off!

Now and then Ron used to bring down one of his acts, a double act from the North of England called the Mighty Atom and Roy. Roy was very thin and Mighty

Atom his wife was not so thin shall we say and was destined later to become one of the Roly Poly's.

During this time when I was still only 16, Ron got me a slot on a television show doing two numbers. It was only when I got to the television studios to meet the producer that I discovered I had to sing the songs in Welsh. I ask you pop songs in Welsh! One was from The King and I, a brilliant version of Hello Young Lovers. The other song I had never heard of in my life and just had to learn it. Luckily it didn't take me long as it was a relatively easy song and of course from a Welsh speaking family it wasn't too bad.

I relished the experience of singing with what was the great Benny Litchfield orchestra. One of the cameramen approached me very seriously prior to filming and informed me that if I made a mistake it would cost them a thousand pounds, as they would have to stop recording.

Of course this was a wind up but I believed him, consequently I was such a nervous blubbering wreck that I did make a mistake and they did have to stop. I was distraught! I apologised to the producer profusely for costing him a thousand pounds which baffled him. The cameraman seeing my consternation did apologise. He hadn't thought for a minute that I believed him!

What I do remember which is such an endearing memory is that my Father bought a new television for the occasion and we had a few people round to watch. Of course there was only the one showing, no such thing as recording devices or catch up TV then, so once you saw it that was it, gone. My appearance caused quite a stir and even made the local papers! Mother took me out to buy a dress which I remember the younger element of my friends and family thinking it could have been just a little bit shorter.

In 1967 Nicky and the Teensters went along to the local auditions in Wales for Hughie Green's Opportunity Knocks which were being held in this big hall where lots of other hopefuls were sat around anxiously with their little amplifiers awaiting their turn. I sang a song called 'Love Me With All Of Your Heart'. I got to about sixteen bars into the song when Hughie Green shouted out "Thank you!" and that was that, our hopes dashed.

I had seen a guy before us playing the piano beautifully who got exactly the same response after only a few bars. I told everyone who would listen for ages afterwards what a rude man Hughie Green was!

Towards the end of our time together as a band, we were doing a few gigs at a holiday camp, when something happened that undoubtedly changed me forever.

Prior to this, the way I perceived rape and my definition of rape was, "A person, most likely a stranger, first attacks you, probably overpowers you and then forces you to have sexual intercourse."

This is true in many cases but what I never realised at that particular time was that my experience of meeting someone, willingly going back to his chalet room to be with him privately and for it then to happen within that context still constituted rape, hence my feelings of guilt to this day and also feeling partly to blame.

I got friendly with one of the entertainment staff at the camp and being young and somewhat naive I accepted an invitation to this guy's chalet for a drink. He seemed nice enough and I just thought it would be lovely to go to his room for a bit of an innocent kiss and a cuddle. Of course when he wanted to go further, I asked him to stop but he wouldn't. I kept asking him to stop becoming increasingly panic stricken but still he wouldn't. I was very frightened and upset by now and was crying and begging him to stop but he continued on doing what he had to for what seemed like an eternity.

I remember exactly how he restrained my body which I don't want to put into writing as it could be deemed offensive but suffice to say it was so easy. Part of me was a bit afraid to cry out because I felt it was my fault for coming here in the first place. That really sums up how I dealt with it over time. Yet again here I was blaming myself.

I felt a lot of physical pain afterwards and laid in a bath for ages. I only told one person who, I have to be honest, didn't really know how to deal with it, sadly showed a distinct lack of consideration and just wanted to gloss over it anyway. This somehow made it worse. Here I was again, older but not really wiser, totally ashamed and feeling dirty but telling myself it was my own stupid fault for being alone with this guy and I had asked for trouble.

I subsequently blocked it out of my mind the best I could, put it to one side and moved on in my own way. Everyone deals with things differently and that was my way.

It was only many many years later when I heard of a particular case in the news that I realised rape can take many forms and it didn't have to be the stereotypical way that I thought it to be. The subject is highlighted in the news and talked about on radio and television documentaries far more now so there is a greater degree of understanding of this horrific crime.

As I write about this and try to explain it to you as honestly as I can, there is currently one of these government promotional adverts being shown on television with a man supposedly watching his younger self through a window having forced intercourse with a girl. He is banging on the window with the voice in his head saying

"If you could see yourself........you're actually raping that girl. She's saying no and you are forcing her to have sex."

When I first saw it I thought, oh my god that epitomises everything I went through. All these years I haven't been able to tell anybody because I thought it was my fault for going there. But he forced me to have full sex with him. I was raped but I never realised it fully at that time and it will never leave me.

Many years later, I was to bump into this person at one of our concerts. He remembered me and of course I recognised him straight away. He came up to me to say hello and asked if I remembered him as if he had done absolutely nothing wrong and that we were old friends from way back. I just shrivelled up inside and felt sick to the pit of my stomach. All I remember thinking was oh please god don't tell anybody you had sex with me, 'cos I will die.

Luckily for me he got drunk and got thrown out of the place! The Manager actually came up to me to tell me this almost apologetically as he thought I knew him. Well I have never felt so relieved. Even now writing all this down I don't feel it was rape, yet I know it was. It WAS rape end of. I was raped and it will never leave me.

Nicky and The Teensters were together as a band for a few years in total until Ron decided to get a trio to back me. Three boys this time, Steven on drums and Michael Tranter and Clive Guyatt on guitar. Clive, funnily enough went on to be my younger brother's best friend later on in life. They never knew each other back then but just happened to have a chance meeting years later.

I can't remember if we had a name. I suspect I just went out as Nicky Stevens with the boys backing me. With this new line up we began to go further afield, now travelling up North. I remember seeing places like Birmingham, Manchester and Sheffield for the very first time.

Here were big cities where it was all happening that I had only ever heard about. They had night clubs the like of which I'd never seen before, and not just a few, there was loads of them. Well for someone like me who came from a small town in South Wales with just one small club, The Townsman in Swansea, I thought these places were unbelievable and suited me and my character down to the ground. I was out there now in the big wide world and having a ball. There was no stopping me and I loved every moment of it.

This really was where my apprenticeship in the business began, because there was (and still is) a vast amount of working men's clubs up there and our Manager would put us with an agent for a week and we would do a different club every night, staying in pro digs and getting to meet other artists. If we ever got the chance we would also go and watch the other artists perform where I would pick up invaluable tips. This proved to be a steep learning curve and boy was I eager to learn.

One night we arrived at this club and the Concert Chairman came up to us and announced somewhat pompously that he understood our band would be backing the main singer who was on that night. Well we knew nothing about this and of course I denied all knowledge of it but he insisted that our keyboard player would be backing this singer. I tried to explain that we didn't even have a keyboard player but he was having none of this. Apparently there had been a slight misunderstanding and the agent thought we were still the line up of my previous band Nicky and The Teensters, and that Heather on the organ could back this guy.

So now we had a situation where this male singer whose name I can't remember and was singing songs like 'The Impossible Dream' and such like, has suddenly got no backing, so without a second thought, idiot here pipes up with....

"I can play the piano..."

The piano turned out to be a big Hammond C3 Organ. I had never even sat at one let alone turn one on! The singer who remains nameless and was none the wiser, proceeded to give me all his music, and, - this shows how much front I had, more front than Brighton - I actually sat up on the organ, on this high wooden bench, where my feet couldn't even reach the pedals! I started fiddling and twiddling with these sliding drawbars, with no clue of what I was doing, making all these strange noises and literally making a mockery of this poor guy's act!

Well imagine if you will. It was like there was a demented idiot behind him like something straight out of the muppets trying to play this flippin' Hammond c3. He came off and let rip, screaming at me all manner of accusations about ruining his act and how dreadful I was to which I replied...

"Oh I'm sure I'll be better in the second half....!" Youth is a wonderful thing!

Then it was our turn. I went on with my band and we did the first song which was ok, but as I went to start the second song there was nothing, no music. I turned round and looked at them mouthing, "Start the song."

"We've forgotten it...." they replied. They had actually forgotten how the song went and they didn't read music!!

Well it was an absolutely nightmare after that as they had totally forgotten how all the songs went. By now the Concert Chairman came in and started screaming his head off saying how absolutely crap we all were. The audience was in uproar, jeering and booing, the singer was still gunning for me, so I did the only thing I could think of and just slipped out of a back window leaving them all to it and made my own way back to the pro digs!

Despite leaving the boys to take the flack, for some reason they thought the whole episode was quite funny! Looking back I suppose they were young inexperienced musicians and our Manager's attitude was if you can play guitar a bit, you're good enough to get out there and strum along, not realising what it all entailed.

Now we all loved larking about and playing pranks on each other, as you do when you're young but on one particular occasion amidst all the fun and games, we were walking along the beach in Sunderland enjoying a peaceful and calm walk and we were looking out to sea when we saw these lights coming towards us in formation, moving very quickly and then flying over our heads and disappearing.

We were all a bit taken aback by this and wondered what it was. We waited to see if it happened again, which of course it didn't. I was convinced we had just seen UFO's and voiced this to the others. It was just the speed at which they were flying and how low and the fact they were silent. There was no noise at all so it wasn't like they were air force jets or such like.

It was really uncanny as we all felt a bit unnerved by the whole incident and we were more than happy to return to the digs albeit in more sombre mood. We all felt we had seen something out of the ordinary. This was certainly no joke. I had never seen anything like it before or since and it is something that cannot be explained away easily. This happened in about 1968 or '69. I've often told this story throughout my life and years later in about 2003, I met up with Clive Guyatt again for the first time and the first thing he mentioned was the 'lights' we saw. He too had kept it in his mind all these years and we still cannot fathom out what it was.

My ex-manager Bobby Pattinson

Ann McKay in 1970
She gave me great inspiration

Me as Princess Balroubador in Aladdin at the Grand Theatre, Swansea in 1971

Chapter 13: Goodbye L Plates

We soon began to get into our stride touring the Northern clubs and somehow managed to acquire a white transit van which in those days was hip. We were cool, can you believe? Carlsbro equipment and a white transit van meant we were on our way!! However we always came back owing our Manager money!

This happy state of affairs continued until all change again and I was teamed up with twins Michael and John and now known as The Michael John trio, again doing regular gigs in the North East.

Whilst we were performing in Sunderland I got myself a boyfriend! He introduced us to this new pro digs that was opening in Sunderland and being run by a chap called Jimmy Butler. I got to know Jimmy and when I eventually parted company with Ron Watkins I returned to Sunderland with the intention of getting myself some work. I was going to get music written for me this time and use the resident bands in the clubs to back me.

Jimmy was absolutely fantastic, taking me round and introducing me to all the major agents in Sunderland from which I got plenty of work. I was now working for myself and very grateful to Jimmy Butler who became a very dear friend, always looking out for me. I even lived at his pro digs for a time.

It was about this time when things really began to kick off. I signed up to an extremely good and reputable agency who I believe are still operating now. Anyone in the business will have heard of Beverley Artistes. They were one of the big agencies and booked so many acts all over the North East, but were also booking for Night Clubs as well.

This resulted in my working seven nights a week in working men's clubs and sometimes I would be on what they called a 'double' which meant after I finished at the working men's club I would go straight on and do a spot at a night club. I would often work Sunday lunchtime too so on many occasions Sunday would see me doing three gigs. It was absolutely great.

My eighteenth birthday passed by fairly uneventfully. I was working in Newcastle upon Tyne doing the usual of performing at a working mans club then on to a nightclub afterwards with Michael and John. Of course I celebrated with a good few drinks. Not because I wanted to but because I felt I had to now I was 18!! The major thing that sticks out in my memory about my eighteenth was the pale blue Ford Anglia my lovely kind parents bought me. I can even remember the registration number YBX 938. Its funny I seem to be able to remember the registration number of quite a few of the cars I first owned.

Returning home for a visit one day, my Dad asked me if I would go with him to have a look at a car. When I saw it, I honestly thought it was a new one he had bought for himself. I really could not believe it when he said it was for me. It was a complete surprise and it was to become invaluable for travelling around the clubs and getting from A to B.

My Dad naturally taught me to drive, as he had some experience of teaching people to drive when he had a school of motoring. Dad had a Ford Zephyr which in those days was classed as a big car complete with column gear change and one continuous seat in the front. To me driving this thing was like driving a Sherman Tank, it was just so enormous and I stalled it on many an occasion in the middle of Carmarthen with a huge build up of cars behind me and Dad shouting in my ear, ".....Slowly, let the clutch out, slowly...!"

He actually got very irate and began to lose it a bit but eventually we would get going again. I think everyone goes through a bit of that when they first start driving. I can't remember why exactly, maybe Dad's nerves couldn't take any more but I went on to have further lessons with local driver Dai Mot. When I questioned his funny name with Dad he had to explain to me that Dai had a sign on the back of his car reading M.O.T.

Of course Mot was not his surname but it's quite common in Wales to give people the surname of their trade and maybe those of you who have read Dylan Thomas's Under Milk Wood will have seen some classic examples of this. We still do it now down in Wales and I am proudly known as Stevens The Voice or Thomas the Tonsils!!

Anyway with Dai Mot now teaching me it didn't take me all that long and happily I passed my test the first time. Dad was a perfectionist when it came to keeping the bodywork gleaming. We would polish the car which I found boring beyond belief and just when I was thanking GOD that we had finished this laborious chore, he would stand back, look at the car and say "Mia", reverting to his pet name for me since I was a baby.

"Mia," he would say, "we can get it better than this," and off we would go and start all over again.

I remember when I took off in my car up the Swansea Road out of Carmarthen, and back up to the North East, oh boy did I finally feel so independent and grown up. The world was finally my oyster!

So the car and I returned to the North East and my pro digs in Sunderland where I was living permanently at this stage. Being a pro digs it was full of acts, groups, comedians, male singers, female singers and by living amongst them and talking with them 24/7, I was now getting a proper chance to see how other artists work and what I learnt was invaluable. Also being young I continued having a ball. Each club in Sunderland would have its own special 'night'. Tuesday night was the 'in' night for the Manhattan Club and a group of us would regularly go along to see the John Miles set in the days before he made it. We thought they were brilliant and we were proved right!!

Because there was such an abundance of night clubs and working men's clubs, the mass of talent concentrated in that part of England was absolutely immense and if you couldn't learn your trade there and then, with all of that at your fingertips, you may as well forget it.

I heard about a showcase being put on for an agent called Dick Ray in Jersey who wanted artists for about five venues on the Island that were doing summer seasons, which was a lot for such a small island. I went along to the audition and was subsequently offered my very first summer season in 1970 in a small cabaret room in St Johns called La Belle Etoile which means the beautiful star. I've been there since and sadly the building no longer exists, it has all been flattened and there are houses there now.

The season started in April and finished in October and the highlight for me was the 'Battle of the Flowers'. For those of you who have never seen or heard of it, it really is something to behold. It is held annually, traditionally on the second Thursday of August and consists of music, funfairs, dancers, majorettes and of course a parade of flower floats flagged by various street entertainers.

Leading the parade that particular year were six mini cars each with a girl on top holding a letter of Jersey. I was in the leading mini holding the letter J, dressed in a bikini and trying to keep my balance as the car moved along the front in St Helier. I'm afraid even in those days I would not have made it as a glamour model!!

I was to share the bill with dancers, singers and two comedians and was fitted with the most amazingly beautiful costumes. I started busily rehearsing as not only was I doing my own stuff but singing and performing with the dancers. Big show numbers such as 'Before the Parade Passes By' from Hello Dolly. It was another massive learning curve. Mam and Dad and Dorrien flew out to see me for a holiday. My father was absolutely thrilled. I mean this was a big step up now from the working men's clubs and to see his daughter in a show with dancers made him so proud.

Whilst I had been working at the clubs I had been earning extremely good money. I worked hard for it of course but at the same time I was gaining a good solid reputation as a singer so I was able to command good fees. Unfortunately I had the worst fashion and make up sense you can imagine. I was absolutely hopeless. So now here I was amongst all these glamorous girls and scrutinising the way they applied their make up and how they dressed and from that every week I would use some of my hard earned cash to update my wardrobe. Out with the old and in with the new. I also quickly learnt how to do my make up properly.

There was a professional photographer on the island who used to come to La Belle Etoile and during the interval of the show I would have pictures taken with various members of the audience which would then be displayed on a board for the guests to buy. I didn't get paid as such but the photographer, apologies to him as I have forgotten his name, owned a hairdressers and I was able to have my hair done as often as I liked.

Well as you know ladies that is worth more than just a few pennies. I could have gone every day if I'd wanted to. I had numerous hair pieces in numerous styles, the lot, it was absolute heaven.

What I found hilarious and which totally cracked me up was upon my return home after the season, Mam proudly announced that she had "done a nice album of my summer season in Jersey," but when I was looking through it I wasn't really recognising anyone in the photos. Of course they must have been random audience members and when I questioned her about it, her explanation was, "Well I thought they were such lovely pictures of you so I bought them..." Cracking!

One of my favourite hair pieces was a long piece styled in masses of curls like Ann Mackay. Ann was a female vocalist who was appearing at The West Park Pavilion in St Helier and after seeing her work, became an artiste I really looked up to. I learnt a lot from her and she was really the only other female singer on the Island that summer.

She actually got married whilst we were there to the cousin of Ian from the Krankie's and I had the honour of being her bridesmaid. I think the original bridesmaid opted out and I was second choice but as anyone who knows me will testify I will take any chance to pose and strut!! I provided my own frock and wore it on stage afterwards no problem!

Ann's dress sense, make up style, song choice, and everything about her I admired. My act at the time was just drawing popular songs out of the top 20, so nothing very creative, but Ann was singing stuff I would never have thought of. I considered her to be so far ahead of where I was and certainly where I was trying to get to. I actually did nick her opening number for my new act! A song called "Get Ready"! She won't mind I'm sure!

She was about my age but she never went on to become famous. She doesn't even sing anymore and sadly the marriage was not to last! I last saw her a few years ago when we were doing The Best of British tour with the Krankies and she came along to see me. I also took the album of photos from that summer along to show Ian who immediately recognised his Aunty in one of them!!

Working at the Belle Etoile was a Welsh receptionist by the name of Pat Tipples. I know it sounds like something straight out of Hi De Hi but that truly was her name and what a great name! Pat was lovely and we got on fabulously well! At first I had my own room and I can't quite remember how it came about but I must have invited her to share my room. Well two girls sharing a room, you have never seen anything like it. Oh my god you should have seen the dressing table in that room, it was like World War Three. At that time I used to wear false eyelashes, two lots on the top and two on the bottom. If I leaned too far over, I fell over!! I looked like Spiderwoman! I used to have them all soaking in this half tumbler of water to get the glue off and it used to look horrendous.

We just weren't tidy, we were absolutely dreadful, but who wanted to be tidy! We were young and having fun but also working flat out. I worked every night of the week including Sundays and only had every other Sunday off. One night off in two weeks isn't much and I certainly wasn't going to spend it tidying my room. Instead we would spend hours on our night off getting ready and then out we would go. Jersey didn't know what had hit it!! Pat and I were incorrigible together. So much so that I managed to get her a job during the following year of 1971 as receptionist at the Maison Royale in Bournemouth where I was working and again we shared a flat for the summer.

It was a wonderful season though and I will never forget it. I would even say it was one of the most memorable years of my life in the music business outside of 1976 which was the year we won the Eurovision, as a) I was only 20 years of age and b) all the acts in our show would socialise together with all the acts from the other shows which was fantastic. People like Alan Fox who was very famous in the North East at the time. It's funny you could be extremely famous and popular in the North East but never heard of down South. There was also a wonderful sound impressionist called Mike Carter who could replicate the sound of jumbo jets by using just his hands and the microphone. People used to think he was miming but he wasn't. This was where I first met Bernie Clifton who was in another show. He and I had so much fun that summer and over the years whenever I've seen Bernie he always says 1970 was the best year.

I remember vividly on one occasion us all being down on the beach all night and watching the sun coming up. Somebody had brought a little cassette tape player and was playing 'Here Comes The Sun' by the Beatles whilst we were all being totally silly and carefree. We even had a chair sitting out in the sea and were cutting Bernie Clifton's hair. I don't know why, we weren't on drugs or anything. It perhaps would have been more fitting if we had been!! Going to bed and sleep was the last thing on our minds that memorable summer.

For me that summer was also a big turning point in my career because top of the bill in our show was an exceptionally good Northern comedian called Bobby Pattinson who offered to be my manager. He wasn't managing anyone else but thought he could get me some really good work. At the same time he arranged for the choreographer of the show, a lovely guy called Ken Wayne who became a good friend of mine, to put an act together for me. Goodbye to piddly piddly pop songs, I was now singing fantastic show songs by Streisand and the like. Not for me your top twenty hits anymore. I had medleys and choreography to learn. Ken taught me how to move and how to present myself on stage. I was developing class!

Jersey 1970

Mum, Dad and Dorrien making sure they have front row seats

Me with my lovely Dad

Me in my finale costume with
Ken Wayne our choreography man

Jersey 1970

Leading the parade of the Battle of the Flowers

Me in my Bathing Belles costume

Bournemouth Maison Royale Summer Season 1971

Chapter 14: Busy Road Ahead

After the Jersey season finished in 1970, Dick Ray, who was the only agent in Jersey at that time, took a few of us artistes and musicians to perform at the American bases in Germany, staying in Frankfurt. Whilst there my twenty first birthday passed by virtually unnoticed. One of those big cards with a satin covering in a white box that were very popular at the time arrived for me from Mam, Dad and my two brothers. I still have that card having kept it all these years. Other than that I didn't celebrate or mark the occasion in any way.

I didn't care though because I was enjoying myself so much. Oh how I loved performing to the Americans. We made good friends with some of the officers and were treated marvellously. One unforgettable night I had a standing ovation and luckily someone took a photograph so I could have it as a keepsake. Afterwards this enormous black guy who was at least six foot tall came up to me and in his lazy American drawl said:

"Honey, if I was closing my eyes, I swear you is BLACK..."!!

Oh well I was so chuffed wasn't I? I mean vocalists such as Aretha Franklin were my idols and I was trying my best to be a black singer, or at least emulate one.

While I enjoyed listening to any type of music or any artiste who was good, I was still struggling to find my own style and by now I'd gone through being Shirley Bassey, having bought a lot of her albums and sung quite a few of her songs. Perhaps a lot of you won't know her album material but whoever had written those songs was absolutely fantastic. Way back I used to sing a song off one of her albums called 'Yesterday I Heard The Rain' and at the time my Father would come along and watch me perform at a Night Club in Gorseinon.

He'd sit there in the front row while I was singing this song, and I could see the tears streaming down his face. I wasn't mature enough to recognise that he was genuinely touched by my performance. I've gotta be honest I think I was a bit late maturing generally. I'm just about starting now really! Anyway when I came off stage, I questioned why he was crying. No tact at all, straight in there with the brutal questioning. He then told me gently that I had sung this most beautiful song so beautifully that it made him cry. That moment changed a lot for me. I realised that music could reach deep into people's souls like nothing else could.

Next I moved on to Streisand. On her albums besides the obvious choice of songs that everybody knew might be a hit or the musical numbers like 'Don't Rain on My Parade', she also had really good quality songs. I like to think at that particular time, that singers going round the clubs doing what I was doing a few years previously were taking their material straight from the top twenty whereas I was looking for class now, hence looking at album tracks to find sophisticated songs that no-one else was singing on the circuit, and then have all the arrangements done for a full seven piece band, piano, bass, drums, lead guitar, trumpet, trombone and sax.

I quickly learnt that turning up at a night club with material like that gained you a lot of respect. I'm a great believer that in this business you learn by watching and listening to other people. Other people become your teacher. I always say to others or youngsters just starting out: "Never be afraid to watch, learn and listen, even if it is just for three minutes of your show, and you will learn something." And that is the philosophy I live by.

Anyway by the time I got to Germany I was very much at my Aretha stage. Consequently that comment from the lovely black American made my day and I haven't stopped telling people ever since!

I returned home with a new manager who was now getting me work in some of the top night clubs, places like Batley Variety Club, Wakefield Theatre Club, The Fiesta at Sheffield and supporting big names including Frankie Vaughan and Matt Monro.

One night whilst I was working at Batley Variety Club and supporting Neil Sedaka. As I came off stage, Neil himself came up to me and told me he thought I had the most amazing voice. He then told me he listened to me every night over the Tannoy whilst he was preparing for his own spot and he thought I was absolutely fantastic. Well I was bowled over by this; I thanked him graciously and explained I hadn't yet had a chance to see him work because I had to dash off afterwards to another club. However I didn't have to rush on Friday nights and promised I would stay behind to watch his act that Friday. That's great he replied and invited me round to his dressing room afterwards to say hello and have a drink.

Now Bobby was excited about this development and the fact that the great Neil Sedaka liked me and thought I was brilliant. He urged me to tell him that I had a recording contract but needed a song, convinced now that Neil Sedaka would write me a song. I had it all sorted out in my head and planned meticulously what I was going to say.

At the agreed time I went round to his dressing room. "Neil," I began, "I absolutely loved your show, it was brilliant. You know I'm on the verge of signing this big record deal myself but I'm having a problem finding an original song which of course has to be top quality". I went on to explain, barely pausing for breath.

I waited with huge anticipation for the offer I felt sure was coming my way as he turned round and replied, "Good luck honey when you do find your first...." Gutted isn't the word!

Another time Frankie Vaughan came up to me after hearing me sing.

"Nicky," he said, "I have to tell you I really believe one day you will be a big star!" Well can you imagine how I felt? I mean the great Frankie Vaughan!

It was only to be about four years later when I met him again, this time I was in Brotherhood of Man and we were doing a gig for the St John's Ambulance Centenary which I will come back to later, with the Queen in attendance. I went up to him excitedly, keen to reintroduce myself and prove to him that his prediction came true, only to discover he didn't remember me at all!! Not a flicker! I reminded him of our previous encounter of course and he was very polite but it was obvious he didn't know who on earth I was and I was certainly brought back down to earth that night! The fickle world of show business!

Bookings kept steadily coming in and the summer of 1971 saw me appearing at the Maison Royale, Bournemouth, a new cabaret supper club as they called it. I was met at Bournemouth Station upon my arrival and immediately taken for a costume fitting. What I hadn't realised was that besides doing my own act in my own outfit or whatever I wanted to wear, I was going to be involved in production numbers. The year before in Jersey whilst I was involved with the show numbers and wore lovely costumes, this was going to be a much bigger and greater extravaganza.

It's difficult to describe but oh boy what a luxurious and plush venue that was, it was beautiful. Everything was brand new, so much so that when we were rehearsing they were still finishing laying down the carpets. It all smelt brand new and as for the ladies toilets, they really were something else. There was this huge expanse of mirrors with a beautiful stool in front of each mirror.

In fact I am going to take the opportunity and confess right here and now that yes Father I did nick a stool from those toilets and took it home for my bedroom in Carmarthen! It was so beautiful; I just had to have one. I'm not quite sure how no-one noticed me but I do remember the show finishing and I just sneaked out of the back exit door. Pat Tipples my partner in crime was there ready and waiting with the boot of my car open!!

Local impresario Jackie Vincent was producing the show which was shaping up to be a flamboyant show with plenty of dancers and other artistes including Nigel Hopkins, trumpet player of Opp Knocks fame and my manager Bobby Pattinson. The costumes made by John Anthony were absolutely stunning. I had never worn anything so glamorous and beautiful. Jewellery, sequins, feathers, high heels, we had the lot.

We used to alternate weekly between two shows. For me my entrance for the second show was pure show business! I was dressed in a long velvet fitted dress, a plunging neckline adorned with rhinestones and slit to the thigh, with a long white fur stole, whilst being carried forward horizontally by two male dancers dressed in top hat and tails and singing that famous song 'Let Me Entertain You'. Move over Natalie Wood I truly felt like a Hollywood Star!! I have a photograph of this costume and when some years later I was to show it to my husband he actually said I looked like a Drag Act, so perhaps it was more a case of move over Danny La Rue darlings.....!!!

As I mentioned previously Pat Tipples and I rented rooms in somebody's house. We shared a bedroom and bathroom and then they let us have another bedroom which was turned into a lounge come kitchen. I say kitchen it was a case of two little hot plates. We were still just as untidy!

Amidst all this glamour and trash I met a rather lovely American man who came to see me in the show. He was a lot older than me and just happened to be a multi millionaire. He was also just happened to be married and so to save hurting anybody he shall remain nameless and I will refer to him as Simon.

I suppose you could say I was gullible or naive to fall for his charm but he obviously took a shine to me. Suddenly I was being showered with expensive gifts and flowers and being introduced to Dom Perignon Champagne!! Heady stuff for a young girl from the Valleys!!

He also took me to a Casino for the first time in my life and taught me what to do if I wanted to gamble. Everything he happened to put his money he won!! Anyway at the end of the night he told me I could keep the money! Well I was straight out to Chelsea Girl the next morning thinking I was the richest person in the world and bought every bloody polo neck that was going in every conceivable colour!

I knew he was married and that this wasn't a good idea but he persisted and kept sending me flowers to the dressing room. Bobby wasn't very happy about it either but by now I was getting a taste for this lifestyle.

When the season ended I was booked to do some gigs back home in Wales for twelve pounds a night. Simon insisted on driving me even though it cost him double my fee to drive me there in his Rolls Royce. He would travel from his house in Hampshire to pick me up from London and take me all the way home to my gigs and back again afterwards!

I duly introduced Simon to my parents, not daring to say he was married of course. When he picked them up in his Rolls Royce to take them to my gig, my Father thought this was amazing. It was hilarious because Dad would get in the car, having bought a cigar especially for the occasion to smoke in the Roller!! Frowned upon now of course, a cigarette was bad enough but there's Dad with a great big lardy on and suddenly he would totally change his accent and start talking like bloomin' Prince Charles!!

Mother meanwhile was in the back with her friend who could not stop laughing and referred to this as Father's 'egg in the throat voice'. He kept that Prince Charles "egg in the throat voice" up all flippin' night!!

From a Ford Zephyr to a Rolls Royce is a big step and Dad obviously just felt he had to buy a cigar and talk posh. That was typical Dad though. Even when we first got a telephone, his voice would change to his 'egg in the throat voice'. I still laugh out loud thinking about Dad in that car with that flippin' cigar. By the time we arrived at my gig that night, my Mam was a wreck in absolute hysterics. Simon meanwhile was appalled because the place didn't sell champagne which was also funny. I mean my parents were from an ordinary working class background and weren't used to going to places and asking for champagne. Mother would go to chapel and perhaps have sherry or wine with communion and Father would enjoy a pint. Champagne wouldn't impress them!

From then on I had a bit of a reputation for turning up at gigs in my Rolls Royce and they would all pull my leg about it! It didn't really last long but was great fun while it did!

As it was nearing my 22nd birthday, Simon was staying at a hotel in the Midlands on business and he asked me who I would like to see on my birthday. My wish was his command and he would arrange it, transport the lot. I named my few close friends of the time and lo and behold they all had first class tickets paid for on the train and overnight accommodation.

On the day itself I was booked into a Steiner Salon where I had my hair, nails and make up done, the works. Simon bought me an exquisite evening dress and shoes and at about 5pm he picked me up and I just felt like a Princess. I have to be honest at that point rightly or wrongly I didn't give a damn that he was married. I was lapping all this attention up and really enjoying this lifestyle.

We arrived at this beautiful hotel in Wolverhampton and I asked him what we were having for dinner. He told me prawns and caviar followed by roast pheasant and dessert of choice with cheeseboard etc. washed down of course with the obligatory Dom Perignon champagne and Gevrey-Chambertin wine, very nice too.

As I walked in to the restaurant still feeling like a Princess, there were all my lovely friends seated at tables. What I didn't see was a slight slope in the floor and as I made my big entrance posing and strutting, thinking I was the bee's knees, I promptly fell flat on my face. I got up very quickly I can tell you and shouted, "Who put that there....?" then carried on walking as if nothing had happened. I wouldn't mind but I hadn't had a drink at that point!

We then got on to the meal. Back in the 70s starters were invariably, orange juice, prawn cocktail or melon so I was quite familiar with prawns. When it came to the pheasant I turned to Simon, trying to be all posh and sophisticated.

"I thought we were having caviar..." to which he replied in his lazy drawl:

"Honey you've just eaten it..."

"Really...?" I questioned.

"Those little black things on top of the prawns...that's your caviar."

Well how the hell did I know? As luck would have it I hated the pheasant, it was far too rich for my liking but it really was a lovely evening all the same and my friends thoroughly enjoyed themselves.

Looking back at my time with Simon, I genuinely believe that although I was flattered by the attention and enjoyed the lifestyle he could offer me, I was also a little bit in love with him. I was always very happy in his company and certainly wasn't going to say no to his generous gifts. It did however run its natural course and no hearts were broken.

Years later in 1983 when I came back down to Bournemouth with Brotherhood of Man, I was at this bar with Ruth Madoc and Su Pollard and the rest of the Hi De Hi mob when suddenly I froze as Simon walked in with his entourage and a glamorous woman on his arm who certainly didn't look like his wife even though I had never met her.

Bearing in mind that I was now looking totally different to when we went out together, I kept my back firmly towards him when he suddenly began talking to Ruth who was next to me. He then asked her if she knew Nicky Stevens? Ruth although bemused was very good and she must have seen the expression on my face. She replied cagily that yes she knew me and he then told her that he had lived with me for two years. Did he heck! That was a bare faced lie from him but of course now I was famous wasn't I? I wasn't famous back then. I didn't dare turn round as I really did not want to speak to him.

At the end of 1971 Bobby got me the lead part in Aladdin, the pantomime at the Grand Theatre, Swansea. I didn't want to play a bloke and true to form told them so in no uncertain terms. I said I would be willing to play the Princess though. The producers reminded me that this wasn't the leading role but I didn't care. They then tried with, it's not as much money, but I insisted I didn't care and it was the Princess or nothing to which they reluctantly agreed. And so it was that I was Princess Balroubador and I was well happy. Not for me a thigh slapping bloke, I just could not have handled that at all. The panto was a marvellous success and ran for a very long season. Everyone said it was the best they had put on in years and referred to it for a long time afterwards. I lost count of the number of times my Mam and Dad came to see me in it, god love 'em. I could see Dad's face up there in the circle, he was so so proud.

They gave me the greatest support you could imagine. When I had first turned professional in 1967, Mother was very dubious about me working in places where people were drinking and smoking, even though she happily let Dad play the clubs! When they could see I was making a success of my career though she was fine about it and they were my biggest fans closely followed by my brothers.

We had Reg 'Confidentially' Dixon as the Dame, Eddie Caswell played the Emperor, and they ended up casting a male as Aladdin thank goodness. My inner Princess would have been mortified if it had been a woman! As it happened Barry Hopkins got the part and I quite fell in love with him until I found out he was gay.

Noel Talbot a very famous welsh comedian played Wishee Washee and a group from Liverpool, The Fourmost, were the Chinese policeman. In Aladdin the wicked baddy is Abanazaar and at one point in the pantomime he comes around selling his new lamps for old as anyone familiar with the story will know. Now I had a mischievous side to me and was very very naughty and if there was any opportunity to play a prank I'd be first in the queue to help anybody. On one occasion when Abanazaar came on with these lamps I just turned round and in my best exaggerated comedy Gladys Pugh voice said, ".... Ohh a pedlar how exciting......" and the whole theatre just erupted with laughter, even though this was years before Hi de Hi!

The next day there was a curt note on the notice board "Would Principals playing straight parts please play them straight". The point was taken!

That didn't stop us from having our fun though. Whenever The Fourmost came on stage and caught Aladdin and I together they would rush around blowing their whistles, waving their truncheons, and separate us. They would have to grab hold of my arm and pull me to one side. However they would also do stuff that wasn't necessarily in the script like grab hold of my arm and then swing me round five times. Well I must have liked it because I ended up in a relationship with Billy from The Fourmost, and we were together for some time!

Chapter 15: A New Direction?

By now Bobby was really trying his best for me, aiming to secure record deals and sending me to various auditions whilst I was still working the clubs but it just wasn't happening. I wasn't getting signed by anybody. It seemed like nobody wanted me.

Through Bobby, I had the honour of being invited to Northern Ireland in 1972 to do cabaret for the troops. When I told my parents, especially my Father, he asked me not to go because of course at that particular time the situation was extremely volatile and my Father naturally was very worried for my safety so I agreed not to go.

However the devil in me that always encourages me to do the complete opposite of what my parents want, just took over and I went anyway but didn't tell them! When we arrived at Belfast and came out of the airport I turned to the keyboard player and remarked that something must be going on as there were so many soldiers.

I then turned to this one particular soldier and asked if there was any trouble in the area at the moment to which he answered no, the reason they were all here was for our protection and that we were the responsibility of the British Army whilst we were there.

We had a military escort along the whole route to our hotel, with a lorry full of officers and soldiers up front then us in a transit style van and what they called a pig van behind us with the gunner on top. Once we arrived at the hotel I was told not to leave the premises at all and there would be soldiers in the car park all the time.

We were treated so well but did experience several episodes of hostility from people opposed to the troops being there. As we were driving through the streets, people would decide to spit at us or throw stones which left me with an overwhelming sense of sadness.

Our very first show was a hoot! I performed my first number which went down very well even though I felt quite nervous. There I was a young cabaret artiste with my little short frock, the only woman in a room full of red blooded soldiers. I needn't have worried though as they were absolutely fantastic. During my next song this alarm went off and the whole place just cleared. There was obviously trouble of sorts that they were all needed for but it only left a handful of people in the room! I just carried on regardless as if nothing had happened. A real trooper!!

The next day we had a very nice afternoon tea, held for us by the Officers. They showed us around the camp and we were allowed to climb up a ladder up onto this platform vantage point on the top of the high fence around the perimeter. As I was surveying my surroundings I was told that all of this was the notorious Creggan Estate and to be extremely careful as anyone could take a pot shot at us!

That's how severe the situation was out there at the time and we had performed our first show there the previous night with no idea of this! We were only there for a few days and when I returned I came clean to my Mam and Dad! I think they forgave me and were just glad I was home safely!!

It was explained to me while I was out there that the soldiers couldn't really enjoy spending the money they were earning while they were stationed there on social activities. They couldn't just go to restaurants or pubs or clubs as normal and let their hair down. Instead they would pool some of their money in a kitty and save it so that when they returned home from their tour of duty they would have a lovely big night out. This particular regiment had a dinner dance and they invited me which made me feel very proud and honoured. I was invited as a guest but must admit to getting up and giving them a song after a few vodkas! It was a great evening!

Also in 1972 and some 5 or 6 years after my original audition I went along with some trepidation to try again for Hughie Green's Opportunity Knocks. Luckily for me this time Hughie Green wasn't there and it was the Producer of the show holding the auditions instead. Anyway I got the gig and I was on the show. My song choice was Barbara Streisand's version of 'Happy Days Are Here Again', a fabulous big ballad.

What with that and my choreography courtesy of Ken Wayne, they were so impressed that they actually asked me for the song I would be singing the following week should I win which was that great number from Jesus Christ Superstar, 'I Don't Know How To Love Him'.

Now at this particular time on Opportunity Knocks an act that kept winning week after week was a young six year old boy playing the drums and his Father on the organ. They went under the name of Steven Smith and Father!! Well I had no chance did I? I knew it.

The way Opportunity Knocks used to work was that each act appearing would have what they called a 'sponsor', basically a close friend or family member who would introduce the act and give a little bit of background information on them. Hughie would talk to the sponsor and generally ask a few questions about the act we were about to watch and ask what the connection was and so on and so forth.

My manager elected to be my sponsor so I asked my Father's advice about what he could say to Hughie and if there was anything interesting in our family history perhaps. After a brief pause Father then revealed to me that my Great Great Grandfather wrote the famous song 'Men of Harlech'. I was absolutely astounded at this revelation. I mean this was brilliant and something I had no idea of at all. I told Bobby who was equally impressed and before we knew it Hughie Green was introducing me as, "Ladies and gentleman, the young lady whose Great Great Grandfather wrote Men of Harlech ....Opportunity Knocks......."

I had no idea at the time that this was one of my Dad's almighty wind ups did I!! In fact I didn't find out the truth until after my Father had died some years later! Apparently he was laughing his head off about the whole thing and couldn't believe I had fallen for it and then told Hughie Green who broadcast it to the nation! It was my older brother Elvyn who finally told me. When the results came out and incidentally I came second to Steven Smith and Father, there was Hughie announcing that in second place yes its the young lady whose Great Great Grandfather wrote 'Men of Harlech'.

Hot on the heels of my appearance on Opp Knocks Bobby took me for an audition in London to play the part of Carmen in a new musical just coming out called 'Rock Carmen'. I was recalled three times for this but I was up against another girl who was a very good singer called Terry Stevens.

On the final call back it was down to the two of us and I remember listening to her through the door and thinking she was so good that I didn't expect to get the part at all. I went in to sing my piece and one of the guys holding the audition noted I was Welsh and asked me to confirm this. He then asked if I knew a song called 'David of the White Rock'. Well of course I did. He then asked if I could sing it in Welsh. Again, and feeling quite pleased with myself I confirmed that yes I could.

I went on to sing it for him and often wonder if it was that song that got me the part? It was so close between us and I thought this other girl had it in the bag. So maybe it just tipped the boat a little in my favour? Although I got the part the money was a pittance and I couldn't possibly live on it. My Ford Anglia had sadly gone to Ford Anglia heaven and I had a brand new Vauxhall Ventura, on hire purchase, so I would not have been able to afford any accommodation on the money they were offering me and I reluctantly turned it down. As far as I know 'Rock Carmen' never took off. We were told it was going to start off at The Roundhouse Chalk Farm, the legendary venue in Camden, but I never heard of it after that.

That same day Bobby took me to see a guy called Don Arden who as many of you may now know is Sharon Osbourne's father. Bobby knew Don and thought it would be a good idea to go along to his office and play the tapes of my songs to him. While Don was playing my tape a chap called Eric Hall walked in. We made our introductions, exchanged all the usual stuff and that was that.

The next thing was we got a phone call from a chap called Tony Hiller who was Eric Hall's Uncle. Eric had immediately got on to him saying he had found a great girl singer and he wanted to know if I would be interested in auditioning to join a group called Brotherhood of Man. Bobby and I discussed this. Of course I knew of Brotherhood of Man as they had a hit with 'United We Stand' but I was unsure as I had no idea what sort of group it was going to be. I didn't really want to get involved in a group again with long haired rocking guitarists projecting that sort of image. As far as I was concerned I had done that and was ready to move on in my career.

Tony Hiller phoned a couple more times and we found out that the group would consist of four members: two boys and two girls doing vocal harmonies with no musicians. I liked the sound of that. When I look back I always find that strange because there I was trying to forge ahead with my solo career, so why did I suddenly want to dive into a group?

I've never been able to answer that question, I was earning tremendous money and definitely on my way up. Why take the risk? I couldn't help thinking though when I heard 'United We Stand' how fabulous they sounded with terrific vocals. Maybe in my head I was yearning to be a recording artist and this was a way in for me, I don't know.

I met up with Tony Hiller and found out what it was all about. The

Brotherhood of Man as they were at that point, were all session singers comprising of Sue and Sunny who were two sisters, Sunny later went on to become a solo artist in her own right and perhaps best known for Doctors Orders. Johnny Goodison, and Russell Stone completed the line up.

They were the best in the business at the time, you couldn't top them. They also had a few records in the charts simultaneously under different names including Edison Lighthouse. Brotherhood of Man came under the Tony Hiller umbrella. Of course there was mileage to be made from the name because 'United We Stand' had been a huge hit. The session singers were being paid great money and didn't so much as have to leave London. They had done a few television appearances but from what we could gather they weren't interested in travelling, at least that's what I was told at the time.

Tony was therefore looking for four singers to take their place. He already had Martin Lee and Lee Sheriden who were known to him as song writers and artists and were already professionally involved with him. I duly met them both in Tony's office and we hit it off immediately. He'd now found myself and another girl singer called Eleanor Keenan. We tried out a few songs in the studio, working out new concepts to see what we sounded like and if our voices blended.

However Eleanor decided that with her current work load she could not commit to the time involved so Martin, Lee and I carried on as a three trying out different styles and rehearsing together when we could. In the meantime we all had our own commitments. I carried on as a cabaret singer, Martin was with a big dance band called The Johnny Howard Band and Lee was in his own resident band at the Top Rank in Bristol, singing and playing guitar.

In Northern Ireland with the Troops, 1972

Chapter 16: All Change

As luck would have it at around this time I was given the opportunity of working in South Africa. Bobby told me I would be working in what was then Rhodesia and which is now Zimbabwe. I would be working in Salisbury which is now Harare, Bulawayo and Durban! This was now new territory indeed in every sense! I had never even been to an airport before! I'd flown from Cardiff to Jersey on a little propeller job but that was it!!

Here I was, 22 years of age going away for several months all told, and that is all the information I had as I boarded my flight to Africa. That, and the name and telephone number of the agent Miles Knox, who would be meeting me at the other end when I arrived. Good job I was also adventurous and totally fearless!

Elvyn and now boyfriend Billy saw me off at Heathrow airport. I remember ringing my parents first and being in tears whilst on the phone to my father with my brother next to me telling me not to start him off or we would all be crying. This was a big big deal in those days, unlike now. However my overriding thought was I was out in the big wide world and about to embark on the adventure of my life.

I checked in, said my goodbyes, got through passport control and stood there alone and totally at a loss as to what to do next. I didn't have a clue where to go or what to do. I recall going up to this man and asking where I should go to catch a plane to Salisbury? Luckily he kindly explained about the whole process for which I was very grateful and when I eventually got on the plane I thought it was never ending as I walked along looking for my seat. Of course it was a jumbo and unlike anything I had seen let alone been on before! I could not get over being served food and having a small bottle of wine with the meal. It was wondrous. I didn't know things like this happened on planes. What an eye opener that trip proved to be. It was like I'd come from cave land!

I sat next to a friendly chap by the name of Bob Tanner who was the Manager of the Queens Hotel in Leeds. We got talking on the long journey which helped pass the time and he and his fellow passenger ended up coming to see me work! It's funny what small seemingly insignificant things just stick in your mind and yet at other times I have a memory like a sieve?!

Our plane had to stop en route to Salisbury, I can't remember where, and thankfully we were able to get out and stretch our legs a bit. The plane was on the tarmac and we were able to go for a drink. Looking back it must have been quite a small airport because we had no big walk ways. As I came down the steps of this plane, I just kept walking backwards in awe as I was just trying to absorb the enormity of this jumbo up close as I hadn't actually seen it on the ground back at Heathrow. I knew absolutely nothing about planes and I really could not get over it. It quite literally took my breath away to think that I was up in the air on that.

When we eventually landed in Salisbury, Miles Knox was waiting for me, everything went to plan, and he took me to my hotel. Within a day and a half I started to lose my voice and began to have a lot of difficulty performing out there, struggling with a bad throat. As hard as I tried I could not get on top of it, and it was spoiling things somewhat for me. I wasn't very happy about it. Here I was in South Africa, a huge chance for me and I wasn't able to give it my all. I was later to find out because of geographically where it is on a high central plateau, a lot of people have had similar trouble with throats. I think it has something to do with the oxygen level and altitude or something along those lines but all I knew at the time was I couldn't shake this thing off and I was gutted.

On the plus side I was getting to meet a whole new load of other acts again who were also all out there working from the UK. My social life out there was fantastic. One morning a load of us got up at 5.00 am and off we drove out to a game reserve to watch the sun coming up and see all the animals, which I found so exciting. There was lots of serious partying too but it was all good clean fun with genuinely lovely people, including a great comic called Lol Crockett who was incredibly funny and I used to find tremendously entertaining.

On the final night of my stint in Salisbury I had a leaving party and after my last singing spot a crowd of us went along to this nightclub owned by a chap called Uppy, and ended up staying there for the entire night. This resulted in me being driven straight from the club to the airport first thing the next morning, to fly down to Durban for the next leg of my 'tour'. I got changed out of evening dress into jeans and tee shirt in the back of the car, got to the airport, onto the plane and promptly slept all the way to Durban.

Once there all I knew this time was I had to go to the Mayfair Hotel in Smith Street. Again totally fearless, because of course by now I was a seasoned traveller wasn't I? With two plane flights under my belt I knew the deal now! I got a cab to the hotel, they showed me to my room and I was told my band call would be at such and such a time the following day.

This particular venue was a small cabaret room/restaurant within the hotel. I was now shattered as I had been up all the previous night so thought I would go to bed and unpack later. I hadn't been asleep long when there was a knock on my door and this larger than life girl came bursting in. She introduced herself and announced that she lived at the hotel too and that she had a hairdressing salon on the beach. Apparently she had been looking forward to having a girl singer for company and was keen to help me unpack immediately.

Suddenly I was being totally organised by this very bubbly girl by the name of Robyn that I actually got on very well with. She promptly showed me around Durban, took me down to the beach and showed me where her shop was. I was there for a few weeks in total at the Mayfair and literally spent every single day on the beach.

My new friend Robyn knew all the beach guards, of which there were many as Durban had lots of surfers. One day I was happily sunbathing as per usual only to be rudely interrupted as a bucket of water was poured over me by these particular beach guards who I had not met before, and who obviously thought this was hilarious. Harmless fun and I soon got friendly with them hanging out together every single day thereafter. They even brought their girlfriends and parents to see my show.

They would often take me out on the water and taught me how to body surf. They would help position me so I would really catch the wave and literally come in on top of the wave all the way. What a feeling! One day they were busy doing something and I decided to go out and do this body surfing thing on my own. I mean how hard could it be I reasoned to myself? All seemed relatively calm at first until all of a sudden I looked behind me and "OH MY GOD", it was like Mount Everest was thundering towards me. I could see the gigantic wave start to froth at the top and started desperately paddling backwards as fast as I could knowing I had to catch this.

Needless to say I totally missed it and what I can only describe as a tonnage of water totally crashed on top of me, tossed me round like a rag doll and then pinned me down on the ocean bed, taking me all the way in whilst still pinned down. I was very lucky not to drown and when I got to the shore line, my bikini bottom was off and my top was hanging around me. A small embarrassment to suffer when I think what could have happened. That was it as far as I was concerned; I never went out again and have total and utter respect for the sea. In fact just recently I heard this same thing has happened to a friend of mine in Australia, but he wasn't so lucky and he broke his clavicle.

After my lucky escape I was even more intent on having as much fun as possible, so what did Nicky do? What I do best of course, I met somebody and fell in love while poor Billy was still at home waiting for me. I was very naughty but I was young....what can I say? Like all young girls I could fall in love at the drop of a hat. I have always admitted that about myself, that I fall in love much too easily.

Life was good and I was relishing every moment. As my contract finished, an agent out there called Peter Hubbard who booked acts for the Southern Sun Hotels offered me a two year contract singing at all his hotels. I was sorely tempted mainly because I had a new boyfriend who lived there and by now I was staying at his place, with his Mam.

Strangely I wasn't really missing home and was seriously considering staying on there. I loved South Africa with a passion. I learned to accept apartheid because I had to. The way I saw it was if I loved the country, I had to love the way that it was. I did find it very sad though when I saw benches for 'whites only' and toilets for 'whites only' but took the view that there was absolutely nothing I could do about it and I just had to go along with it. However, something niggled and I was unsure if I really wanted to stay for that length of time, so didn't give Peter an immediate answer.

After Durban I moved on to Bulawayo thus wrenched away from my new love. I also left behind this great social life only to find myself staying in the most dreadful place with one room, no carpet and an iron bedstead. The bathroom was on the floor below. I spent most of the time in tears and felt very alone.

My life saver was a chap back in Carmarthen called Doug Maynard who owned a Sports Shop near where we lived. Once he'd known I was coming out to South Africa he told me that if I ever went to Bulawayo his brother Gary lived there and I was to make sure I looked him up as he'd be thrilled to see a Carmarthen girl out there. Luckily I remembered this!

So there I was in this dive of a hotel if you could call it that and I made the easy decision to try and find Gary Maynard. I phoned him only to discover he was just around the corner! We sat down over a cup of tea and I explained who I was and where I was staying. He thought this was fantastic and immediately packed up work for the day taking me around all the Welsh contingency of Bulawayo, introducing me to various people and insisted I went home with him to meet his English wife Margot.

Their beautiful bungalow was in its own grounds with a swimming pool, a necessity in the blazing heat. As we arrived Margot was sat out on the balcony with some friends and in that brief moment she must have wondered why her husband was bringing home a young girl?

Gary introduced me to his family, we had a meal and they all came down to the show to see me working and when I came off stage after my act, Gary and his neighbour Geoff immediately came up to me and told me we were going back to my hotel room but that I wasn't coming in. I wasn't sure what they meant until they announced that I would never step foot in that room again and that they were going to pack up all my things. They insisted from that moment on I would stay with them while I was there. How could I refuse such a generous order?

We soon settled into a routine. Gary went to work every day. I would do two shows a night, an early and a late and he would take me down each night, sit there while I did my first show, bring me back home, we would have a meal, then he would take me down for my late show and bring me back home at the end of the night. I will always appreciate their kindness and hospitality and making my stay so much better than it could have been.

They took me sightseeing including a trip to a game reserve called 'Wankie' which of course I found very very entertaining. I even got a sticker saying "I've been to Wankie" which I proudly displayed on my car until it disintegrated!!

Gary was also keen to arrange for me to go to Victoria Falls whilst I was there or Vicky Falls as the Africans call them. He wasn't able to accompany me but he thought it would be a great experience for me to go there, stay a couple of nights, see the Falls and then come back. He knew an old chap who was well into his 70s who worked for the tourist board there and was a good friend of his. Apparently he was a bit doddery and couldn't walk so well but he was going to meet me and sort me out regarding the tour. I was due to fly from Bulawayo to Victoria Falls and was told that this chap would have my name and hold it up on a piece of paper so I would know it was him. Unbeknown to me this was a big wind up and there to meet me was this very handsome thirty year old guide! However, I can't say I minded too much and when I explained to this 'guide' what I had been expecting we both agreed this was typical of Gary.

The Falls themselves were absolutely spectacular. I believe I am right in saying they are wider across than Niagara Falls but don't drop as far down. In the evening there was a Sundowner cruise up the Zambezi River. We set off as the name suggests at the time of evening when the sun was still up but was getting low in the sky. We had a few American tourists on board with us and I suppose the trip lasted about one and a half hours in total with drinks were served along the way.

The sounds of the African night and the array of different animals that could be heard was absolutely incredible and will remain with me for life. We could see hippos and crocodiles in the water minding their own business and enjoying their natural habitat as we cruised past them. I was in awe of the situation I found myself in and I remember incredulously thinking to myself that I was only 22 and leading the most amazing life, getting to see places I had only ever heard of and never in a million years dreamed I would visit. All the way to Africa from Carmarthen. Not bad for little Helen Maria!

However I was Nicky Stevens now and in true Nicky form I got carried away with all the wonder of it all, drank far too much and ended up fully clothed with all the Americans in the swimming pool at the end of the night. But hey I was young!

I had my 23rd birthday whilst there and the Maynard family arranged a marvellous birthday cake for me, which had Carmarthen iced on one side and Bulawayo on the other side. Some friends of theirs owned a Chinese restaurant and we all went there for a wonderful slap up buffet. They really did push the boat out for me.

They had a lovely black maid/cook called Maggie who lived in a little one roomed bungalow, in their grounds and whom they treated extremely well. She crocheted me a little white dressing table set comprising of a big mat and two little ones. It was a beautiful present which I still have today.

Gary was a highly respected man in Bulawayo who knew a lot of people and somehow got me an invite to the Mayor's Parlour in Bulawayo where I was given a greetings letter from the Mayor to take home to the Mayor of Carmarthen and read out to the people of Carmarthen which I thought was a lovely gesture.

Eventually I returned to Durban and over the moon to see my new found boyfriend again. While I was happy to be back it was now crunch time. The contract was up and it was time to fly home. Should I stay or should I go? Should I take the two year contract with Southern Sun Hotels or return and take a further gamble with my career.

Two things helped me eventually decide. I had the first chance in a long time to spend Christmas with my Mam and Dad. I must admit I was on a bit of a guilt trip about not having been home for Christmas for a few years. When I later told my parents this my Dad assured me I could have stayed and it would have been alright, they would have understood. However, for some reason I couldn't shake the guilt. The other thing I kept thinking was that I had started on the whole Brotherhood of Man project which I was still interested in pursuing.

Were both these things enough though to drag me away from my new found love? Answer, yes!! And I have never regretted it. Career wise 'Brotherhood' began to gather momentum. Billy and I, how shall we say, didn't rekindle our relationship and I'm not proud of the way I behaved towards him. But lastly and most importantly it was to be the last Christmas I was ever to spend with my Father.

On the Zambezi River with a local guide 1972

Robyn and me in South Africa 1972

Club Royale Carmarthen 1972
Taken after handing a letter of greetings from the Mayor of Bulawayo
Left to right: dad, Mum, me, Dorrien

Bulawayo 1972

Receiving a letter from the Mayor
to bring home to Carmarthen

With my lovely friend Gary Maynard

Taking a bow at my show in Club Royale Carmarthen
after returning from South Africa

Chapter 17: Clear Road Ahead

Settled back in the UK, I picked up exactly where I left off and began to throw myself into my new venture with Brotherhood of Man. Martin, Lee and I had been playing around with songs and had done a couple of recordings, such as 'Where Are You Going To My Love' done by the original Brotherhood of Man to see how our voices blended, but we were still minus our second female vocalist. We had a radio broadcast booked for the BBC and Martin had sent a tape along of the song we were going to record to Sandra a female band singer he had come across previously. Martin remembered seeing her singing with a band, thought she would be perfect to complete our line up and managed to get in touch with her. I was the only one who had worked as a solo cabaret artist.

The song was meant to be a male and female duet vocal with the chorus line. Martin would sing the male vocal, and I was to take the female vocal which was very high and soulful. As Sandra has since said, when she heard this tape she immediately assumed I was black, just like the American soldier a few years earlier! She'd thought she would contrast well with a black singer as she was very white and blonde. Of course this pleased me greatly didn't it! I mean just call me Miss Franklyn! Again!

Sandra in turn was delighted that Martin had recommended her. They had spoken at length on the phone and Martin was very enthusiastic about the whole idea.

My first ever memory of meeting Sandra was priceless! It was 1973 and we were in our Manager, Tony Hiller's office in Denmark Street in London or Tin Pan Alley as it was known in those days, when in walked this very and I mean very bubbly blonde with Carmen heated rollers tucked underneath her arm. I thought to myself, hello what do we have here.

"Oh hello I'm looking for Martin Lee..." she opened with in this broad Yorkshire accent, "and where can I plug me rollers in I need to do my hair....!"

I immediately thought she was so different from anybody I'd met before. All these years later and knowing her so well, that meeting summed up Sandra totally and she is still the same! Sandra herself loves to tell people that when we met I towered above her. This was because on that very first meeting I was wearing probably my most favourite shoes of the 70s which were pastel pink brogues with six inch platform heels. They were to die for! God knows how, but I used to drive in them with no problem! The second time we met I towered beneath her as for some reason I had hush puppies on. She couldn't believe how much I'd shrunk!

The end result of that meeting was a unanimous decision. Her voice blended exceptionally well with the rest of us, it was a lower pitch to mine which created a good sound and gave the treble and the bass with the boys covering the alto and tenor. It was the perfect four. We liked her very much as a person too so she was in. Three became four and we embarked upon a tight schedule of rehearsals.

Sandra and I initially rented a bedsit each in Streatham which consisted of one room and a shared bathroom and toilet. I thought Sandra's was better than mine but she didn't like it at all. I had my very own fridge and kitchen units and I recall going out shopping and buying enough food for three weeks just to fill that fridge up. Utterly ridiculous I know but I had my own pad now and I had to buy food! It didn't occur to me that I might not eat it all before the sell by date. Having lived mainly in pro digs up until now and going back to my parents in between times, I now felt very independent, but we were both homesick.

We discovered a friend of my cousin had refurbished a very large Victorian style house in Brondesbury Park, London with huge rooms, so Sandra and I decided to move in together into the downstairs flat. Two very large bedrooms, a huge lounge, kitchen, bathroom, it was ideal. We were the first tenants so everything was brand new as well.

We were rehearsing our dance moves in a scouts hut in Enfield, Middlesex daily so of course it was important that we all had to be in one spot. I stopped all my solo cabaret work and Martin got me a job as a soloist in the band he was with, The Johnny Howard Big Band.

Martin was also a soloist along with a couple of others. Lee bless his heart was at the Top Rank in Bristol with his own band and he would travel up from Bristol every morning to North London, rehearse with us and travel back ready for his evening gig.

We rehearsed with our drummer Paul Robinson who also happened to be Sandra's boyfriend at the time. Eventually Tony brought in Guy Luteman who was working on a programme called Lift Off with Ayshea Brough and those famous puppets Ollie Beak and Fred Barker. Guy came in to do the choreography for all our songs. That was very much the thing in the 70s. If you were a group you were choreographed. Lee wasn't very comfortable with the dance moves as he freely admits to this day. He wasn't a natural mover and really had to work hard on his bit. He did marvellously well and it all came together.

We had these moves called crutch bumps, which I suppose are hip thrusts, and a bit like the move in the Time Warp. We had so many laughs about trying to get the hang of this move and even now just thinking about it brings that familiar uncontrollable fit of giggles rising to the surface. After forty years together I can honestly say I do not laugh with anybody else the way I laugh when the four of us are together. We truly are like a family, warts and all!

Once we had our own flat the boys would come round there every day to rehearse the vocals. In those days we used to have a tape recorder, a little square box with a microphone, where we could play and record what we were doing.

There was this one particular song called 'Do Your Thing' where I had quite a high part to sing. When I got to that section I really went for it and used to overpower everyone else's vocals, subsequently when we played it back on this little machine all you could hear was me belting this out with everyone else muffled in the background.

Now we weren't in a 24 track recording studio so the others just kept making me stand further and further away from the microphone until eventually I ended up in a cupboard in the lounge. The balance was perfect! Those vocals back then were certainly very high! It's a wonder Martin is still talking now from those high notes he used to have to reach!

We got to the point where we had rehearsed and rehearsed and rehearsed and thought we were absolutely perfect. We were confident and ready for our band and Tony brought one in. The whole set up complete with microphones and leads fell apart as we got tangled up in wires whilst trying our dance moves. We hadn't thought to rehearse with microphones and leads! And so we were back to the drawing board to resume rehearsing but this time incorporating the microphones and leads and feeling a little deflated. As we know now, that's all part of getting a show together and getting it right, and is also the part that the audience doesn't see. They see the end result which may only be only 45 minutes and probably wish they could earn similar money for that period of time. They don't realise the hours and hours of preparation involved.

I suppose it took us around three months to get everything polished and ready to go on the road, with just under an hour's worth of material. Not bad for four people who had never worked together before, and had to learn harmonies and dance steps from scratch. We were ready now to go out and get ourselves kitted out in our first stage outfits.

Sandra and I headed straight to Oxford Street and the Kings Road and got ourselves some lovely Ossie Clarke creations. Ossie Clarke was the big designer name of the day and his designs were made with the most wonderful fabric, always bordered with silk round the edges. The boys ended up with outfits which were typical of the day with ruffles up the front of the shirt and the piping down the side of the trousers. We were very much in control of what we wore then and have been ever since.

That's more than I could say for the act itself though, although luckily I thought it was brilliant. It was already written and scored and we were told what we were to sing. Colin Fretchter, a brilliant musician, was our Musical Director and arranged all our harmonies. He helped us a heck of a lot in the early days of our career and was somebody that we looked up to enormously. He arranged the harmony vocal and the orchestration for what I still think is one of the best Brotherhood of Man vocals that we have ever done. 'He Aint Heavy He's My Brother' was on our very first album, and is a close four part harmony vocal all the way through. I know it was at the beginning of the 70s and later on we recorded loads of other great songs on our albums but when I hear that one in particular, our voices when split four ways sound so pure somehow, almost virginal. That's the only way I can describe it. For me it's the raw Brotherhood, and absolutely spot on. Nobody as far as I know has done a version like it since, I am so proud of it.

Anyway in our original act we covered a lot of the older material like United We Stand, Where Are You Going To My Love, Reach Out Your Hand which were all from the original Brotherhood of Man. Later, after the success of Save Your Kisses for Me, then obviously the style of songs were to change immensely.

If I knew then what I know now, recording wise and act wise I would have spoken up more. However, back then I always thought that what I was told to do and what I was told to record was set in stone with no room for negotiation.

When we got down to the business of recording further down the line, I didn't believe I had any right at all to voice my opinion which of course was rubbish. I know better now! There are some songs that I would never ever have been part of, if truth be told, if I had just had the strength to say "No I am not recording that!"

As the weeks went by we realised we couldn't really afford our flat and Sandra suggested that we go and talk to Mr Morgan who was our welsh landlord, and ask if he would reduce the rent. Now one of the many things I love about Sandra is she is not afraid to put her point across and say something is unacceptable, and to ask for an explanation if she feels an injustice. I on the other hand thought it highly unlikely he would reduce the rent. Everything was brand new, the furniture, the carpets. No way was he going to suddenly take a cut in money! Sandra insisted we go anyway. We had nothing to lose as we knew we couldn't stay there any longer. She said that I was to do all the talking as I was so good at it! I agreed and we walked in through the door, I said hello and then didn't utter another word as Sandra never drew breath!

Mr Morgan was a lovely man and I think he indulged us for as long as he did because he found Sandra so amusing and enjoyed the fact she had the gall to tell him we couldn't afford his rent and could he bring it down a bit please! She explained our whole sorry tale so honestly and with such sincerity, hoping that he would see our plight that I could see where she was coming from and I was mesmerised by her story. Both Mr Morgan and I listened intently to every word she said. I nodded encouragement whilst he smiled affectionately until she had completely finished, and didn't seem at all annoyed.

"I see," he said eventually, "so you can't afford the rent, it's too much is it?", as we nodded vigorously, all wide eyed innocence. He then promptly dashed any glimmer of hope we may have had by flatly refusing our plea. Believe me when I say Sandra should have won the case on honesty and sincerity alone. It truly was a five star performance and I have never forgotten it although she probably has!

Meanwhile Tony Hiller got us our first gig in April 1973, which was actually a television show in Belgium called The Knokke Television Festival. From what I can remember it was a competition of various TV variety programmes and we were representing Belgium! For the life of me I can't remember why?! The Fortunes were also on the bill.

We just did the two numbers for that, but our first major gig was in the late autumn of 1973 and was to be our first live performance on stage in Baileys, Hull. We stayed in pro digs and I'm not exaggerating when I say we were just like little kids. You would never have thought we were all in our 20s. It was like staying away from home on a school trip, spiking each others beds and silly pranks like that. I think we put coat hangers in Sandra's bed, made an apple pie bed for one of the boys, all daft things and very childish.

The first night we went on stage I was being a bit of a Jack the lad and thought I knew it all as I had done cabaret before, whereas the others had been band singers. I mean I was an experienced cabaret artiste imparting my expertise by trying to build up their confidence, telling them to relax and how much they would love it and people would be actually watching them and not just dancing to their music.

My words of wisdom worked!! Martin, Sandra and Lee did the act perfectly and I cocked up?! It was a choreography mistake where I went one way and the others went the other! The most glaringly obvious mistake you have ever seen in your life. I will say this when I make a boo boo, I really make them! The worst thing was seeing them trying not to laugh on stage at me Madame Big Mouth!! I deserved it and boy did we laugh afterwards.

The one thing we did establish from day one of rehearsals in the Scout Hut was that we were all four very different characters but all on the same wonderful wavelength sharing the same sense of humour. When I am with them I can be crying with laughter within five seconds flat, silly things that probably others wouldn't find funny. Just lovely 'in group' humour which I'm convinced has kept us going strong over the 40 plus years we have been together now.

Joking aside, I had stayed in pro digs before and was used to how it worked but it was all new to the others. We have very fond memories of a lovely lady in Liverpool called Anna Hall who provided Bed and Breakfast only, meaning in theory that we had to sort out our own evening meal.

However our schedule meant we used to get back to the digs so late at night and then subsequently get up so late that we made a deal with her to have our breakfast at dinner time which was 5 o'clock in the afternoon!! It was a great arrangement. We also got to know her son Derek very well and he still comes to see our shows to this day along with his lovely wife Sarah.

Len and Irene Beech were another couple who took us under their wing, and we stayed with them in Erdington, Birmingham. I introduced them to everyone as I had stayed there previously when I was on the road on my own. Indeed many an artist stayed there over the years and not surprisingly as it was the most beautiful place and Irene the most wonderful cook. It was like being at home with your Mam and when you are away from home for long stretches at a time, you certainly appreciate home comforts and home cooked food. Of course not all pro digs were great, some were distinctly average and some you would try out but never return to. People like Anna Hall and Len and Irene Beech were the crème de la crème, they made sure you were welcomed and felt properly at home. This meant a lot especially for a woman on her own.

By now we were working pretty constantly up and down the country with barely a night off. Some of you may be old enough to remember the Bailey's Clubs which were dotted around the country. We worked a lot of those, where you would open on a Sunday night and finish on a Saturday. In those situations it was just us appearing on the bill. Occasionally you might have one other artiste, but usually it was just us.

We would do our act for about an hour, sometimes going on as late as 11pm.

Club land in those days was really big business. Not only was work available for seven nights a week but there was also a full audience seven nights a week. It was a place people could relax and have a drink, eat dinner, watch an artiste perform, then perhaps round the evening off with a bit of dancing. The whole scene was flourishing, not just for artistes but for the club owners themselves. We worked in some wonderful theatre clubs all over the country and all open seven nights a week. This current work schedule was all on the back of United We Stand and the fame that it had given to the name 'Brotherhood of Man' at this point.

Although I was taking recordings home for him to listen to, my father only ever saw one of our gigs and that was in a club in the Welsh Valleys. Unfortunately the sound wasn't very good, it was playing up a lot that night and when we came off stage my Father told me that it was apparent something was wrong and he could see things weren't right for us on the stage but nevertheless he could also see that we were a very good act.

Sandra often recalls when she was at the bar that night ordering a drink, this man came up to her and offered to buy her one which of course she declined as she didn't know him from Adam. He slammed his hand on the bar and insisted..."Yes, I will buy you drink!" and she looked at him puzzled, "because I'm Nicky's father!"

That sadly was to be the only occasion they ever met him. However when we released our first single in January 1974, 'When Love Catches Up On You', the big single as we called it, and I took it home, Dad played it over and over again on the record player, constantly lifting the arm and placing it at the beginning again. I even overheard him saying to my Mam, "Blodwyn they're good you know."

Incidentally a week after the single was released I rang my Manager to ask what number it had got to in the charts. Talk about how green is my valley!! How green was my mind! I truly believed that if you released a record it automatically went into the charts. Suffice to say that particular song didn't make it.

My older brother Elvyn was by now divorced but still living in Wales as was younger brother Dorrien. We didn't really see much of each other just basically when I was home for a quick visit which was a feat in itself as we would have to ask for time off! I didn't even have the time to get home sick! Of course I kept in touch constantly with my parents and they knew where I was every week and would have a phone number for me. Somehow we managed without mobile phones or Skype!

Like any young girl I had my share of boyfriends at that time. Usually they were in the music industry purely because I never went anywhere to meet anyone else due to our punishing work schedule. We had a manager who was well known and respected in the business, we also had a recording contract and so were constantly recording bits and bobs whilst trying things out.

Looking back now I never ever wondered for one minute, then or now, what happened to Nicky Stevens the solo artiste. The whole situation and how it came about felt natural and absolutely right. Life was good, busy and very exciting but little did I know what was just around the corner.

Chapter 18: Getting Lost

1974 started out much the same with us appearing at the Wakefield Theatre Club. This was somewhere I had worked as a solo cabaret act and we since found out that as I finished on the Saturday night, Sandra started as the resident band singer on the Sunday night. Apparently everyone was telling her it was a shame she hadn't been there the previous week as there was a fab girl singer called Nicky Stevens who she would have got on great with and would have really liked. The fact her name is Sandra Stevens is pure coincidence but even more bizarre as Stevens is her stage name as was mine.

Some gigs were good, some not so. We went up to Scotland and there was one night we were booked at this place called The Doocot. Well we could not find this place for love nor money so had to stop to ask somebody for directions. We were in Martin's little VW Beetle at the time and wound the window down to ask this chap who was passing by. He came out with a load of directions which seemed to go on for ever but all we could understand was, "Yer canny miss it!" We didn't dare ask him to repeat it so were still none the wiser as we drove off. That has stuck with us all these years, if we are in Scotland one of us will inevitably say, "blah blah, yer canny miss it..." One of our many "in" jokes.

Now throughout this time I had still retained my own personal Manager, Bobby Pattinson, although paying two managers proved a little difficult financially. While we were working in Wakefield I was staying with Bobby in his home. One February morning I received a letter from my Father which I read and was lovely. I then decided to go into Leeds shopping but every time I went to say goodbye, I'm going now see you later, Bobby would stop me saying, no no you can't go yet, I need to talk to you, and then he'd disappear off into his office for half an hour, come back out, then I'd try and go shopping again and he would stop me again.

After a few times of this I was really beginning to wonder what the heck was going on and what he wanted to talk to me about. I went to my room and he and his wife were in their bedroom talking and when they saw me coming up the stairs they closed the door. Something was definitely going on that they didn't want me to know about and I was a bit worried.

Eventually Bobby came downstairs and gently explained that he was going to have to take me home to Wales as my Father had been in an accident and was unconscious. The Doctor's thought it best if I went home to be with the rest of the family. I went to pieces immediately and they gave me a brandy as I tried to gather my thoughts.

Bobby was still a comic, so all this disappearing upstairs into his office and closing the doors on me was him cancelling all his gigs so he could take me home. He'd been on the phone to Tony Hiller explaining what had happened and that the other three would have to carry on without me. The motorway network back then was nothing like we've got now and basically it was a non motorway journey all the way from Wakefield to South Wales.

When we got to Carmarthen we had to pass the hospital and knowing that is where my Dad would be I tried to get Bobby to stop so I could go in and see him immediately. This was about quarter to twelve at night and Bobby became very insistent that we didn't go in as it was too late and I should go straight to my Auntie Lol and Uncle Ken's where my Mam was. When we pulled up outside, all the lights were on in the house and I remember thinking how strange that was. I rang the doorbell and I heard my Auntie's voice in a very sympathetic tone saying, "Oh bless her, here she is."

That's when I knew my Dad was dead. I just knew.

I walked in to the lounge and everyone was there looking at me and I knew for sure. It turned out the letter I had received that very morning had been posted ten minutes before he died.

I was to later find out that the GPO (General Post Office) as they were known then had been laying some cables down and hadn't guarded the trench adequately. People had already complained about it as it was very deep.

We have never known exactly what happened but my Father's body was found in this trench the next day covered in rain water. Auntie Lol and Uncle Ken's next door neighbour had been passing by and as he looked down saw a hand above the water.

As I said we don't know what happened but the coroner's result from the post mortem concluded that he had knocked himself unconscious when he fell and then drowned in the rainwater at the bottom of the trench. This one man told me afterwards that Dad had been standing right by the trench when he waved to him and said he'd see him over the pub. It must have been seconds after he turned his back that it happened but we'll never know how he came to fall in the trench. All we do know is that no foul play was suspected.

Mother at that particular time wasn't sleeping in the same room as Father because of his dreadful snoring, which incidentally I have inherited. My brother was sharing a room with him. He had woken up very early and because it was February, it was still very dark. The lamp was still on in the room which was odd as Daddy would normally have turned it off when he came to bed. Upon realising he wasn't there he became a bit worried so went in to wake Mam who went outside and discovered his car was still there so he couldn't be far. Dad had said earlier that evening that he was going up the pub to see Colditz on a colour television 'cos we only had a black and white one.

When it got a bit lighter outside Mam decided to go up the pub to see if they knew what had happened to him or where he was. As she turned the corner and walked up the road a bit she could see the ambulance and police and a crowd had gathered. As she moved closer she recognised the fabric on Dad's coat from his elbow which was sticking out from under this cover they had put over him.

It was such a dreadful shock for all of us and was something that should never have happened. He was only 59 and a perfectly healthy man who was dearly loved by everybody, friends and family alike. It was such a terrible terrible time.

I look back now at how different my grief was compared to losing my Mam in recent years. At the time of losing Dad I had become very spiritual and believed in life after death. Part of me was thinking, oh well he'll come to me anyway, just because he's shuffled off this mortal coil, he'll come to me in spirit. I suppose I expected that one day he would appear as I knew him as a vision in front of me and when I eventually realised that wasn't going to happen was when I began to find it very difficult.

I had a lot to occupy me and managed to hide a lot of my grief. Tony Hiller couldn't believe how well I seemingly got over my Father's death. Of course he never saw how I was when I was on my own. The nights were endless because I couldn't stop crying but I never once showed my grief to anybody else and kept it from everyone. And that's how it was, I had my way, Mam had hers and my brother's had theirs. Everyone copes differently in grief. The one thing we didn't do which we perhaps should have done was unite as a family to discuss and share our feelings so we could find some common ground.

We all functioned as separate units which I now find tremendously sad. I feel that I myself could have given my younger brother more support and maybe my Mam too but I was only 24 and having trouble understanding and coming to terms with what I was going through, let alone find the strength to help others. Hindsight is a wonderful thing.

If it was now as my older and wiser self I would react totally differently but it was an extremely difficult time. And so it was that I threw myself into work and was away most of the time. Elvyn lived and worked away. It was only Dorrien who was left at home. I always feel sorry and very sad that I wasn't mature enough to realise that as a young teenage lad he was left at home without his Dad. His older sister and brother were both away and he bore the brunt of responsibility of looking after Mam with no-one to take care of or support him. My Mam later told me that he used to disappear up to his room every night and just shut himself off by playing music through his earphones. That was the way he dealt with it. I am eternally sorry that I never helped him but I just did not understand then that he needed help or for that matter that any of them needed help. I was so wrapped up in my own grief.

Mam in turn was heartbroken. The weight fell off her. I suggested taking her and my brother with me on a gig to Scotland. We were going to be there for a few days and I asked them if they'd like to come up and stay with me which they did. Sadly the visit didn't go as planned. Mam just could not understand that I would be working till late then be straight off out for a bit of partying with other groups who were up in the area. It was only a case of going back to the hotel for a few drinks and sitting round chatting, nothing wild but we fell out over this as in her eyes Mam accused me of having no respect at all for my Father and staying out till 3.00 am drinking every night. Respect didn't come into it. That was the only way I could cope.

As a family we all handled it so differently and I always found it very very sad that we couldn't comprehend each other's grief. I've learned since that grief is a very individual and personal thing and everyone arrives at points on the journey at different times. No book has ever been written that can fully prepare you as each persons experience is unique. There are definitely phases of grief and when I have read books on how to deal with it, they have more or less hit on everything I have been through such as the overwhelming feelings of guilt. The one thing I wished above all else when my Father went was that it had been me instead of him. I told Elvyn that I wish I had died that day instead of my Dad and his reply was, "Helen, he'd have never got over it."

I suppose really I had youth on my side and I say this because the difference in how I have felt recently and still now after losing my Mother in my 50s as opposed to losing my Father in my 20s is very different. Life has dished out a lot more in the last thirty or so years and some experiences leave scars that have healed but are still tender and I believe make you a different person.

It's only now when I look back and think if only I had gathered us all together. The worst thing I remember was when my Mam was crying one day soon after Dad had gone and we her own children had the nerve to turn round, the audacity to turn round and tell her to pull herself together. How ignorant we were? Dorrien and I even said that if it had been the other way around, Daddy wouldn't have been like this. What a dreadful thing to say and only serves to show our immaturity and dreadful lack of understanding at the time of what it must be like to lose a husband, let alone the shock of losing him under such circumstances.

Like I said though I kept my grief to myself. To everyone else I was just the same old Nicky. They never witnessed me behind my own closed doors. I don't know if that was necessarily a good thing but I don't think I would have known at the time how to share my grief or show it publicly. I just didn't have the right vocabulary to express my feelings adequately. Plus I was worried about what people would think of me as well. Whereas nowadays I could easily ask for help if I need it. And so I carried on, business as usual.

My Father as I have previously mentioned used to play the keyboard and organ down at the RAF Club in Carmarthen or at the Milford Arms and of course the Welsh are renowned as a nation of singers. Now my Dad knew, as well as anyone, that at the end of a good night out there are certain songs guaranteed to get everyone singing. One song in particular, a welsh hymn, which because it is so well known people will use as a good old sing a long song, 'Un Bob Un Sydd Ffyddlon' was one of these, and I insisted this must be played at Dad's funeral.

His funeral was held at the local crematorium, Park Gwynne Crematorium where all my family have been cremated. I myself have already made arrangements that my ashes are to go there and put in the same plot as Mam and Dad so I can end my days in Wales where I belong, albeit in ash form!! The crematorium was absolutely packed and probably the only thing I remember clearly from that day was the minister standing there before me and asking the congregation to please sing this song as if Ozzie was playing the organ, which they did. It was wonderful and very moving, a lovely and befitting funeral.

Everything else about that time just felt so surreal. Losing someone you love especially so unexpectedly is such a jolt to the system and so dreadful that all your energy and emotions are taken up just trying to come to terms with what has happened, let alone think about the funeral. And the fact I had read a letter from him the morning I found out and knowing the exact post box where he posted it which was literally moments away from where he died was absolutely heartbreaking. For me bereavement is the worst thing anybody can go through. It is a rollercoaster of emotions and a cruel part of life.

The rest of the band were wonderfully supportive. When Martin first saw Mam, he came into the room to say hello and offer his condolences. He was later to confide in the others that he couldn't see her surviving much longer as he truly felt she was dying from a broken heart. She appeared to be giving up on life but was only in her early 50s. Little was I to know that what came next, winning Eurovision and all the ensuing fame and success, would give Mam a wonderful new lease of life.

Brotherhood of Man
The Early Days

One of our first ever publicity photos

1973

Cavendish, Birmingham

Chapter 19: Back On The Road

Life continued on and we were as busy as ever. That summer we were booked to go to Portugal working in a Casino in Albufeira.

We stayed in an apartment complex which also had a pool. Sandra and I shared a room, Martin came out with his first wife and Lee brought his wife and children.

Again being away we got up to loads of mischief, once more behaving like naughty children. After what I had been through I was more than ready for some fun in the sun! Polaroid cameras had just come out which afforded us many a laugh. One day I was in the shower and suddenly the curtain was whipped back and click goes Sandra with the bloody camera accompanied by my screams of laughter!! Childish but we thought hysterical at the time!

The days were spent around the pool or down on the beach which was nearby. We had all just discovered 'Piz Buin' which was new out at the time and we all thought it was the 'in' sun tan oil to have. We would lay there on the beach or by the pool smothered in the stuff, dozing whilst gently frying in the blazing sun. Martin had a little alarm clock and every half an hour, the alarm would go off and we would all turn over in unison. We were so well choreographed it was hysterical. It's another standing joke today and if we ever go on the beach together we laugh about who's got the alarm clock.

It's strange the things you remember in your life. I will never forget Sandra saying all she wanted was to wake up with brown legs!! We would even have competitions every night to compare limbs and see who was the brownest! I mean this was serious stuff! I did quite well in this as my skin tans well. Even as a young girl my hair was coal black and my skin had a Mediterranean quality about it! People would refer to me as that little foreign girl and ask where I was from to which I'd reply hands on hips in my best Gladys Pugh voice, "I'm from Carmarthen, I'm not foreign!!"

Often since in my adult life whenever I have been in Italy or Spain people have stopped me to ask directions!

During our time in Albufeira Martin was suffering with a bad throat and on one particular night really struggled to get through the show. As we finished the audience were shouting for more and as you may or may not know, in the business many performers invariably do what is called 'false tabs' which is where you pretend you have finished, take your bows, hopefully receive big cheers and a standing ovation before coming back on stage to do another couple of well prepared numbers.

Our false tabs number was a medley from Jesus Christ Superstar but by then Martin's voice had almost completely disappeared. He really couldn't manage another note so we just left the stage and didn't go back on. The next minute Tony, our Manager, came flying through the door. I cannot bring myself to repeat here what he called us but he let it be known in no uncertain terms that we must never take audiences for idiots and ordered us back on the stage. He really let rip and screamed all sorts of foul and abusive language at us. He stormed out of the room leaving a deathly silence in his wake, only broken with Lee piping up, "Well, there was no need for that..." and we all just collapsed with laughter.

Anyway we went back on and I made a big speech to the audience apologising for not returning on stage immediately and asking them to bear with us as Martin had lost his voice and these things happen blah de blah de blah. He then went on to sing 'Oh Happy Days' in full voice better than ever!! It was most peculiar. I think he had had such a fright and was shocked into it!!

Just before we had come out to Portugal Tony had secured us a record deal in a number of countries and we had released our second single called 'Lady'. One day whilst keeping to our usual routine of pool, oil, set alarm, lie down, cook, turn over, and repeat when Martin suddenly disappeared. I presumed someone must have called him away. Anyway when he returned it was like a scene out of Glee or an American kids programme. He jumped in the pool and shouted with excitement, "Hey gang listen to this, you'll never guess....."

Of course we didn't know what he was on about but it turned out we had received a telegram telling us we had made the charts in Belgium and a TV crew were coming to film us! We were so excited!

When the Belgian crew arrived we were filmed by the pool and when we looked back on that footage we all looked Turkish!!! Our skin was now so dark from our daily alarm clock sessions, so much so that my Mother didn't recognise Lee. She actually thought he was a Turkish man!

The following year 1975, we were again booked to go to Portugal but this time at the Casino Estoril on the Algarve for a month which was something quite new for us. This was and I think still is the biggest Casino in Europe and has been for forty odd years. It is also the Casino that Ian Fleming based Casino Royale on because of its glamorous and sophisticated ambience.

On the first day of rehearsals all the dancers were gathered and I remember one very glamorous and elegant young black girl in particular who stood out and captured my attention immediately, and just happened to ask the choreographer who this beauty was.

"That's not a girl, that's Billy," came the reply.

It turned out that Billy was French with American parents and from that moment on we hit it off and got on so incredibly well that we were inseparable. We would often go clubbing and it never really bothered me that blokes would elbow each other and snigger as we went by. Billy planned to have a full sex change when he returned home to Paris but his parents knew nothing of this so every time he rang home he had to lower his voice to become more masculine, it was hilarious. Sadly I never knew if indeed he had the sex change as we never kept in touch. Not long afterwards we were having hits in France all the time so he couldn't have missed us. However for that short time he was my best friend.

Night time was show time with a full on Vegas style production complete with a big troupe of dancers and lots of sequins and sparkle. We used to follow on from one of these spectacular numbers where the dancers were dressed as Russian

Cossacks and doing a typical dance that you would expect.

There was an elaborate castle scene on the stage and the dancers would emerge from the castle gates to that famous Russian tune 'Kalinka' doing the squat and kick move which I think is called the Preesyadkee, although that could mean something else entirely!! Anyway I hope you know the dance I mean?

What would happen afterwards was the set would move away to the left and the band would come from the right on their platform to the middle of the stage. As we used to follow on straight away so the intro of our song would be over the far side of the stage and not behind us. Martin would start the first line of the song on his own but he could never hear the key properly because the band was in the process of moving from the right to the centre of the stage.

This was quite a problem and we had endless discussions on how to make the best of the situation. This one night Martin had a brainwave: "I know what I'll do, when the dancers are finished and there's a blackout I'll run across the stage, ask the guy to give me the note and quickly run back as the guy is announcing us so I'll have it in my head."

We were not entirely convinced this would work but we went along with the plan. So the dancers were on stage in full flow giving it the full squat and kick to Kalinka with a final flourish and a 'Hoy', then came the blackout....

Martin went to run across to the MD, he was on a mission now, meanwhile the Stage Manager tried to grab him, missing by about two inches, because now all the lights went back up and the dancers came out through the gates again to 'Kalinka, Kalinka, da da da da da da hoy'.

Martin was now stuck in the middle of the stage in full view of the audience bang in the middle of a huge production number, with all these Cossack dancers whirling furiously past him. He just froze there like a deer in headlights because of course he couldn't move for fear of an accident. The Stage Manager just put his head in his hand and said something which I think was, 'Oh No,' in his Portuguese accent. It was absolutely hysterical, although at the time it was a terrible thing to happen. I really don't know how we managed to go straight out and perform as if nothing had happened.

After the main show there was a club downstairs where we would do our act again and this is where the type of audience would change. Now this time we followed a lesbian act that spent a lot of time cavorting on the floor. Not full on pornography but certainly doing very risqué things!

They were fondling each other to the theme from Love Story! Well, I mean we'd never seen the likes of it! There was a little hole in the curtain backstage which got bigger and bigger each night as everyone took it in turns to peep through and watch although I have to say I never actually caught anybody looking through that hole, funnily enough. How do you follow that? Well we did somehow!

There was another time in that same show where we would play Kazoos during the instrumental part of the Alan Price, Georgie Fame song 'Follow Me'. Afterwards we would tuck them into our waist bands as there was nowhere else to put them.

119

We would then walk forwards doing this bit of choreography to the sound of clatter, clatter, clatter, clatter, where each Kazoo had fallen down through our trousers and onto the floor and of course would inevitably set us off.

Another time as the audience were mostly Portuguese, we used to try and get them joining in and clapping their hands. One of us had this bright idea of finding out what the Portuguese word for 'everybody' was, which was 'todos', pronounced todoosh. I can't remember if it was Martin or Lee but as soon as he shouted it out to the audience, that was it, none of us were rendered capable of singing another note, we had gone completely.

We were always terrible for laughing and getting the giggles and still are. That has not changed in forty years. Not quite so much on stage now though, we manage to control ourselves to a certain extent! We set each other off like no one else and have this humour between us that probably nobody else would find funny.

Just the other day for example we were in our dressing room with what I didn't know was one of these wardrobes that I think you can get from Ikea, where you have the poles and then a cover over it with a zip up. I asked Martin what it was and if it could be moved. Well he tried and the more he tried the more of a disaster it was with poles sticking out through the material and the whole thing verging on a state of collapse with Martin trying his best to keep it together!!! Sandra was in hysterics and shouting, "I'm going to wet myself," whilst I had my face up against the wall, unable to catch my breath I was laughing so hard. We were all quite literally crying with laughter! These are the sort of priceless moments that may not seem much to anyone else but are the glue that have kept us strong and together for over forty years now!

Chapter 20: Preparing to Overtake

On our return back home from Albufeira we were booked to do a guest appearance on The Golden Shot with Charlie Williams, singing one number. For those who don't know, this was a popular game show of the day where you had a target board and someone called Bernie, who was off camera and never seen in charge of the crossbow, moving it around under the guidance of the contestant. When the contestant thought he had the crossbow in the right place they would say 'fire' and how close they were to the target would determine the prize they won.

Bob Monkhouse was another presenter of the show which was very popular and screened on a Sunday afternoon if I remember correctly. That was hard for me as Daddy wasn't there to see it. I had said to him the year before that we were hoping to go on the programme and he was always asking if we'd got it. My Mam bless her, wept when she saw it and it broke my heart to think he was missing it.

Later in that same year found us once more working at one of the Bailey's Clubs. In those days we used to have the resident band from each club play for us. The guitarist in this particular band not only went on to play on all of our hit records but was also to become my husband.

Alan and I didn't really have what you could call a conventional courtship. We couldn't actually go on dates as such, because of the nature of our work and with both of us working seven nights a week it was nearly impossible. We would stay behind at the end of the evening and have a couple of drinks together then when I had to hit the road again we would try our best to keep in touch. I would come back to visit him whenever I had the chance, and of course if it wasn't too far away. In those days I would think nothing of travelling for three hours after a gig. It wasn't a problem.

As Christmas 1974 approached, Elvyn was managing a hotel come nightclub in Rhyl, North Wales and he invited all the family to spend Christmas there, including his own son Mark who was eight years old at the time. We thought was a good idea as it was our first Christmas without Dad. I felt so sorry for Mam as she was still so raw and tender from losing Dad. The plan was, she and Dorrien would meet up with Mark, her grandson at Swansea railway station to make the journey to Paddington where I was picking them up in the car to then drive us to North Wales.

I still don't know to this day what happened but eight year old Mark never got on the train. Whether he had gone to the toilet or to buy a magazine, I don't know, but as the train was pulling out he didn't quite make it on board. Of course Mother was now absolutely beside herself. However when the train got to the next stop Dorrien got off to wait for him and luckily Mark bless him had had the initiative to get on the next train after telling a member of staff what had happened, resulting in them both eventually arrived at Paddington safe and sound together.

I was totally oblivious to all this, and there ready to meet them, very much looking forward to introducing them to Alan for the first time, who was waiting with me. All he met was a poor blubbering wreck of a woman who was absolutely bereft and totally distraught still not knowing what had happened to young Mark and of course her son as there was no such thing as mobile phones then.

It was very traumatic and I have never forgotten it. I really felt so sorry for Mam who couldn't stop weeping. The boys turned up some time later marching along the platform with not a care in the world. Mam was the only one suffering!

Despite this dramatic start we all put a brave face on things and really made an effort to get through Christmas. It was a case of having to really. As anyone will tell you, with bereavement it is the first of everything that is the hardest and most painful and you don't realise quite how many firsts there are to go through. We were on neutral ground though and of course the food was provided by the hotel which meant no cooking. Mam thought it was marvellous when all this food just kept on coming. It was a real treat for her.

Mam told everyone she thought Alan was a 'nice boy', so he had her seal of approval which I was happy about and when we realised the relationship was serious we got a place together in Watford in the early part of 1975, which meant I now had a base to return to at the end of a gig instead of the endless rounds of pro digs. We worked it pretty much ok and in August 1975 Alan and I became engaged.

You know it's funny because for a long time many people thought that Martin and I were an item. I think with a mixed group, people naturally draw their own assumptions. On one occasion Alan even sat behind someone who was convincingly telling everyone that the dark haired girl and bloke with a moustache were married!

Apart from our engagement, 1975 was pretty uneventful and we continued gigging and travelling up and down the country. Of course we would bump into various other bands on the circuit particularly doing theatre shows and such like but much of the time we were on our own as quite a self contained unit, topping the bill at clubs working with singers and comics of the day.

We had our set act to perform which was provided for us and already written. The songs were already chosen although there was the odd song that we would change that we thought would perhaps suit us better and would be good for our type of act.

I personally continued to enjoy listening to music. I have never wavered from the fact that if it is good, then I like it. If it is classical musical and good, I like it, if it's a good middle of the road pop song, I like it and if it's a great heavy rock band and they're good and the musicianship quality is good, I like it. There are only two types of music I don't really like, I'm not a big reggae fan, nor am I a die hard country fan. I like country rock, in fact my favourite group as I write is Rascal Flatts who are enormous in the states but they are more light country as opposed to country and western stuff.

We were booked for a week's stint at the Rendez Vous Nightclub in Workington, Cumbria; as always we arrived in the afternoon, did our sound check, sorted the microphones and lights out, all the usual stuff. Lorna the owner of the club informed us that we would be meeting the Vicar that night and how it would be great if we could give him a mention during the show as he would love it. She explained he was the night club Chaplain and how he was a regular most evenings and we wouldn't be able to miss him. When it came to the show, I was doing the usual chat and suddenly remembered about the vicar in the audience so spouted forth, "Oh, apparently we have our vicar in tonight....where is he now....?"

Suddenly this guy appeared in platforms, flares, long hair and ceremoniously made his way on to the dance floor to just in front of the stage, dropped on to his knees in a praying position and just bowed to us. Well, we couldn't stop laughing at this image in front of us which was to be my first introduction to Idris Vaughan, a very very, lovely, warm humorous human being, who made us all laugh.

I suppose I spent quite a bit more time with him than the others did. We got on like a house on fire and would go out walking or driving around the Lake District, doing lots of sightseeing together. We would often go back to the Vicarage and polish off some of the communion wine. Every night he would stay up late with us enjoying our company as we were enjoying his. Idris was Curate at a Church in Workington and towards the end of our week his Vicar told him he needed to get a decent night's sleep! I think he was enjoying our lifestyle too much and almost nodding off during his services! Idris is a very special man and has become my bestest, dearest, and closest friend in the world. We did lose touch for a short while but thankfully when we were working in Stafford in the 90s near to where he lived, he came along to see us and we have never lost touch since then.

In the winter of 1975, Barry Blue, a well known British singer, songwriter and producer of the day, gave Tony Hiller a song for us to record. When we went into the studio to record some of our own stuff, Tony played it to us to see what we thought with the idea of me and Martin singing the lead. We ended up learning 'Kiss Me Kiss Your Baby' and recording it within one day and to our delight it was a huge hit all over Europe reaching number one in several countries apart from here in this country. Sadly it didn't do anything here.

We went to Holland frequently to perform on the programme Avro Top Pop, a programme similar to our Top of the Pops. As I said Martin and I had lead vocals and Sandra and Lee had no lyrics at all to sing on this track, they were purely backing. As I remember it went 'Aah Ooh' over and over which was in fact a great part of the song and very catchy. It was great how the camera men would do the shots because every time they sang the Aah Ooh's it would flick to either Lee or Sandra. It was all very cleverly done.

With the huge success of Kiss Me Kiss Your Baby I found myself for the very first time walking down the street and being recognised! Oh my god I was ecstatic that someone actually shouted my name! Of course I stopped my shopping immediately and rushed back to the hotel to tell everyone! It was great fun and so new. Whenever Sandra was recognised people would say or sing to her 'Aah Ooh'. Now when we do a show or concert in any of the European countries especially Belgium or Holland we open with this song. It really is a great upbeat song and I love singing it.

123

We also received our first ever gold disc for Kiss Me Kiss Your Baby in Belgium which I was so proud of. It was presented to us at Pol's Jazz Club in Brussels which is still going although I do believe he is dead now. I was told at the time that Pol was famous for being a resistance leader during the Second World War and smuggled quite a few of our guys back down the line so to speak.

I recall seeing various photographs dotted around the place of airmen but he never actually told us that himself, it's what other people told us. I have a lovely photograph of Pol and I singing together on stage which I was very chuffed about and another one of the four of us receiving our gold disc.

This I brought home and lovingly put on display on the wall, like a huge solitary exhibit which people would have to file past reverently when they came to visit, to see what a gold disc looked like.

On the back of this success we also did a small tour around Belgium. A lot of the hotels we stayed at then would have huge great advertising boards outside, which you don't really see nowadays, I think it is more of an American idea. When we arrived at our hotel in Antwerp, on this particular board in giant red letters it said "Welcome Brotherhood of Man". Usually you would arrive in a hotel and perhaps in the foyer on a nice discreet stand the hotel would welcome the cabaret act but now we had this bloody great sixty foot billboard announcing our arrival.

Tony was due to arrive shortly after us. Now Tony is an East End Jewish guy who used a lot of cockney rhyming slang and one of his favourites that he often used was 'Niagras', as in Niagara Falls for balls, that of the male anatomy not the tennis variety!!

I don't know why or what came over me but I had a word with the Manager of the Hotel and explained that our Manager was arriving and as we were so grateful at how welcome we had been made to feel with our name on the huge advertising board, would he consider doing the same for Tony and welcome his 'company'? The Manager was happy to oblige, "Certainly Nicky what is the company's name?" To which I replied, "Niagras."

He seemed a little baffled by this but undeterred went along with it and after convincing him it made perfect sense in English, at my request he arranged for "Welcome Tony Hiller's Niagras" to be emblazoned on the board. The others couldn't believe what I was doing!

On the day of Tony's arrival, we were all having breakfast as they began to change the sign. The lovely Manager approached me to ask how to spell Niagras. How I and the others held it together I do not know. You can imagine Tony's reaction as he was driving up to the hotel; there half way up to God's heaven is this huge sign basically welcoming his bollocks to the hotel!! He was stunned!!

Some time before the trip I had mentioned to Alan about flying over with us and accompanying me on this tour. He said he would, we were all prepared and on the morning we were leaving, he decided for whatever reason that he wasn't going to come, we had a big argument and I walked out of our apartment and slammed the door. I was in a right temper.

Anyway, we finished the gig that night in Antwerp and the others were wondering what to do and whether we should go back to the hotel as it was still quite early. I suggested we stay put for a while as there was a rather nice bar, which we did, and socialised for a while.

Eventually we returned to the hotel, which was a Quality Inn Hotel, a bit like a Holiday Inn nowadays, and I went into my room which was in complete darkness. As I opened the door I could see there was a box of Milk Tray on the floor which I certainly hadn't left. My eyes quickly scanned the room and I could make out this lump in my bed. Heart pounding I quickly ran back out, closed the door, then ran to the others panicking that there was a box of chocolates on the floor and some stranger in my bed.

They thought I was winding them up but humoured me and came back with me to my room. I gingerly opened the door and walked in and there was the Milk Tray still in place on the floor. I looked towards the wardrobe space which was basically just a rail and I recognised Alan's coat. "Oh my god I don't believe it," I shouted and immediately put the light on and we all jumped all over him.

Apparently when I had slammed the door on him that morning in a fit of temper, he had leapt straight out of bed, got all his stuff together and literally rushed to the train station and caught the next train over! He had told the Manager who he was and was allowed in my room!! These days that would never happen of course. He could have been anyone and probably wouldn't have got in the hotel never mind the room. And all because the lady loves Milk Tray! That was typical Alan though. In the very first flat we shared together it had like a square bay window from ceiling to floor and half of it was frosted glass. One evening when I thought he had gone to rehearsals with his band and it was pouring with rain outside, I was sat in the chair watching television. Suddenly I was startled by this ladder coming up against the window and gradually Alan appeared carrying a box of milk tray. He was very funny and would often do things like that.

After Antwerp we were scheduled to go on to Paris and I persuaded Alan to join us. We were already booked on a flight so he caught the train and remained with the four of us for the rest of the trip. On our arrival at Charles De Gaulle Airport, Paris, our record company had sent a limousine for us which was incredibly long and quite different to the British style limo. The name of our chauffeur was Jean Pierre who spoke extremely good English with this wonderful French accent, the sort that everyone imitates. He drove us everywhere we needed to go, whether it be the TV studios or the hotel, he'd always be there waiting for us.

I have very fond memories of Jean-Pierre, especially one particular evening when we were in the cocktail bar at the Concorde La Fayette, a luxury hotel with the most incredible views of Paris. This cocktail bar on something like the 33rd floor was our first real taste of 5 star treatment. We were all in our element, enjoying this new found fame and indeed new class of bar so to speak!!! By now Kiss Me Kiss Your Baby was number one all over Europe.

Jean-Pierre was regaling us with a whole load of jokes which when translated into English didn't really work and weren't at all funny although he thought they were hilarious. We all very politely falsified our laughs on the tag line which did not make sense whatsoever. I often wondered if we laughed in the right places!

He was such a great character and a lovely lovely man. If you had put a beret on his head and placed him on a bike with a string of onions and a striped shirt, that combined with his voice you have the epitome of what most of us think of as a typical French man.

Another time we were driving along in the limo and suddenly I could see all this smoke. I quickly told Jean-Pierre who immediately stopped the car and opened the bonnet. The car was literally on fire. I can't remember what happened next but we managed to get another car and never set foot in that limo again which we were quite disappointed about as we thought we were the bee's knees in that car and had really 'arrived'. I never did find out what happened to that limousine.

I love all the memories from around this time. They were such carefree fun days. We were taken around Paris by a lovely lady, who was one of the executives from Vogue Records our record company in France, called Michelle Robique. She took us, along with Sacha Distel, to Maxim's in Paris, which by then had become one of the most famous restaurant's in the world and if I remember rightly one of the most expensive as well. It was a memorable experience and we couldn't quite believe we were here let alone in Paris. I mean let's face it if you are going to do anything anywhere in style, Paris is the place to do it.

On another occasion, in Germany this time, we were doing a show with a few other British acts of the time, The Rubettes being one of them. We already knew them as they were a very good resident band at a club in Ilford and we had met them when we were doing the club circuit.

We were getting ready when suddenly we had all these fans screaming outside our dressing room door which we thought was fantastic. We decided unanimously to show our faces and perhaps graciously sign a few autographs, but unfortunately for us when we opened the door smiles at the ready the fans didn't even notice us as their backs were turned and they were all screaming at the door of the dressing room opposite ours for The Bay City Rollers who were also on the bill and of course at their height then. We met the Rollers briefly at that time but never socialised with them. We always laugh at that!

Years later a similar thing was to happen in Dublin in 2012. We walked out of a venue through the automatic doors to a horde of screaming fans which was lovely, but older and wiser now we looked over our shoulder only to see Jedward on the receiving end of this adoration!!

I was just enjoying our whole experience in show business and going with the flow. We were well known in Europe and getting loads of experience both on stage and television and you're talking good quality stuff by now. We were really learning our trade. Nowadays of course it's the other way round, someone will go on Britain's Got Talent or the X Factor and become a star immediately, then learn the trade afterwards.

We on the other hand had been working together for four years and each one of us had vast experience in the business on our own merits too, all of which stood us in good stead for when we competed in the Song for Europe at the Albert Hall. We were confident and more importantly we were ready. Although quite what we were ready for we were as yet unaware!

My mischievous work!

Singing a duet with Pol 1975

Talk of the Midlands, Derby, 1975

Receiving our first gold discs for Kiss me Kiss your Baby
Pols Jazz Club, Brussels 1976

Chapter 21: Nearly There

From the beginning our song-writing team (Hiller, Lee, Sheriden) consisted of Lee Sheriden, Martin Lee and Tony Hiller. Lee had written a song some time previously although I can't recall exactly when, called Oceans of Love which he had taken to Martin and Tony to see what they thought. They didn't show much interest in it at the time but Lee persevered and brought it to the fore again at one of their song-writing sessions for another listen. This time round they kept the tune as it was but put their heads together, came up with totally different lyrics and now called it 'Save Your Kisses For Me'.

It suddenly worked and Tony immediately thought we should record it which we all agreed. When we first went into the studio, Lee sang the lead however Tony wasn't sure and suggested it might suit Martin's voice better. Of course he was proved right and if you asked Lee right now he would totally agree with that.

Once we had recorded it, it was entered for Song for Europe 1976. When we received the phone call from Tony to say the song had made it to the final twelve in the Song For Europe competition which was to be held at the Royal Albert Hall, we could not contain our excitement and were all jumping about and yelling with delight. At the time we were all staying at these pro digs run by an extremely nice family and the poor owner had to ask us to calm down as his children were in bed fast asleep. He was as thrilled for us as we were though.

The final twelve had been decided by a panel who back then didn't know who the artists were. Martin himself in later years was to sit on the panel himself and told us he would just hear a selection of songs and mark them. The performers would remain anonymous. The concept was also going to be different that year. Instead of having one artist singing six songs like Cliff, Lulu, Clodagh Rodgers or the New Seekers did, the songwriter/s were now able to choose exactly who would sing their song. This was the year it changed and I always say we had the best year. Apart from anything else it was so exciting to have a brand new format.

From the moment we found out we had got through to the big night at the Albert Hall we spent all our available free time preparing. We rehearsed so much at every given opportunity with barely a chance to put a cup of tea down before running the routine through again. Every single day, over and over and over again, to not only get it just right but to get it perfect; we lived and breathed that song.

Guy Luteman was brought in for our all important choreography. When he gave us the dance routine I remember thinking how strange it was but when I saw it all whilst we were rehearsing in front of full length mirrors I actually thought it was great and so different from anything else. Bearing in mind we were all different heights, we saw that when we were bringing our heel up to our knee, all our knees were at different levels and so we had to work out how far each of us had to bring our knees up so the end result would be perfect along the line.

I mean who would ever have thought of doing something like this and that it would work so well? We weren't out to look for a gimmick; it was purely what Guy had choreographed for us to suit that song, end of. If you sing that song to anyone now they still remember those moves and dance along! Bucks Fizz was remembered for ripping the skirts off; we were remembered for our dance moves.

In many ways I like to think we paved the way for future artists to try and find a gimmick or something in their performance that was very memorable and different. We also started a new craze in berets which came back into fashion after our Eurovision performance!! I often wonder what would have happened with future artists if we hadn't done that dance routine.

Our stage wear was equally important and Sandra and I were soon out looking for outfits in Knightsbridge and saw the suits we liked almost immediately, a white one and a red one. Sandra chose the red for her and said the white would look good on me and she had the great idea of scarf and berets to match. We kept the berets going for quite a few television appearances after Eurovision and they were our trademark for a while.

It was then the boys turn. Of course we needed them to blend in so we all went out shopping together for the jackets in beautiful water silk and again Sandra came up with the idea of them having flowers in their lapels.

The day of the Albert Hall dawned and boy, it was a phenomenal day. We arrived bright and early along with all the other acts for rehearsals with the wonderful orchestra conducted by the great Alyn Ainsworth who sadly is no longer with us. I think the excitement must have been overwhelming because I don't remember much about that day. It is all a bit of a blur really.

When it came to our spot the routine started with the four of us with our backs towards the audience and as the music began Martin would turn round to start singing the lead and I just remember feeling so glad it wasn't me. It was a huge responsibility on Martin's shoulders and he did it fabulous!!! It was flawless and I was so proud of him.

Apart from that I held my nerve really well. The whole event was televised live and the voting was done by panels dotted around the country in quite a similar way to Eurovision itself, with the head panellist giving the results from that area. When it came to the voting though, I couldn't bear it. I just stuck my fingers in my ears. It just meant so much to me and indeed all of us by that point, as it probably did to everybody else competing that night and I just could not bring myself to listen. There was one more vote to come in and it was neck and neck between us and a group called Coco, one of their members being Cheryl Baker of the then future Bucks Fizz.

The next thing I knew I was being almost physically thrown up in the year by my fiancé shouting, "You've won, you've won." I could hear this roar going round the Albert Hall. All I could say was, "Have we won? Have we really won?" over and over again. Honestly it was a wonder nobody slapped me. I was like a broken record that was stuck. So elated and so euphoric was I!!

When it came that we had to go back on stage and perform it again, guess who did the leg movement wrong at the very end. Yes, yours truly cocked up yet again just like that very first show together where Mrs Gobby let the side down. We had to cross one leg over the other and I went the wrong way. I was forgiven though because we had done the job and secured our place in the 1976 Eurovision Song Contest representing the United Kingdom and were duly presented with commemorative medals from Garrards the jewellers of London. We were on our way!

The pendant made for good luck for the Eurovision Contest

The morning after winning the Song for Europe 1976

Receiving our Song for Europe medals at the Albert Hall 1976

Chapter 22: Destination Eurovision

After the excitement of the evening we went back to our Manager's house in North London for drinks and a bit of a celebration. We were driving up the Edgware Road with Tony hanging out of the window shouting, "We won the song for Europe," at the top of his voice to bemused passers by who must have thought we were lunatics or drunk!

When we got to his house all his family were there to welcome us and they immediately put the record on and we had to stand in a line in front of his fireplace and perform it again!

The following morning we had a big champagne reception at a hotel just off Marble Arch. All the press were there and the place was absolutely buzzing. Management, agency, and record company, were also all there. We had become enormous overnight! Now we all know the press love a good love story don't they and as such they suddenly became very interested in Alan and me. We were photographed together and later when I was able to return home and have breakfast in my Mum's kitchen, she got up as usual when the daily paper was delivered through the letterbox and I heard her laughing away. She came in and threw the paper down in front of me and there we were, Alan and I taking up the whole front page of the Daily Express with the headline "Nicky Saves Her Kisses For Son of A Gun"!

It's these sort of things that when I look back now make me realise what we achieved. I just didn't register at the time when I was caught up in it all. In fact it's only really now at this point in my life when things are calmer and quieter that I can look back at all my newspaper cuttings and reflect properly on the enormity of what happened back then. At the time I couldn't appreciate it properly, it was like being on a high speed train constantly. Bang, bang, bang, onto the next gig, interview, show, press call, radio or television appearance. There was simply no time to sit back, let it all sink in and think 'flipping heck we must be huge now if I'm on the front page of the Daily Express'. It was just unreal.

Alan was over the moon with it all. He was in a group called 'Son of A Gun' who had enjoyed a degree of success by winning New Faces, and appearing on the Bay City Rollers' television programme Shang A Lang, although they hadn't had a hit record of their own.

He seemed to really be on the up and in fact I had always thought he would make it before I did. Despite being headline news though Alan remained in his residency with his band in Watford and sadly they never really managed to capitalise on their achievements thus far.

He was always very supportive of me though and when I had first played him 'Save your Kisses For Me', he had said straightaway with no hesitation, "You will win the Song for Europe with that and then you will win the Eurovision Song Contest."

That has always stuck in my mind. He was one hundred percent confident. He played guitar on the recording of the song too which was great for him. Strangely everybody that heard the song seemed to have this gut feeling that this was the song that would make us, and it would be huge.

Prior to winning Song For Europe we had taken in a booking to perform at this nightclub in Bedford on our old fee, which we honoured, even though by now of course our fee had gone up considerably. We always say the owner of that club must have been thanking god that day because the place was absolutely heaving. What we found incredible and couldn't get over was that people were queuing all around the club for our autographs. It was all those little 'firsts' and some of course not so little that were really special to us.

The record itself was released and the first week it went into the charts at number 14, then to number 4 and then number 1 for six weeks. When we went to The Hague in Holland for Eurovision we had already been number one for two weeks. We truly felt that the whole country was behind us. It was a marvellous feeling.

There was only a relatively short period of time between winning Song for Europe and going to Holland, and with that an ever growing sense of excitement at this new group on the scene. One day we had to go to a store on Oxford Street to do a personal appearance. We all met at Tony's office and went together in a big black limousine. We were taken to the store where we were due to appear on this makeshift stage which had been erected for us.

The press were there in full force along with a huge crowd of well wishers and it seemed like Question Time. I could not believe the interest from the public, especially young girls. Questions such as, "When are you getting married?", "What will you be wearing?", "How many bridesmaids will you have?" The interest shown to me as a person was unbelievable! I was due to be married in June shortly after Eurovision which was to be held in the April that year and not only did everyone know about it but they wanted to know every little detail.

Another thing we were asked to do in this interim period was film a video of the song which we did in Holland Park. This was quite a new concept. We weren't actually singing the song but it was being played whilst we were filming various different scenarios and different routines.

Also as anyone who watches Eurovision is probably familiar with, before each country's entry they showed a snippet of the group or country they were from. For this bit they filmed us in Trafalgar Square with all the pigeons and walking along the street wearing policeman's helmets and jumping on a London bus. Both of these videos were shown on the evening of Eurovision just before our performance.

In those days if your record made it into the charts, the chances are you would appear on Top of The Pops. And so it was with us, we went to the BBC Television Centre in Wood Lane which is no longer, for our first ever TOTP. I was really nervous about this. I mean TOTP on home ground? This was a whole new ball game and very special. This was UK fame now at last. Marmalade were on the same bill that week and I told one of the guys how nervous I was feeling as this was our first appearance. He didn't realise this but reassured me I would love it.

Of course he was right. There were three or four different stages set up in the studio and as one song finished it would switch to the DJ of the day, perhaps Noel Edmonds or Tony Blackburn. I can't actually remember who was presenting on our first appearance. As the camera turned to them for their bit of chat, we were waiting on one of the other stages and suddenly all this crowd of youngsters surged around us. Oh my god it was so exciting. The stuff dreams are made of.

Peters and Lee were also on that show and came rushing up to us offering their congratulations and saying how thrilled they were for us and how they were dying to meet us. I mean they wanted to meet us? I was completely star-struck myself meeting all these other groups and artists.

Video players had literally just come out and I videoed absolutely everything I was on. I telephoned everybody I knew, friends and family alike and told them to tell everyone they knew to watch everything we were on! Everyone was told to watch Helen on Top Of The Pops.

All my friends and family were equally excited, especially the townsfolk of Carmarthen. What you have to understand is Carmarthen was a little town where basically everybody knows everybody and is still much the same today so of course they were so very proud of me. Here was one of their own making good! More than one person has since said there should be a plaque outside the house I was born in to say I lived there which absolutely cracks me up as I have never felt I was that important!! However at that time there was a huge buzz around us.

We travelled to Holland a week before the contest, to prepare for the big day. We were all booked on the same plane. Lee had his family with him, and Alan of course was with me. Also with us was the film crew from the BBC, including Bill Cotton, bless him, who was Head of Light Entertainment for the BBC at the time and was later to be promoted to Controller of BBC1.

One of the producers travelling with us said that he would be quite happy coming second and I thought at the time, what a thing to tell me when the four of us were getting on that plane with such sheer determination that we were going to win that contest come what may, only to be told it's ok we'll happily settle for second. Of course there was the little matter that if we were to win the United Kingdom would have to host the competition again, with everything that would entail financially, and I remember being quick enough to say to him that just for that reason alone we would do our damndest to come first!

Upon arrival we began rehearsing the routine to the song rigorously and made the conscious decision to miss out on a number of receptions that the very hospitable Dutch people held in our honour leading up to the contest itself, because we wanted to be to totally rested with no hangovers! We would just eat a quiet evening meal at the hotel and have early nights to try and keep ourselves looking good and fresh. The last thing we wanted was to be tired or worse look tired, because it meant so much to us.

Prior to this we had no clue what we are up against with the other countries so when we had finished our own rehearsals we would sit out in the auditorium and watch everyone else rehearse their songs to suss out the opposition so to speak. I must admit there were a lot of good songs that year however I'm being very very honest when I say that in my heart, I genuinely felt that ours just pipped the others to the post.

I wasn't being big headed or anything like that, and I certainly wasn't on an ego trip, it was a feeling deep inside that there was something about our song and the way we were performing it, and that inner feeling would not go away. As we watched everybody do their bit we all felt the same way, that we just had that bit of an edge.

There were endless rounds of magazine, newspaper, radio and television interviews during the week and on the morning of the contest we went up to Sir Terry Wogan's 'box' to be interviewed live during his morning programme for the listeners back home. I remember mentioning to him that my Mam would be sat at home in Wales in her kitchen now listening to this which was an extremely proud moment for us both.

Late afternoon they ran through the whole show and all the panels from each country got to see it, meaning they could see you and hear the song more than once which I think is right and very fair. They ran the whole programme exactly as it was to be that evening. We all agreed that the run through had to be absolutely spot on, as it was the first time they were seeing us and we had to make a lasting impression. We were on first which I for one was glad about, because then that was it over and done with, and we could relax.

People kept saying to us that being on first was bad luck and how it was a shame but we took the view that the first impression was the lasting one. You could of course think first seen first forgotten but we chose to look at it as a positive.

The whole day has and will always remain etched in my mind, even down to getting dressed and the endless fussing with my hair. A local Carmarthen man Terry Johns thoughtfully made us these beautiful wooden pendants with BOM on one side and the comedy tragedy masks of the theatre on the other. We all made sure we had these on us during the performance and needless to say I still have mine.

Most importantly I remember amongst all the excitement and craziness, ringing my mother during the afternoon and just crying. Crying to her that my Dad was missing this. I get upset now just thinking about it. Mam was very good though and stayed strong. I told her that not only would we win it but we would win it for Dad. It was thinking this thought that carried me through. When we went on, my quarter of the performance that I could give, I just kept thinking this is for you Dad.

There are quite a few interviews since that still have copies of that quote "When Nicky Stevens went out on that stage she was singing for one person". I have said that many times over the years.

The great thing is, to Dad I was always successful no matter what. Nothing better demonstrates this than the time I dyed his grey hair orange! I had to do his eyebrows and moustache to match! Bless him, it was an absolute disaster. It was truly awful. Love him, he went down the RAF Club that night and everyone was taking the mickey out of him. His answer to all their ribbing was, "Helen did it." End of. If

Helen did it, it was fine. That was my Dad. He loved me and he was so proud of me. I think what made this time so very sad was the close time span. If we'd lost Dad perhaps eight or ten years before the contest, it might have made it easier but to be so close and having only ever seen us perform once it was tragic.

After the run through we had a break with time to eat, gather our thoughts a bit and have a cup of tea after which it was show-time and time to go out live. I felt absolutely fine at this point because we had rehearsed so much. We knew for certain that we could not perfect the routine any more. It was reassuring that we had each other for moral support, to boost each others confidence and gee each other up when necessary, so none of us were on our own. Our whole team were around us, manager, agent, publishing company, record company, all routing for us. We were more than ready.

The atmosphere in the Green Room was great. Everyone was very friendly and polite and as each artiste or group came back into the room after performing we would all applaud them.

We were first though and when it was time for us to go on as in all television shows, a runner came to get us and took us to the edge of the stage ready to walk out and take our places. We were like racehorses just waiting to be let out. We all looked at each other and I can't remember who said, "This is it gang, if we win this, we will never have to go back to some of those dreadful clubs," but we all agreed. Of course not all the clubs were dreadful but this thought certainly spurred us on!

The next minute we were there on the stage with our backs to the audience in our starting position. We could hear our little promo film with us on the bus and featuring the pigeons playing, then Alyn Ainsworth being introduced and our last words to each other were, "Good luck gang!!"

The intro started and that was it. I could see the shadow of Martin's hand with just a slight tremor to it and once again I thanked god that I wasn't singing the lead!!! Because we had run that song more than once every single day for what seemed like forever, it paid off. We were able to go on auto pilot. We were one hundred percent confident with our choreography and our vocals. As we finished, the applause was deafening and fabulous so from that alone we knew it was good which gave us a huge boost. Then of course we had to come off and sit there and wait through the entire contest which seemed like flipping weeks!

During the voting I had several brandies to try and calm myself down and I tell you what, those brandies were like glasses of water. They had no effect on me whatsoever. I was so hyped up and jittery. The votes started coming in with the 10s and 12s. Dix points and douze points, and I thought to myself oh yes this is looking good. Bill Cotton and everyone else was gathered round us now with a sense of mounting excitement and we got to a certain point in the votes where people were saying that's it we had it in the bag, no-one could catch up with us now. It was then that a buzz went round the room and one of the television crew started rounding us up in readiness even though at this point there was still another couple of countries left to vote, it was merely a formality. I, however, couldn't or wouldn't believe it.

I don't do second I remember thinking. I can't do second; it means so much to the others and me to win. For the most part I just kept my fingers in my ears until the presenter announced over the microphone....

"And so ladies and gentlemen, the winner of the Eurovision Song Contest 1976 is...." I held my breath waiting for him to actually say "United Kingdom and Brotherhood of Man" and then I felt myself lifted upwards to this almighty roar. I just threw my hankie up in the air and let out an almighty scream. That was it, it felt absolutely unreal and was such a fantastic moment.

Incidentally at the time of writing this we still hold the Guinness record for winning by the greatest majority of votes. There may be more countries competing now as opposed to the eighteen back then and consequently more votes involved but we still hold that record for the greatest majority of votes. I am also proud to say that here in the UK we hold the Guinness record for the biggest selling Eurovision winning song ever. I have the certificate pride of place, on the wall in my office at home to prove it!

I heard a lovely story later from one of the locals in Carmarthen. The pub where Dad used to play the organ was showing the contest on their television. Apparently, all were gathered round watching and for what was normally a rowdy pub you could have heard a pin drop. They all knew my Dad so well and they were all too aware that he had missed this great occasion. There was a palpable sense of community sadness.

My Mam also told me that all the family were with her and glued around the television back home shouting encouragement and my Uncle Ken screaming at the top of his lungs that we had won as we couldn't be beaten now!!

My Uncle Ken also joked that Dad would have given up his job to become my personal assistant and chauffeur me around everywhere. These stories mean so much to me.

Anyone who remembers or has since watched footage of us going back on stage to perform again will know just how elated the four of us were. A lot of our party were sat in the audience, including Danny Betesh our agent from Kennedy Street, and some of the BBC producers and upon realising they were the British contingency the camera zoomed to them waving their hands in the air totally delighted for us which was a great shot.

The previous year's winner Teach-In from the Netherlands, who sang Ding-A-Dong, came on and presented us all with flowers. Tony Hiller came on stage as the Eurovision medal was presented to the song-writing team. It was all so wonderfully surreal.

We then had to put our flowers down and perform once more. As we sang, the credits rolled and I grabbed Tony and started waltzing around the stage with him. We finished by picking up the flowers again and waving them in the air. Our careers and lives were about to step up another gear!

Part Two

Leads Us To Who Knows Where

1976, after winning the Eurovision Song Contest a return visit to the Mayors Parlour with the family. Sadly no Dad.

Chapter 23: Life In The Fast Lane

We came off air and somewhat reluctantly off stage, as I wanted to savour that moment and feeling forever, what happened next was just so manic I couldn't take it all in. We were instantly surrounded by a throng of security guards and ushered to a huge room where we were directed to this stage with a table and microphones for a question and answer session with the world's press! This was crazy!

It was quite literally a sea of flash bulbs and I thought my god, this is it. This really is the big time. However, we were aware that Sandra had disappeared and we couldn't find her anywhere. Tony who had a knack of really making me laugh went straight in to drama queen mode and shouted out that was it, she had been kidnapped! Of course she hadn't and she eventually turned up and we were whisked off immediately to the foyer for our first press call as Eurovision winners!

It transpired that a photographer from a Dutch magazine had cornered Sandra and was taking various pictures of her in different poses. It turned out to be THE Dutch pop magazine of the day and one particularly odd pose ended up as the front cover with Sandra pushing down on this giant pen. Very strange! I think it was some form of advert. I have to say though it was a fabulous photo of Sandra with her Farrah Fawcett Major blonde locks!

After the press meeting we were taken back to our hotel and walked in through the foyer where all the staff greeted us with applause. We went up to our rooms to get changed and made our way to a reception being held for us and as we walked along this corridor I heard a voice saying, "Here they come...." and these double doors opened in front of us to reveal this most incredible buffet laid out and the centre piece was this wonderful stand with this enormous salmon on top with grapes cascading out of its mouth, surrounded by more equally wonderful displays of food, endless bottles of champagne and yet more press! My feet just wouldn't touch the ground. We were on a different level altogether now and were having to come to terms with it fairly quickly. Many more interviews followed and lots of celebrating.

I think we managed to snatch a little bit of sleep that night and the following morning we were due to fly back to Heathrow. We boarded the plane and the Captain announced, "Ladies and Gentlemen, we have the Brotherhood of Man on our flight with us this morning. On behalf of myself and the rest of the crew, and I am sure all the passengers as well, we would like to congratulate them on winning the Eurovision Song Contest last night." With that the whole plane applauded!!

The plane duly landed and would you believe it seemed like yet again the world's press were waiting on the tarmac for us!! We obligingly posed for photos and the next day's headlines read "Britain's Heroes Return Home"! It absolutely cracked me up! As if we'd been to war and back as all conquering heroes! As we walked through the airport there were shouts from all around of "Well done!" and "Congratulations!" as well as little pockets of people bursting into spontaneous applause. It was just so incredible and demonstrates the popularity of the contest at that time.

So now I was on a high and my thoughts were something along the lines of, Ok, I'm a pop star now so obviously when I get back to my flat, it's going to be surrounded by press and fans because lots of people know I live there? How wrong I was! There was nobody there, not a soul in sight! I was quite disappointed and felt let down. I was ready to act the part of the big star returning to Watford and there wasn't anyone around.

I believe it was the same for Lee, but Sandra and Martin who were living in Wakefield, Yorkshire at the time, were greeted with bunting and the whole street as well as press and television crews, out in force to welcome them. They had a fantastic reception and were both carried shoulder high to huge cheers.

When I pushed open the front door it would hardly move for the piles of beer mats and pieces of paper with messages of congratulations that people had shoved through my letterbox. The telegrams and cards I had received from the people in Carmarthen of congratulations and best wishes was overwhelming and humbling. It seemed everyone I had ever known was wishing me well including teachers who had taught me at school. It was wonderful. Whatever I did big or small they whole-heartedly gave their support and for that I am eternally thankful.

So there I was alone with nobody waiting for me which brought me down to earth somewhat. What I didn't realise at the time was they were all in Wales at my Mother's house! Press and fans alike. Mother was holding court and announcing to all and sundry that she couldn't possibly tell anyone where I was as I was resting! As if I'd just come out of a long running West End musical or something! I thought that was priceless! I absolutely loved it!

Mam then invited the press and television crews inside her house and gave them a mini guided tour, showing them the room where I was born, the latest photograph, everything! My Mam had suddenly become a famous show biz Mam. She did radio interviews, the lot and of course she couldn't set foot outside the door without being stopped!

A lot of people, Brotherhood of Man included felt that after we lost my Dad, because of the terrible circumstances, and the ensuing shock of it, that Mam really wouldn't be long behind him and that basically her heart was broken.

Even to this day our Minister Mr Davies of the Tabernacle Chapel, who conducted Mum's funeral, told me I had given Mam a new lease of life and a lot of the townsfolk echoed that same sentiment. As far as I'm concerned, it is the greatest gift I have ever given to anybody, a new lease of life to my Mother when she was most in need of it. Out of everything I have achieved in my life that is the single greatest thing I have ever accomplished, without a doubt the greatest achievement in my life. The success of Brotherhood comes second although obviously without it I couldn't have done that for her.

As for me I experienced such extremes of emotion during that period in my life. Pure elation at what we had achieved that night combined with my struggle to get through the bereavement process and cope with what was still raw grief at losing my Dad so suddenly.

On the Monday, we had been pre booked to do the whole week at the Golden Garter in Wythenshawe which was to be our first show fresh from Eurovision. We now had our own Musical Director, David Mellor and as such he was to conduct the resident band. This was pure luxury for us to have an MD who could read music and knew everybody's parts. The two guys who we had previously, Simon Burn and Paul Robinson, as good as they were at drumming, if a musician didn't understand his part or notes, they wouldn't have been able to help, whereas David could write scores and had all the knowledge required which is what we needed then.

The place was packed and as the curtains opened what greeted us was absolutely phenomenal and I will never forget it as long as I live - a packed room and sea of people waving Union Jack flags. It was incredibly emotional. There was a write up in the newspaper about that show and the writer of that review was gobsmacked at the quality of the show and our vocals, having preconceptions that we were just put together for Eurovision.

One of the highlights of our act and always a showstopper was our cover version of The Hollies song, 'He Ain't Heavy He's My Brother', which was scored for us as a four part harmony all the way through and it used to tear the place apart. He obviously realised hang on a minute these guys can really sing and we received great critical acclaim from this journalist for the quality of our harmonies for were described as 'pure class' which meant a lot and made us all so happy.

Amidst all the madness and the ensuing work engagements that followed, Alan and I finally got married. We had set the date the previous year when we got engaged and it just so happened it was in the June of that year. We had jointly decided on a registry office ceremony. Neither of us were church goers even though I had been brought up attending chapel and had been baptised, we felt it would be hypocritical to get married in church, bearing in mind we had been living together as well and Martin joked that if I turned up in white he would fall on the floor laughing! I did tell him years later that was the actual reason I didn't have the big white frock!

However it didn't matter as Sandra came with me to help choose my wedding outfit and as can often be the case it was the first dress I put on. Sandra said I need look no further. It was just a fabulous designer dress in a biscuit coloured voile. The bodice was completely sheer but with a wonderful lace design strategically placed which covered my vital parts! It was an absolutely stunning dress with a matching brimmed hat. I had a yellow vintage Rolls Royce as a wedding car and Tony played the part of giving me away even though it's not quite the same as walking down the aisle in a church.

This was the long hot summer of 1976 so the weather was glorious. The ceremony was held at Watford Registry Office with all the family on both sides in attendance along with a huge crowd of fans and well wishers, press from all over Europe as well as Britain and a noticeable police presence!

My Mam and Sandra were getting quite annoyed as the poor guy doing our official wedding photography couldn't get a look in against all the press determined to get their photos!! I could hear Sandra shouting out, "It's her day, it's her day," to no avail. The next day our wedding photo made every single national newspaper and many European ones too. Again I can only really appreciate how famous I had become at this time in my life now, when I look back. These days I have time to reflect on the whirlwind of events at that time.

Our wedding reception was held in a hotel in St Albans and when we arrived all the staff were outside awaiting my arrival and applauding before rushing in to take up their posts. It was like a scene from Downton Abbey! I was quite overwhelmed to be at the centre of so much attention and how everyone had come out to see me.

Whilst all the rest of the guests were arriving Tony, Martin and Lee were crammed in a phone booth. I think some gig had come in but I was getting all irate with them because everyone else had come through and there they were negotiating a gig! We had arranged for some of our musician friends to play for us in the evening. However I sang for most of the night and Alan played guitar! But that was me in my element, I was enjoying myself!! The very next day we were straight back to work as we were scheduled to appear on Top of The Pops to perform our next release, 'Sweet Rosalie'.

Our honeymoon wasn't till a couple of weeks later. We managed to snatch a week in Lake Lucerne in Switzerland. It was a package deal with a daily itinerary and there were a few other people on the tour with us. I think I must have started to become a bit of a diva because I told Alan not to tell anybody who I was! By the end of the week though I was really miffed that no-one had recognised me!! On one trip I actually said to this couple, "You don't recognise me do you? You don't know who I am?" I cringe now when I think about it! Their response was, "Oh we all know who you are but we didn't like to say anything as we thought you would value your privacy!"

Joking aside, being a Welsh girl there were no airs and graces with me and we all had a great time and ended with a good few drinks on the last night. Not so long ago one of my fellow passengers on that trip sent me a photograph of us all in Lake Lucerne. We happened to be working at a club near the resort and they kindly sent the photo along which was a lovely memory.

This photo was taken by Patrick, Earl of Litchfield

Just married, with hubby and the rest of the Brotherhood.

Chapter 24: Travelling First Class

From then on it was new bookings all the way and our work schedule was so manic that as I have said before we just did not have time to appreciate and realise our success. Suddenly we were being given the 'star' dressing rooms, these large rooms with lovely furniture and unheard of before. We have always preferred to share a dressing room as a four and if Sandra and I ever need to strip off the boys just turn around. It works for us and has never been a problem. It would be strange to be any different now. These dressing rooms were also guaranteed to be full of people after each show especially when we were in Yorkshire! We also now had our own band and were focused on performing and keeping up with the demands of the new workload on the back of our success.

There was one time when we were booked to perform with Andy Williams in Manchester and we were driven up from London in a limousine for that particular night. As you can imagine this was a very prestigious gig for us. I mean Andy Williams, Tony Bennett and Jack Jones were right up there in a class of their own and Andy Williams was my very favourite singer, so this was incredibly exciting. Afterwards we all went to this big supper that was laid on for us which meant it was quite late when we returned. By this time our poor chauffeur was getting more and more tired and as we were driving down the M1 we could see he could hardly keep his eyes open so for fear of and ensuing accident Martin ended up taking over the driving while the chauffeur gratefully fell asleep next to him practically snoring on his shoulder. We thought that was hilarious!

We were scheduled to appear at the Golden Garter for a week's run. About half way through this week we had to get up at about 6.30 in the morning to catch a private jet which was to take us to Cherbourg in France where we were booked for a lunchtime television show on the beach, then it was back to the airport, board the jet to Holland for a live teatime show then back on the plane and across the channel to Manchester, on stage at the Golden Garter, quickly return to the airport and fly down to Heathrow ready for the Cilla Black television show the next day. We finished that and the limousine was waiting to drive us all the way back to Manchester to continue with our week at the Golden Garter!

That type of punishing schedule began to show in all of us in many different ways. However, I can only make comment on how I felt and one afternoon we were in London for another television appearance whilst we were simultaneously working at the Lakeside Country Club, Bob Potters famous club in Camberley where the darts comes from today. I felt so exhausted at this point that all I wanted was to sit down and not have to move.

I was in the kitchen ironing my outfit for that evening's show and Alan must have realised that something was wrong because he came into the kitchen and asked if I was ok. I remember looking at him and thinking 'good god he's totally expanded outwards from the waist'. In my mind he looked like Bluto from Popeye and I told him how big his muscles were getting and how it must be all the work he was doing on our house that we were buying. Worried now he asked again if I was alright and with that I cried out that no I wasn't and just burst into tears. From then on I couldn't speak. Every time I tried, nothing would come out whatsoever and the tears were just streaming down my face. I was panic stricken. Alan tried to calm me down and realised that I must be suffering from exhaustion. He called a friend of ours who was a nurse and as luck would have it lived next door and she made me lie down immediately. When I could eventually speak I couldn't put the words in the right place in a sentence. I could form words but still couldn't string a sentence together in the right order. I suppose I lay down for about an hour before I started worrying about getting to the gig. By now I was able to speak properly and managed to get there and go on stage. It was so bewildering and to be quite honest I was petrified in case it should happen again. I really didn't know what was happening to me and had seemed to lose all control over my speech. The next day I saw the Doctor and with no hesitation he told me I was mentally and physically exhausted and ordered two weeks of complete bed rest.

So what did I do? I stayed in bed every day and went to work in the evening! I can't remember where we were working at that point but luckily I was able to stay at home. Alan was a great support, he did everything, the cooking, the washing, housework and I didn't move from my bed until six o'clock in the evening, then I'd get up, shower, do my hair, put my face on and go and do the gig. I would then come back go straight to bed and stay there until six o'clock the following evening and that's how it was for the two weeks. We did however speak to Tony and ask if we could lighten up on the work as we all agreed it had become too much for us. From then on even though the work was still in abundance and we worked extremely hard, we were able to cope with it.

I laugh when I think that these days I'm in bed by 10pm most nights. Back in our hey day the night was still ridiculously young at that time, bearing in mind a lot of the time we weren't going on stage until 11pm if not later.

Another big highlight of the year was meeting the Queen for the very first time. We were booked to perform for the St John's Ambulance Centenary Concert at what was then The Talk of The Town in London. This truly was a glittering occasion with an array of stars on the bill. Nearly all the Kings and Queens of the world were also in attendance and we were fortunate enough to be introduced to them.

We were prepped beforehand about the protocol of meeting the Queen herself and were told that we must not speak to the Queen unless she speaks to us first, that we would be introduced to her and we would curtsy and say, "Your Majesty." If she spoke to us that would be fine but other than that we were not to say anything.

I began practising my curtsy and was really worrying that I wouldn't do it right. I wore my wedding dress as it fitted the occasion perfectly and was positioned next to Peter Cook and Dudley Moore in the line up awaiting my turn. As each dignitary approached I was frantically asking Dudley Moore who they were. His reply to me was just to curtsy and smile, they will soon go past.

Suddenly there she was, the Queen herself, now only three people away from me. It really was an OMG moment. It was a case of forget the curtsying and thank god the frock was long. I just put my feet apart and bent my knees down in a slightly undignified Dixon of Dock Green bob. I remember her glittering tiara appearing in front of me. It was just truly amazing. The Duke of Edinburgh and Princess Anne followed behind and my impression of the Duke was that the Queen had got him in the bath and really scrubbed him hard because he looked so shiny and clean with his white starched collar. He looked immaculate. Funny what goes through your mind at these moments!

The Queen and all the other dignitaries were then led into the big function room itself accompanied by a fanfare of trumpets, for a sit down banquet. I spoke to one of these guys afterwards and he was showing me the detail on his outfit which was all real gold thread. It was absolutely exquisite.

Frankie Vaughan was also on the bill that night and I remembered that time a few years ago at Batley Variety Club when working with Frankie and he had told me I would be a star one day. I couldn't wait to go up to him to let him know his prediction had come true. I excitedly introduced myself and asked if he remembered saying that. Unfortunately he didn't. He didn't even know who I was. When I prompted his memory he just said, "Oh darling I am so thrilled for you." Another Neil Sedaka moment and Nicky put in her place!!

Douglas Fairbanks Junior was compèreing the show which was being televised. We were asked to do 'Save Your Kisses For Me' plus another which was fine. We picked 'He Ain't Heavy He's My Brother' as our second song as we were quite keen to show the British public what we could do vocally and let them know we weren't just about 'Save Your Kisses', as wonderful as that was for us, it didn't show us vocally at our best.

However what happened, and in fact used to happen so much it really annoyed me, was when the programme went out the second song was cut and we were down to one number. The same happened at the Silver Jubilee concert the following year and really was quite frustrating.

We were extremely honoured to be booked for a week long stint at the London Palladium with American stage and screen actor, singer and dancer Joel Cray who many of you will best know for his role of Master of Ceremonies in the stage and film adaptation of the musical Cabaret.

My family made the special trip up from Wales to see the show. Mam didn't see us performing live that much and mainly watched us on television which we were on nearly every week at the time, sometimes two or three times a week. Living where she did in West Wales it was usually miles away and a difficult journey. Of course if we were anywhere nearby like St David's Hall, Cardiff, she and my brothers would come along.

But this was different. I mean now you're talking, this was the dizzy heights of The London Palladium! It doesn't get any better than that. Suffice to say my Mam was disappointed with the backstage area! She thought it would have lovely plush

149

wall to wall red carpet throughout and as anybody reading this book who has worked the Palladium will tell you, the backstage is very different to front of house!

The end of 1976 saw us appearing on the Christmas Top of the Pops which would feature number one hits from that year. 'Kisses' was the biggest selling single of the year and we earned ourselves a platinum disc. In those days it was very much a singles market unlike now so in order to earn yourself a silver disc you had to sell two hundred and fifty thousand copies. A gold disc was five hundred thousand and platinum was a million so we bagged all three! At one point we were still one of the top one hundred best singles of all time although I'm not sure where we are now.

Chapter 25: A Different Road

I don't know why but I suddenly became disgruntled with my appearance and lost all confidence with the way I looked. This centred around my teeth and hair and as I couldn't change my teeth every five minutes my hair then became the main focus for change and experiment.

I don't know what was wrong with me, it was very bizarre and I just wasn't happy. It was almost like I was going through an early menopause! We would have a publicity photo taken and there I would be with a different hairstyle and colour. I met a guy some time later who said he fell out of love with me the day I cut my hair! I would be happy for a while with a new style and then lose my confidence again. Once I started I couldn't stop, constantly seeking the perfect hairdo! The silly thing is it had taken me so long to grow my luscious long hair which was in beautiful condition. A member of the public actually wrote in to one of the newspapers or magazines and asked if I had left the group because I was constantly changing and they obviously didn't recognise me. I think it's because Sandra kept to the same style and of course Martin and Lee couldn't or wouldn't make such drastic hair changes! It is something maybe women will understand!

I was dying my hair all different colours. One minute it was red, the next week it might have blonde bits in it and eventually I treated and coloured it so much that it went like cotton wool. I think it was 1977 and we were in San Diego staying with my in laws at the time. Elvis Presley had died and I just couldn't do anything more with my hair. It was literally ruined. When I came back home, I had it all cut off really short and dyed it back to black. That was the end of any radical changes. I still experimented on occasion with colour but nothing too drastic. And then as soon as I decided to have my hair in the way I wear it today, the 'Cher' look, that was it. It felt right, I felt fabulous. The 'Cher' look (or one of them) gave me confidence to be me and I have stuck with it ever since.

I did actually go on to have some work done to my teeth at a later date. My two front teeth were always slightly larger than the rest of my front teeth and one was slightly crooked so I went along to a top dentist in Kensington, London and had four crowns put in the front. It was the best thing I ever did because from that day on whenever I smiled I did so with full confidence. It cost me a heck of a lot of money but was one of the best large cheques I have ever written in my life.

As a band we always styled ourselves. Sandra and I stuck to trousers and jackets which seemed to be our signature style. There was only really one time when Sandra wore a skirt which came to just below the knee. We did have a few people who designed and chose some outfits for us and they would consult with us and show us the drawings which were fantastic but I have to say they cost an absolute arm and a leg.

We did the Rolf Harris series at the beginning of the 80s which was six shows in total and screened every Saturday night at different schools with school children. We had our outfits made for that series and I remember writing the cheque which back then was for over a thousand pounds. I think there was also a little bit of when you are a 'name' people think they can add a few noughts on. Admittedly they were fantastic clothes and beautifully made, you couldn't fault them, but we couldn't afford them either! Not long term anyway. Nowadays we stick to the principle of wearing the same colour theme. Being older, if we all wore exactly the same it wouldn't work. We dress for our age but I like to think we are still stylish.

Although we were now earning considerably more and as a band we were doing extremely well, I was also enjoying spending it. I was absolutely terrible and so was Alan which didn't help. If only we had been a little wiser and more cautious. Out of the four of us I can categorically say that I was the worst manager of money. Going back to earlier in the book, when we had our first record out and I had naively asked what number we had reached in the charts, I now equally naively thought that as I was a pop star having all these hit records and earning this good money then that is how it would always be, I would always have money at my disposal and it would never end. We earned big money and paid high taxes like everyone. I suppose we were very fortunate though in the respect that we could trust the people around us. I was just a victim of my own naivety. I had a posh home and an upmarket car, I could treat my Mother and the family occasionally. It never occurred to me to question whether I needed that new car or whether I should be putting some by for a rainy day. I spent money like water but certainly had a lovely time whilst doing so!

I was very short sighted in that respect and really wish I had been more savvy and given it more thought. I mean I bought a Rolls Royce purely because Martin and Sandra each had one and for no other reason. I was keeping up with the Jones' which was utterly ridiculous. As songwriters, the boys were in a totally different financial bracket to me anyway but that didn't deter me. My Rolls Royce was second hand because in those days they were the cars you could buy that wouldn't depreciate in value; in fact they would go up in value so my argument at the time was that I was making an investment. Something happened though, which I can't quite remember, and the bottom fell out of the market. Lo and behold the gear box also packed up on it, which we had to replace, and I ended up selling it back to the very same guy I had bought it from for a fraction of the price plus a brand new gear box. I should never have bought that car! It happened though and I can't change it now. I'm sure most people if they are totally honest with themselves, no matter what earning bracket they are in or what success they have achieved, and it doesn't have to be in the music industry, can look back and wish they had done some things differently for whatever reason. I'm sure we can all apply that to ourselves in some way. All I know is that when we achieved our success and started earning big bucks I should have let my Mother take complete control of my finances from then on. I would have been rolling in it!

My social life in contrast at the time was very simple actually. It was based at the local pub, The Unicorn at Abbots Langley. I was in the darts team and I loved it.

We didn't really have any close friends in the business. We weren't ones to do 'the circuit'. While other celebrities would want to be seen at the right clubs and mixing with the rich and famous that just wasn't us. I think the first and possibly only close friend I have in the business is Ruth Madoc.

We were so fortunate at that time to have the most incredible set of friends and neighbours all of whom were outside of the entertainment industry were and were very proud of us and always quick to congratulate us. I think that is partly because they knew Alan and I were regular down to earth people.

We hadn't put ourselves on any sort of pedestal and for that in many ways I thank Alan because I actually remember questioning whether I should be seen in the pub now that I was number one in the charts. His reply was swift and to the point, that I would not change because of this and I would still go down the pub, still play in the darts team and I would of course still mix with everyone the same as I had always done and to not be so bloody stupid.

He was right, just because I happened to be number one in the charts didn't mean I dropped my lovely friends and unfortunately didn't mean I was number one at darts either. It was a great piece of advice. Whatever success we had there was no jealousies from anyone in that pub; they were always so pleased for us.

It was really heart-warming as well because whenever I entered the pub, if we were number one in the charts the whole place would applaud and many a drink would be bought for me. It was brilliant! Come closing time it would often be everybody back to mine and I'd be cooking bacon and eggs at one o'clock in the morning. No one ever took advantage of us though and they all had the greatest respect for our home. There was never a cigarette burn or a drink spilt and we had the most wonderful fun times.

I loved being in a position to spend money on the family, although I had to twist my Mother's arm to let me buy her things. It made me feel so good though to be able to do this for her much as she protested. We had the whole family to stay for our first Christmas and spent a fortune on Christmas presents. Looking back with hindsight maybe some members of the family were just a tad embarrassed to receive such extravagant gifts. For us though it was a joy to be able to do it.

I remember spending a hundred pounds on our best friend's Christmas present which back then was a small fortune and still is! I also enjoyed buying clothes and all the usual girlie stuff. Alan and I also very stupidly would have a brand new car each every August which was totally over the top and unnecessary. We were big Toyota fans and I still have one today. We were just so bad with money. We had it but enjoyed sharing it also. Whenever we were out for a meal I would always offer to pay. Not to show off or be a Jack the lad but it just seemed lovely to be able to treat friends and family and for them to share some of our success.

Unfortunately we didn't invest in more property. As far as we were concerned we already had our own home and set about doing lots of home improvements such as a new kitchen, new bathroom as well as re landscaping the whole garden. We never really spent money on holidays either, I suppose because we were both travelling so much with work, as Alan by then was part of our backing band.

There is only one holiday I can recall having at that time which was going to California to visit Alan's Father in San Diego. Other than that whenever we had time off, I didn't want to go anywhere. My holiday was being able to sleep seven nights continuously in my own bed.

There I was newlywed, riding on the crest of the wave of a successful career. I had everything I had ever dreamed of. To some maybe, having a family would be the next natural step to take. However the fact remains that I never ever thought for one minute that I would actually achieve what I had done and although I hadn't at any point consciously made the decision not to have a family, it became apparent to me that I didn't want to have children in case it would ruin my career and for me my career came first. I have to be honest it was as simple as that. Alan thought the same way and it wasn't a problem for either of us and I have no regrets about that decision.

Also at that time I had a wonderful cleaning lady called Audrey Onion. A wonderful name although I think if you delved back far enough in that family's history it would have been pronounced *Oh - ny - on* although I couldn't say for sure. Audrey, who incidentally taught me how to make fantastic Yorkshire puddings, was also the cook at The Unicorn. We heard she was looking for some other part time work to subsidise her income which is how she ended up cleaning, washing and ironing for us three days a week from 9.00 am to 1.00 pm. A real treasure!

We also had a dear gardener George who like Audrey came three days a week from 9.00 am to 1.00pm. We just did not have the time to keep our home and garden how we would like to. There was absolutely no time whatsoever as we were so busy working. The first day George came he called my husband 'Sir' and myself 'Madam'. We were having none of that and told him we were Alan and Nicky.

We struck up a close friendship with George and whenever we called round to see him he would pour us about half a pint of whisky. He was so thrilled that we were there that he couldn't give us enough.

Likewise we became great friends with Audrey and her husband Harry who was a retired railway worker. They actually lived on the platform of the fast rail service from Euston to Birmingham. It was a little station cottage and their lounge window was about three feet from the platform and the fast train would whizz by the window. Whenever we went to visit, we would get into the habit quite easily of sitting there and as soon as we heard the roar of the express train we would automatically stop talking, wait for the allocated amount of seconds and then continue again with our conversation once the train had passed by. It's so funny how everyone just got used to it and reacted accordingly without thinking as the train passed by many times daily.

Audrey had these glasses which were like Pyrex dishes to look through and one of our favourite party pieces was when everybody was up dancing whenever we were out anywhere, Alan would grab hold of her, waltz around the room but put her glasses on. Neither of them could then see a thing! It was so entertaining and funny every time.

We absolutely loved their company and many a Sunday we would take it in turns to visit each other for Sunday dinner. We would go mental over this one card game called Solo and after Sunday lunch we would sit down and play Solo for about six hours. If we were home on a Friday, Harry would invariably be working behind the bar at the railway club in Watford and we would go along and play bingo, then as per usual everyone would come back to our house and the grill and frying pan would be on the go again, the works. If it so happened that the pub crew came back to ours after early closing on a Sunday night which would sometimes happen, I would joke to Audrey not to make too much mess as it would be her clearing it up in the morning and I'd still be in bed!

On one of these nights Audrey, bless her, had had too many gin and bitter lemons and sat there in my lounge she announced that she was going to be sick. I quickly rushed to the downstairs toilet and threw a towel at her just in time for her to throw up in the towel. Poor Audrey couldn't apologise enough, but it didn't bother me as I have a strong stomach and I took this towel, emptied the contents down my waste disposal, threw the towel in the washing machine and thought nothing more of it.

Ten minutes later Harry's broad Yorkshire voice asked, "Have you seen our Audrey's teeth?" and he proceeded to explain that when she was sick her teeth came out. I knew then they had clattered down the waste disposal. Harry without hesitation dutifully put his hand down the waste disposal and lo and behold fished out her teeth which had about three missing. She continued to wear them with the three missing teeth until the day she died!

Audrey was such a lovely lady and I loved her dearly. They were such down to earth good Yorkshire people and I will always hold a special place in my heart for them. Along with George they played an important part in my life during the 70s, not only as friends but in helping to look after our home for us whilst we were away. We were close friends for many many years and I was extremely upset when they died in the 80s.

With fame and success there is always a flip side but luckily ours was minimal. In the very early days of fame we had about three young girls who were obsessive fans and one in particular who one night had to be admitted to hospital because she stood outside the club all night in sub zero temperatures with snow on the ground, waiting for us to come out. We have had a few strange fans along the way. It was nothing we couldn't handle though and was never a huge problem; they soon dropped by the wayside or got fed up with us!!

For every performer in the public domain there is a strange breed of fan living their lives through that performer and being totally consumed by it. I admit to feeling a bit sorry for that type of person as they clearly can't find satisfaction elsewhere in life. You hear about it on television and read about it in the papers all the time now and it must be even more difficult for those in the spotlight nowadays who are so accessible to anyone through Facebook and Twitter.

On the whole we have been truly blessed with some lovely genuine fans who have remained loyal throughout our career and regularly send us all birthday cards and Christmas cards, year in, year out. When I lived in Abbots Langley there was a group of little girls who lived nearby and I would often come out to find little posies of flowers underneath my tree which was very sweet and quite touching.

Iris and Margaret were the first true Brotherhood fans that I can remember. Two lovely girls and die hard fans right from the beginning who used to come along to our gigs and sit in the front row, always with one leg crossed over the other. If the right leg was crossed over the left then the right hand would be tapping the knee as they were singing along with us. If they decided to change legs, they did so together and then the left hand would be tapping the knee. One night they completely floored us as they had made replicas of mine and Sandra's outfit so when Sandra and I went off to do a quick change they had the replica of the new outfit underneath the original, velcroed on so they were able to quickly rip it off ready for when we came back on stage! Another time they had a bottle of champagne and when I quizzed them on what they were celebrating they told me it was their one hundredth show. I'm telling you they had seen us one hundred times!!! Such amazing stamina!

There was even a crowd of dedicated fans who would take part time jobs in the evenings so they could travel at the weekends and come to see our gigs wherever we were. Now these ladies don't follow us around anymore, and in fact Iris has sadly died. Funnily enough though it was Margaret who gave me the idea for the title of this book. Another chap Graham Finnigan was brought along by his parents as a young teenager aged about 14, to see us perform at the Golden Garter, Wythenshawe, hot on the heels from our success with 'Kisses'. Graham to this day has remained a fan and is now married, his children are grown up and he still comes to see us perform whenever he can. We keep in touch by email and whenever he is down in my neck of the woods on business, or we are working in Cheshire where he lives, then we will always try and meet up and go out for a meal.

It's the same with so many of our fans who have grown older with us and now have families. If we know they have come to see us we always ask them to come backstage after the show to say hello. Some bring us the most thoughtful and wonderful gifts and cards which we appreciate so much. They have become more like very good acquaintances now which I like to think of as a step up from just a fan. Thank you to you all for your years of loyalty. You know who you are!

Chapter 26: Flying High

1977 was the year of the Queen's Silver Jubilee and we were once more honoured to be asked to perform. Again this was held at the London Palladium with a glittering all star line up. Legends such as Julie Andrews, Harry Belafonte, Shirley MacLaine, Cleo Laine, Johnny Dankworth, and John Williams alongside the Muppets featuring Waldorf and Statler in the Box opposite the Queen.

Alan had previously introduced me to the music of John Williams and in particular I loved Cavatina which became the theme for the Deer Hunter. I was privileged to meet John on this wonderful occasion; he was a lovely man and I happened to tell him that my husband had introduced me to his music and that I was a great fan. I then went on to tell him that Alan had every one of his albums. He told me I should have brought them in and he would have signed them. I could have kicked myself as I never thought of it. Anyway he was then interested to hear my opinion because Cleo was going to be singing to the theme of Cavatina as lyrics had now been written for it and this was the first time it was going to be performed. He was interested to know what I thought about it once I'd heard it.

Well of course I listened with great interest and lovely as it was with the lyrics, I could only say that I preferred his version. The music on its own left so much to the imagination and the tune just did not need lyrics put to it. Don't get me wrong Cleo sounded fabulous of course but my preference was for just the instrumental. It speaks volumes and takes you to places in your mind that lyrics can't. I told him this afterwards and he was very appreciative of my comments.

Tommy Cooper was also on the bill that evening. A couple of years previously my older brother Elvyn had been manager of a nightclub in Rhyl, North Wales which Tommy had appeared at and from what Elvyn told me he and Tommy had become really good friends during the week he was there. At the end of the week Elvyn had raced very late at night to take Tommy to catch his train. Tommy who was known to like a drink or two had his drink in the back of the car with Elvyn speeding along. From out of nowhere the police stopped them. You can imagine the policemen's faces when in the dead of night after stopping this car the window was rolled down to reveal Tommy Cooper in the back! I think they were quickly waved on! Anyway Tommy was very grateful to Elvyn and they bid farewell at the station.

I couldn't wait to see Tommy Cooper and tell him my brother knew him and managed the nightclub in Rhyl. I stopped Tommy in the corridor backstage at the Palladium, introduced myself and proceeded to relate the whole story to him and told him how funny it all was when they got stopped by the police etc.

Well he never said a word. He looked at me as if I was from another planet and walked off to speak to somebody else. I was most indignant!! I went back to the dressing room and in full Welsh diva mode told the others how rude that Tommy Cooper was. Of course they just thought it was hysterical and couldn't stop laughing! Another Nicky moment! When would I learn?!

What a memorable evening it was though and very prestigious to do. At the end of the show everyone came back on stage in lines, there was a drum roll, the audience stood up and those on stage would turn slightly to the left towards the Royal Box to sing the National Anthem. Well as the audience stood up, Tommy Cooper thought we were getting a standing ovation and he began to thank the audience. He was very close to me and all I could hear was, 'Thank you, thank you very much.....' in true Tommy style! Once he realised his mistake he quickly shuffled round to the left!

It was around this time we were doing a radio broadcast and Bob Monkhouse and Arthur Askey were also on the show. As we were performing our song which on that particular occasion was Chanson D'Amour, Arthur and Bob suddenly came on the stage Flanagan and Allen style, Arthur with his hand on Bob's shoulder. Of course the audience thought this was hilarious. Now you have to bear in mind that this was a radio show with a radio audience at home so all they would be hearing is us singing Chanson D'Amour accompanied by all this unexplained laughter. They couldn't see Bob Monkhouse and Arthur Askey clowning around in our act. I was furious. I wanted to go and wipe the floor with both of them but the others managed to restrain me with the argument that Bob and Arthur were veterans of our business and I would have been out of order. I still maintain to this day that I was not out of order and I was absolutely livid.

We did speak to the producer of the show about it and they did a little bit of tweaking with the sound, managing to dull it down a bit so it didn't come out quite as bad as I feared. I did feel though the whole incident was highly unprofessional of them and I was appalled. To be quite frank I suppose I was disappointed and would have expected better of them.

We were now meeting so many famous people on a regular basis, either on the same television show or stage show, and it was usually the same old familiar faces. People like Showaddy Waddy, Mud and Bonnie Tyler and we would enjoy chats over coffee, sharing the news and comparing notes. I never became friends with any of the show biz set at all apart from Ruth Madoc and Bonnie Tyler. They are the only two people in the business whose phone numbers I do have.

Alan and I used to buy our Toyotas from the same garage as Ruth's ex husband Philip Madoc who is now sadly no longer with us. At this point they were already divorced, Philip was a successful actor and Hi De Hi had already started. I have to say Philip was the first actor I ever got to know and when later on he went on to play the part of Lloyd George in a Sunday evening television series I just could not get over how an actor can basically just step into the shoes of another human being and look and act like that person. It just blew me away. Ruth and Philip still had a connection as they had children together and I think Ruth must have heard about me through Philip. It was in 1983 when we were doing a summer season at the Winter Gardens in Bournemouth with Mike Yarwood and Hi De Hi was on at the Pavilion when Ruth and I first met.

Unfortunately audience attendance that year was abysmal and it wasn't a hugely successful summer. We were lucky if the first six rows were being filled, which was such a shame for what was a beautiful theatre, sadly now demolished. We started our season before the Hi De Hi mob and at the end of the show after we had all taken our bow, Mike Yarwood would say, "If you've enjoyed the show please tell your friends and if you haven't please tell them you've been to see Hi De Hi," the usual jokey banter.

He would then go on to ask the audience if they would like a sneak preview of He De Hi and when the audience invariably said they would, Mike would pull me forward and I would say "Hello Campers" in my best Gladys Pugh voice and the audience would fall on the floor laughing. Mike finally pulled that out of the finale and everyone told me after that they thought it was because I was getting such a good laugh! I do remember however Mike saying he was very disappointed the first night that he met Ruth Madoc because he thought that I was more Gladys than she was. He expected her to talk like that all the time!!

As it is with Summer Seasons, there is always a place where all the acts congregate and go for drinks after the show. Ours was the Pier Theatre and eventually Ruth and I began talking. Of course I told her I'd been dying to meet her as I'd heard so much about her and she said the same to me! We both found out later that we hadn't approached each other before as we hadn't wanted to appear too forward or gushing. So there we were being all cool and laid back when all we'd wanted to do was say "Hiya love how's it going...."!!

Anyway it didn't take us long to become really good pals. Often if we were out and about together, people did actually think we were sisters. I made Ruth promise me that if ever Perry and Croft, the writers of Hi De Hi, introduced a sister for Gladys then it had to be me as there just wasn't anyone else for the part!

Many a time through my career I have yearned to do a little bit of acting but I really don't think I am cut out for it. Three years ago I went to Bournemouth University and completed a six week acting course, one of many of these short introductory courses that were on offer with no follow on course available. I was extremely enthusiastic and was quite consumed by it but if I am being honest I don't believe I was much good. The entertainer in me gets in the way. You know the old saying 'Less is More', well I did the complete opposite and always felt I had to be dramatic and over the top. I would start off well and then as my tutor said, 'Our old friend would creep back in,' meaning the entertainer in me and my acting would become a bit 'ham'. 'Less is More' is definitely not for me. However, it made me appreciate how hard acting is and was so glad that I gave it a go. It is something I still hanker after but I am realistic and know the limits to my talent.

Just next to the Winter Gardens was a hotel where we would also go for a drink. The hotel was set up on a bank and on this bank were floodlights directed towards the hotel to light it up at night. Therefore from the road if you were shouting to someone who was sat in the garden, they could hear you but couldn't see you because of the lights.

One night I went across to this hotel after the show for a quick drink and chat with whoever was around. I could see Jeffrey Holland who played one of the yellow coats was there with his family so I called up to him in my Gladys Pugh voice asking him to get me a vodka and tonic.

I then heard his family telling him that Ruth was down on the road and wanted him to get her a drink and saw him disappear inside the bar where I quickly went to join him. Standing behind him as he was ordering and still in my Gladys voice I asked him if he had got my vodka yet. He turned round, saw me and proceeded to call me all the names under the sun. He had completely fallen for it and it totally freaked him out. We had a good laugh about it but he was genuinely shocked at first.

The whole Hi De Hi cast were such good fun, they were a great lot and Sue Pollard was hilarious. On a Wednesday night after 11 pm the local Bowling Alley would stay open just for us lot in the shows and we had a little 'inter show' competition going. I hasten to add it was a member of the back stage crew whose name escapes me, who was our champion bowler. I started off so well and was really quite good but what I used to find was my first game was brilliant, my second game not so, and my third would be worse. I reached the peak in my first game and that was it, I could never be consistent, more's the pity. It was such fun though, a great social evening and way of winding down and relaxing.

We visited a lot of the seaside resorts whilst playing the theatres during the summer and at the time had Cannon and Ball as our supporting act. This was before they had made it. The first time we worked with them we knew nothing about them but had heard on the grapevine that they were very very funny. I would stand in the wings and watch their act and I just thought they were the funniest thing I had ever seen in my entire life bar none. I laughed so hard and so much that I actually gave myself a sore throat! I'd literally laughed myself into a form of hoarseness.

In those days both Sandra and I would use Carmen heated rollers and we would stand in the wings watching them with these blessed rollers in. You just couldn't not watch them. You could not stay in the dressing room and not watch that act because they were so funny and so quick. There was nothing like them on the scene whatsoever. The number of times they threatened they would tell the audience that the two Brotherhood of Man girls were in the wings watching with heated rollers in their hair and that they would drag us on stage!

The worst thing possible was when you were on stage and you happened to glance in the wings and see Bobby Ball standing there watching you. It was horrendous because even now to this very day he reduces me to tears. We were a tremendous combination of laughter and music of the day and it worked so well.

They supported us for many shows until the inevitable time that they found fame in their own right and when they did there was no other act as pleased for them as the four of us. It was so well deserved. There were stories later on that Bobby and Tommy had got quite big time over the years but when we met up with them again a few years ago on a variety show tour, there was no sign of it with us, even though this time it was them topping the bill. After all we had been there first and Tommy took all the banter from me with good grace!!

Another double act I remember working with although this was in the days before the success of Brotherhood and when I was touring the working men's clubs, was Little and Large. I thought they were absolutely fantastic. Years later we were to work together on the Queen's Silver Jubilee Command performance and it was great to catch up again. A few years ago now Syd was doing his solo act at Bournemouth Pier Theatre which went down really well with the oldies. I went along to the show and at the end he came out into the foyer to meet and greet his fans and sign some autographs. I went up to say hello to him and he promptly asked if I wanted a photo taken with him!! He didn't recognise me at all! Mind you it's hardly surprising given the thickness of his glasses. You win some, you lose some in this business!!

1976 promotion picture for My Sweet Rosalie

Sandra and I are on the beach in
South Africa in the late 1970s

The billboard in Thailand with
our slanty eyes

On stage at The Night Out, Birmingham, our backing group taking the limelight
L-R: Mike Holmwood, Mike Hope, Alan Johnson, Brian Auker, Colin Fretchter

Chapter 27: The Sky's The Limit

During the years immediately following Eurovision we performed a few live gigs in Europe but we mainly appeared on television and radio as this was the big thing at the time. We would work on prestigious variety shows of the time that we just didn't have over here. Shows that included acts from right across the board from a local Brass Band to a family singing group Partridge family style, to Julio Iglesias or Sacha Distel to bands of our calibre. We gained a huge European fan base and great popularity on the back of these shows.

However in the late 70s we embarked on one of our first major tours to Thailand. Martin and Sandra who by this time were married had been holidaying in America so they were flying in to Bangkok from there, whereas the rest of us, the band and my husband included all travelled together. This was when I had just had my dental work done because I remember Martin and Sandra rushing to my room in the hotel desperate to get a look at the new teeth!! Martin had always taken the mickey out of my teeth. From what I remember though they met with the seal of approval!

As Lee and I arrived at Bangkok airport there were loads of screaming girls waiting for us to come through! All these fans with the most beautiful garlands of flowers to put round our necks and beautiful bracelets again made of flowers. It was the most fantastic welcome and I couldn't get over it. It still hadn't really sunk in how famous we had become! It felt like something I would watch on the news.

We were driving out of the airport and started making our way to the hotel. I was next to our Musical Director, Colin Frechter, who as I have mentioned before had played a huge part in the early days when we first got together arranging our songs and harmonies. As I looked at our surroundings I passed comment to Colin that this must be one of the worst areas. Of course he then told me that no, what you see is what you get and this is it. This was a huge culture shock for me. I didn't know places like this existed. I had never seen anything like it and was absolutely flabbergasted. After about twenty minutes or so, the car pulled into the driveway of our hotel to a whole different world. I remember being totally in awe of the place. This was to be the first of many such 'awe' experiences.

The fans were just so wonderful and welcoming. I actually did put a little tape recorder on stage and still have the cassette recording in my possession of one of the concerts we did. The fans would allow us to speak but as soon as we started singing, they would start screaming and drown us out. Lee announced this one song, our version of the Bee Gees, 'How Deep Is Your Love' and he asked the audience if they could be really nice and quiet for the song. You could hear a pin drop as he explained it was a beautiful song and to please listen carefully to the lyrics and it was called 'How Deep Is Your Love' blah de blah. Well we started and they were louder than ever, screaming all the way through! This was our first experience of this type of concert. Back home in the UK, everyone would heartily applaud us politely. This was a totally different audience.

In readiness for our visit someone had erected a giant billboard of the four of us on top of a building. When I say giant, it was absolutely enormous and you could see it from flippin' miles away. However although it was us, our eyes were strangely oriental. I think an artist had painted it and copied it from a photograph. But clearly whoever had done it couldn't see us with western eyes and we were most definitely eastern on that billboard! Actually I thought we all looked rather lovely but I fell about when I first saw it.

Prior to coming to Thailand I had contracted laryngitis and was on the last day of antibiotics when we flew out to Bangkok. Because of the time difference which is quite big we arrived in what was their morning so I hadn't really had a good nights sleep. We spent a lot of time sorting out our visas when we arrived and then we had to go straight to rehearsals and sound check ready for two shows that night. Unfortunately this combination of events caused me to lose my voice. It completely went. A Doctor was brought in to see me and he gave me more antibiotics but my voice never returned whilst we were there. Everywhere we went, another Doctor came to see me and more antibiotics prescribed but nothing worked, it was hopeless. It was dreadful not being able to sing. I had to mime everything. The other three carried on but of course there was one voice missing. No matter what I did or how much I rested it, there was nothing there. I could talk softly but that was it, I was stuck half way across the world with no voice.

As part of this Far Eastern tour we moved on to Singapore. It was absolutely delightful and we played at this wonderful theatre restaurant on the waterfront. We used to open the show with a number called 'Big Noise From Winnetka' which was a big four part harmony. My first note of the whole song was a top F! Even when my voice is on fine form, to hit a top F is challenging! Unfortunately any song that featured me and that nobody else could cover just had to be cut out.

Despite the bitter disappointment at not being able to sing there were lots of 'firsts' and wonderful experiences for me. I mean when had I ever been in a rickshaw? The four of us paired up and got in these little two-seater buggies that were pulled along by a bike. I found it highly amusing to look around and see the other two being pulled along by this poor little eastern chap pedalling away as if his life depended on it. I know it is a common sight there but for me at the time I'd never seen one let alone had a ride on one.

When we got back to where they all park up, this dirty little man came up to us and asked us if we wanted to go and see a 'special' show. He then proceeded to show us the most disgusting pictures of people doing things with animals. Our manager gave him a row and told him where to go in no uncertain terms. He was quite protective of Sandra and me.

The tour took us over the Christmas period and on Christmas Day itself we were around the pool. Our bass player at that time was Duane Gwillam. Now Duane for whatever reason never took his blazer off, so there we are around this amazing swimming pool in the scorching heat and there was Duane sat with his blazer on. We always used to affectionately take the mickey out of him and make reference to his blazer but nothing swayed him, he just loved wearing it and took it all in good part!

I can't remember when, but the day came when he got a new blazer. Well, the poor chap never heard the end of it, to chants of 'Oh my god Duane has a new blazer, it's a fashion show' and such like. He really was a lovely man and such good fun. He was with us for many many years and took everything with good humour which is just as well as we teased him mercilessly.

Being in Singapore, one of 'the' things we had to do was go to the world famous Raffles Hotel for drinks and I'm so glad we went when it was still the 'old' colonial style place. The smell of the wood and the whirring of the fans combined to make you feel as if you had walked straight onto a movie set, only this was real and I felt very sophisticated indeed as I sipped my drink! Another fabulous first! My word Helen Thomas had come a long way!

For those who have had the pleasure of visiting Singapore you will know the the uniforms of some of the hotel staff are quite something to behold in themselves. There was one young lad in our hotel dressed in the most exquisite Eastern outfit, looking like a little movie star and if anybody had to be paged, he had a big long pole that he would carry around with a little square blackboard on the top with ornate edging, that was probably plastic but painted gold to look ornamental. Written in chalk on the board was the name of the person who was being paged and he also had a little bell, ding ding, ding ding. You would hear this little bell periodically throughout the whole day ding ding, ding ding.

Alan, as you may have gathered from the Milk Tray episodes, was a great practical joker and he thought it would be funny if we got Mr Bollocks paged. Ever keen to join in a joke, I rang reception and asked them to page a Mr Bow Locks. They asked me how to spell it and I spelt out B o l l o c k s. The member of staff said, "Ahh Bollocks?" and I said, "No, Mr Bow Locks," and he seemed to understand.

A short time later we were all gathered in the daytime restaurant and bar area with other western people. Suddenly we heard this bell in the distance, ding ding, ding ding and of course the giggles started immediately, as it was gradually coming closer. It was just the perfect setting because there were steps from the foyer and then a certain amount of steps going up to this area of open restaurant where we were. We therefore had a prime view of this little blackboard coming up the steps inch by inch followed by this young lad and his bell ding ding!!

We were just sat there biting our cheeks and as he was going around the restaurant you could just see people keeling over laughing and cracking up. Suddenly the ding ding stopped as an arm came out from the kitchen and dragged him in. One of the staff must have realised there was a laugh being had. We were such childish little mites! May I just add at this point that Martin, Sandra and Lee had nothing whatsoever to do with this ridiculous prank but they did enjoy the laughter it generated!

When I eventually came back to the UK I had to see a throat specialist In

London and apparently because I had now been on antibiotics for seven weeks, I had wiped my throat clean of all the natural bacteria that the throat needs to fight everyday germs and therefore had left my throat vulnerable and had contracted thrush of the throat. It had got so bad by now that I felt as if my whole throat was closing up, I could hardly swallow and I was choking. I was also in considerable pain.

I saw a specialist in Wimpole Street who was wonderful. He wrapped a little piece of bandage around my tongue and made me stick my tongue out as he held on to it and then inserted the thinnest of rods down my throat with a little mirror on the end of it. I could not feel a thing! What he was doing reminded me of that game where you have to pass the metal hoop around a winding piece of wire and if you touch the wire it buzzes! His immense skill meant I did not feel anything. I certainly got what I paid for that day. He also took some x-rays but as soon as I told him the details and ran through what had happened he was pretty certain what was wrong and he was right.

The cure was simple, he prescribed some lozenges and I tell you what after taking just one I experienced the first relief in seven weeks. From that point it took about five days to clear up and I was fine! I was so disappointed though about not being able to sing on that tour. It's luck of the draw really. The others don't seem to have had any major vocal problems. Sandra had nodules in the early days but since then her voice has remained wonderful. On the whole I have been lucky and like to think that my vocal training taught me how to use my voice properly. I admit for most of my life I have smoked. Never a heavy smoker, but I am pleased to say I gave it up some years ago.

As a vocalist you are of course at the mercy of your voice and if you do have a sore throat or any minor problem you quickly learn to adapt and duck and dive a bit on stage to compensate. For instance even just recently Martin had a very bad throat at the Tivoli Theatre in Wimborne, Dorset so we left out a few things and Lee sang some of his stuff. Sandra can sing my parts and I can sing hers if necessary, although there are certain things you just can't cover. Whatever happens, the show must always go on!

Chapter 28: Speeding Along

We embarked on another major tour some time later to South Africa. One of Alan's best friends, Mike Foure, a sax player, lived out there at the time and arranged to meet us at the airport. The way our show ran then was that I was the first person to speak so I asked Mike to teach me a little speech in Afrikaans to hopefully impress the audience and also surprise the others as I kept it a complete secret.

It was basically just a few sentences strung together on the lines of "Good evening, my name is Nicky Stevens, it's a great pleasure to be here all the way form the UK to perform for the African people."

We kicked off the tour in Johannesburg and as soon as I started to talk, the others were suitably surprised and everyone appreciated the effort.

Typically Martin decided that he wanted to be a part of this and asked if he could be taught a few phrases too such as good evening or good night, that he could throw into the concert. Unfortunately the next night he got it totally wrong and ended up walking on stage at the beginning and saying, "Good night my name is Martin Lee," to a somewhat baffled audience.

Accompanying us on that tour was a lovely comic, by the name of Bryan Burdon. On the first night he introduced us and as he went to walk off, the lights changed to a blackout and he promptly fell straight into the orchestra pit! We were all behind the curtain unaware of this and wondering what on earth the terrible noise and kerfuffle was. I'm glad to report he survived with no lasting damage!

Our next leg of the tour was Cape Town and I have such fond memories of our time there, one of the loveliest being after the show and going down to Blouberg Beach in the darkness to have a barbecue with the iconic silhouette of Table Mountain in front of us. Alan and Mike reconnected musically at this time and would wade out knee deep into the sea with their instruments so to speak, Alan playing acoustic guitar and Mike his saxophone. We would have a little fire going and it was such a special time. I'm not so sure that legally we were allowed to be there but it will be forever etched in my memory.

We also had a wonderful xylophonist on the bill with us who I shall call Mr X. We would all get together and spend our days around the pool in the hotel and being in swim wear we couldn't help but notice the size of Mr X's lunch box!! It was bloody enormous! So much so that the boys were convinced that he put something down his trunks or underpants because nobody could actually believe the size of it or even that it was real! One day as a joke, some of the boys including Martin and Alan put a toilet roll down their bathing trunks and all strutted down to the pool area. The rest of us as per usual were like children giggling away but Mr X didn't blink an eye. He didn't seem to notice or maybe he thought it was just normal!

On the very last night of the tour having been out there for quite a number of weeks, Martin got his camera out and decided to ask if he could take a photograph to see if his wedding tackle was real. He went along to his dressing room and blurted out, "Come on Mr X give us a flash, we all want to see what the package is like!" He obligingly dropped his trousers to confirm his package was indeed the real deal. Martin was so flabbergasted that his mouth dropped open; he didn't take the photograph and just scurried away mumbling something! To quote Martin, "It just fell out like a baby's arm!!"

The African audiences were extremely warm and welcoming to us and when we arrived in Durban, we were the first band to perform to a mixed race audience. We felt very privileged and honoured to do this. One of the staff working at the hotel we were staying at was so pleased and excited about the mixed race concert that he arranged to pick us up in the hotel minibus whereas we would normally travel back in taxis. However, bless him he did it without permission from the hotel and sadly got the sack for his trouble. We felt terrible about that but there was nothing we could do about it.

Unfortunately since my previous visit to the country in 1972 I hadn't managed to keep in touch with Robyn the hairdresser who had a salon on the beach but nevertheless she had read all the newspaper articles and knew I was coming back so came along with her husband and little girl. We were able to catch up on all the years in between and it was great feeling knowing this time round I had really made it.

I also couldn't wait to show the others the Mayfair Hotel where I had worked and stayed on my own back then which coincidentally was more or less round the corner from the theatre we were working. Sadly when we got there it proved to be a right dump much to the amusement of the others. When I subsequently mentioned it to a few of the locals they all advised us to avoid going in there as it had really gone down hill although back then it was a perfectly fine hotel with a classy restaurant where I would do my act with a great band. I found it quite amazing that in what was only six years somewhere can change so much and on this occasion for the worse.

Whilst in Durban we went along to see a Dolphin Show one afternoon. The people running the event recognised us and asked us if we would like to stay behind after the dolphins had done their act and they would show us around the training pools and generally behind the scenes. We would then get to see the dolphins they were training. Of course we leapt at this opportunity.

The dolphin show itself was absolutely great as dolphin shows always are, then we had the promised tour behind the scenes and whilst the others were busy watching the training dolphins, I wandered back to the big pool where we had watched the main event and two dolphins were still in there. I then wondered idly to myself that if I did exactly what the trainer had done, because I could still remember the arm movements used, would they obey me? So with no one around I stood at the edge of the pool and mimicked the two arm movements of the trainer and to my surprise and joy the dolphins came up out of the pool and lay alongside me!

There I was with these two dolphins at my feet on the concrete and I thought oh my god what do I do now?! I thought the staff would go mad if they caught me. Then thankfully I remembered, the hand movement as if you are throwing something, would or should make them go back into the pool which I quickly did and luckily they obliged. Not a soul witnessed this. I crouched down and was stroking them. If you can imagine solidly filling a wellington boot and the boot being very wet, that is the best way I can describe how it felt. They just stayed there for a while allowing me to do this. It was absolutely amazing.

After that everyone came back and I owned up to what I had done. The trainers didn't appear to mind too much and confirmed how intelligent these creatures are. They then told me to slap the water which I did and suddenly the dolphins came and 'stood upright' in front of me. We ended up staying there for a further hour playing with them.

We would slap the water, they would come up in front of us then spit water at us, do the little chattering sound as if they were laughing, swim off go round then return alongside us on their backs so we could stroke their bellies. They would then spit more water on us, do the laughing noise and we would start over again. I lost count of how many times we repeated this. We were absolutely soaked, but the worst thing was not one of us had a camera to capture this experience. It was such a great honour to be that close and play with them.

Short of being in the water with them it doesn't get any better than that but as the trainer pointed out, if you are in the water with them on your own you really have to know what you are doing because if they nudge you in the stomach, you can be quite seriously winded. Of course they don't realise or mean to hurt you and in their mind they are just being playful but you do have to know how to handle yourself in the water.

Three houses along from where I was born in Carmarthen lived the Jones family, Mr and Mrs Jones and their three daughters Dilys, Jennifer and Leslie. Dilys was the oldest and Leslie the youngest. In fact Leslie had been my very first best friend. They eventually moved to Llanelli and I heard that Dilys had moved to South Africa to live and had gone to Cape Town. During my time there I managed to catch up with her. It was so lovely to go to her home and meet her husband and she had put together the most detailed scrap book for me all about South Africa, information and pictures she had cut out on the gardens, the buildings, and the beaches. It was so kind of her and good to see somebody from back home whilst I was that far away. I have still got that scrapbook.

For those who don't know Africa has THE most amazing sunsets, none more so than from Umhlanga Rocks where you can see it on water. The water picks up all the colours and for a certain radius shimmers with the reflection and light of the sun. As in a lot of countries you actually see the sun moving and it appears absolutely gigantic and almost unreal. It is the most incredible sunset. These are the sort of images and experiences that I will hold in my memories forever. I consider myself extremely fortunate.

Whilst enjoying what the country had to offer in the daytime we maintained our heavy work schedule and each evening would see us performing to highly appreciative theatre audiences.

I tried to do whatever sightseeing I could cram in whilst I was there and we would visit many of the small villages where the locals would sing and dance for the tourists, wonderful African singing in the style of Ladysmith Black Mambazo who we are familiar with now as they have introduced African music into our culture. The dancing was equally moving and I actually saw one guy picking up a railway track in his mouth. The singing, chanting and dancing we witnessed there touched my innermost soul.

As I said it is all put on for the tourists in the hope of gaining a tip. On one trip Martin very foolishly got his wallet out and he was suddenly surrounded by half a dozen bare breasted tribal women. Of course the African ladies think nothing of being topless, to them it is commonplace unlike in the Western world and Martin's face was an absolute picture. It was a mixture of embarrassment and astonishment, combined with a certain appreciation! He did not know what to do, whether to give them money or just enjoy the scenery!

Something I was keen to do this time around was take the others to Wankie Game Reserve before returning home. They were all up for staying a couple of days longer after the tour finished but unfortunately due to heavy rain the reserve was quite washed out and it wasn't a good time to go. Therefore as the tour finished they returned home and Alan and I stayed on with some good friends just for a short break only to find that when we arrived at the airport to return home we had outstayed our visa! I don't think it was by much. It didn't even occur to us to check on things like that! Luckily after apologising profusely they allowed us on our way. After all what could they do, we were on our way home and it really was a genuine oversight.

I did and still do have a great affinity for South Africa. I have often wondered over the years why that is. When I first visited in '72 it was very different. Apartheid was still very much practised and I found it strange to see benches and toilets with "Whites Only" signs on them. It was difficult to comprehend that black people were not allowed to even sit on the same bench as white people.

And yet there was something about the place. Whether it was the incredible wildlife and natural game parks, or the beautiful and dramatic coast line, I don't know. The country for me houses a great spirit, the spirit of Africa itself. There are so many wondrous things about the country. It has tremendous beauty with totally different terrain and climate to what I was used to along with wildlife living free in all its majesty. I absolutely loved it and when I returned with Brotherhood, I can remember walking down the steps of the plane and kissing the ground whilst saying to myself, "Welcome back, so much do I love you."

I could have quite happily lived there, then and still now. Yes I know things are very different now and although there is no apartheid, I hear a lot of stories about the danger in certain areas, but as a country, geographically speaking, I could live there tomorrow. I have felt a similar feeling for other places I have visited, France and Italy for example I also hold a great affinity for, but none quite like South Africa. Who knows why, maybe in a previous existence I lived there.

Chapter 31: No Stopping Now

Throughout all our travels I remained constantly in touch with the family back home, particularly Mam and Dorrien. They always knew where I was and how to get in touch with me even if I was far across the world and they continued to enjoy the success of Brotherhood of Man. Dorrien had left school and was a semi professional singer and musician in his own right, performing in various bands.

One night we were working in Cardiff it must have been about 1979 and weren't due to go on until late so I was able to nip along and watch Dorrien in his band in a working men's club in one of the Valley towns. He went under the name of Bernie Thomas, Bernie because in school he did a great impression of Bernie Winters the famous comedian and other half of Mike and Bernie Winters. The name has stuck and it is really only close family who call him Dorrien similar to me and my real name Helen.

I saw their first spot and must say I was exceptionally proud. He was fabulous but sadly Alan and I had to dash back to Cardiff to be on stage ourselves. Apparently so the story goes, after I left, the Concert Chairman announced that I had been in the club and that I was the sister of the bass player, Bernie Thomas. This woman then piped up, "Yes love and my brother is Tom Jones!!"

As a young lad Martin had lived in Australia for several years but sadly his Mother died out there when he was very small so he and his Father came back to England bringing with them lots of fond and precious memories. Consequently when we were booked to go there on tour for six weeks there was no one more excited than Martin although we were all very much looking forward to it. I mean how much further can you go than seemingly the end of the world?!

The plane journey seemed to take most of my life! At the time British Airways had a tremendous advert on television at a time when they were going through a phase of phenomenal advertising using space ships and such like. This particular one was where somebody was obviously filming it from the plane on the descent into Sydney and capturing the spectacular view of Sydney Opera House as it came in to land. I couldn't believe it and was so excited when we had the exact same view as we landed.

Tony and his girlfriend were with us as were the boys in our backing band, Mike Hope and Nigel Crouch on keyboards, Mike Causey on drums and Duane Gillam on guitar. When we got to the hotel which was in the morning on Australian time, Martin told us that whatever happened we mustn't go to sleep. Well of course our body clocks were now totally out of sync and by the time the afternoon arrived we were dying to sleep so Martin suggested we all go to bed for two hours and then we must get up. Alan and I went off to bed and of course there was no way we could get up. It was horrendous, we woke up at midnight starving and at that time there was nothing to eat in the hotel as it didn't have 24 hour service so everything was closed. We certainly had no intention of wandering around Sydney at that time of night looking for a restaurant. It was awful we were so disorientated and completely upside down. We had to be up early the next morning for our first radio interview at 9.00am!

I would say it took me two weeks for my body to get into the time zone properly. I could not cope with that jet lag whatsoever. Anyone who hasn't experienced jet lag may think it's just a case of staying awake a bit longer then going to bed at the usual time. But your body clock is regimented and finely tuned into knowing when it is time to sleep regardless of where you are and what time it is there. I really think that people do not truly understand jet lag and the effect it can have on you. I certainly didn't. Some people do cope better than others but I can't cope with it at all! Apparently it is easier to adjust if you fly from East to West.

Apart from the perils of jet lag Australia itself was fantastic and first impressions were very favourable. The cost of living was incredible and the beautiful properties for sale at a shadow of the price here in the UK made it a very attractive place to live. Everything was available in abundance and I can fully understand why so many people do emigrate there. We were booked to work at the St Georges Leagues Clubs which are fantastic non profit making clubs. All the profits are ploughed back into the clubs which in return just get bigger and better and grander. Of course now being in the Southern Hemisphere we had very mixed audiences including people from New Zealand as well as Australia which although it is such a vast place, population wise equals that of London.

We had a great reception nonetheless as by now we had hits in Australia and were well known there. The way it worked was that we based ourselves in Sydney and would leave the bulk of our belongings at the hotel there, then pack a small case to travel to various other parts of the country always returning to this hotel. We visited Brisbane and Melbourne where we did a television show with Hinge and Brackett who were there at the same time. It was great to meet them for the first time and to see another British act out there.

As a girl does I had bought myself plenty of new clothes to take with me which included a pair of these skin tight trousers in a silky lycra plum colour. They were extremely figure hugging and didn't leave much to the imagination but I loved these trousers and around the second day we were there I proudly wore them and went out of the hotel for a little saunter down the road on my own to take in some of the sights.

I must say I could not believe how many times I was propositioned on this short walk. I knew we were within walking distance of the famous area The Cross where a lot of prostitutes were known to hang out but this was ridiculous. I was beginning to wonder what the hell I must look like and was actually getting quite annoyed. I thought I was looking quite good but blokes were constantly coming up and asking how much I charge amongst other things! I was so disgusted that I quickly made my way back to the hotel and told the Manager at the reception how appalled I was. I then learned that the trademark of prostitutes at the particular time we were out there was the very trousers I was wearing, in all various colours but that exact style. As you can probably imagine the boys in the band found this absolutely hilarious.

However the tables were turned when soon after arriving the boys being boys decided to have a lads outing to a bar across the road from the hotel for a drink. I think they were in their two minutes before they came rushing out having discovered it was a hard core gay bar with everyone dressed like the Village People. Hilarious!! Yet again we were out of nappies and playing like children!! Great, great memories!

Many years previously back in the early part of the 70s when I was with The Johnny Howard Band, I was going out with one of the sax players by the name of Ronnie Coldfield who I was very smitten with at the time. He got a gig at the time on a cruise ship which was heading for Australia. We kept in touch for a couple of weeks then I never heard from him again.

Our visit to Australia in 1980 had been well advertised as we were having hits over there and consequently Ronnie left a message for me at the hotel to say he was now living there, had got married and he would give me a ring to catch up. I was quite apprehensive about him phoning the room because although we were now both married he was after all still an ex boyfriend. I needn't have worried though because Alan picked up the phone to him when he called and immediately said, "I've got a bone to pick with you. Why did you bugger off and leave her because now I'm left with her!" which really broke the ice between them.

Alan being one of the band and great friends with them, would many a night go out drinking with the boys after a gig once I had gone to bed. One night he came into the room during the early hours of the morning looking for his 'man' bag. We looked everywhere for this blessed bag until eventually he conceded that he must have left it at one of the bars he had been to and returned to the bars to see if it had been handed in. Unfortunately it hadn't and I was absolutely furious that he had taken it out in the first place because it contained all our credit cards and quite a lot of cash.

I got up early the next morning and telephoned all the credit card companies to cancel the cards. That night after the gig we came back to the room and there on the table was his bag intact with all cards and cash. Alan had completely forgotten that on his way out the previous evening he had asked the Manager to put the bag in the hotel safe for him as he didn't trust himself with it. Of course he had got so drunk that he had forgotten this vital piece of information. Luckily the hotel was already paid for and we had cash to see us through! Yet again the others found this highly amusing and the next morning at breakfast I could see everyone biting their inner cheeks in an attempt not to laugh. Not me though, I was most certainly not amused! I was going absolutely mental!

We did the whole sightseeing thing while we were there which included feeding kangaroos and holding koala bears. I saw colours in the sky that we just do not have here and therefore are impossible to describe. The sky at night was also totally different. Absolutely breathtaking. We spent a lot of time trying to explain to Sandra that we were in a totally different hemisphere and seeing a completely different star formation! She just didn't get it!

Again for the umpteenth time in my life I found myself thinking how fortunate I was. There I was walking along the legendary Bondi Beach on the other side of the world being paid to do what I love and all because I have this talent or gift that people will pay good money for. We really have been so lucky. Yes I know there are people in other walks of life who are able to travel the world for various reasons but this is my journey and I like to think I have travelled first class.

Chapter 30: Enjoying The Ride

There was a period in 1983 when Lee decided he didn't want to renew his contract with Tony Hiller as he felt he didn't want to be tied up contractually for any length of time. He subsequently left the group and singer/songwriter Barry Upton joined us in Lee's place. Originally Barry was in our backing band playing keyboards but when Lee left, Martin, Sandra and Tony decided Barry was the one to move to the front line. It was whilst Barry was with us that we did a tour with David Soul.

We got on very well with David and his musicians who were absolutely fantastic and included the drummer Ray Pound who was also Stevie Wonder's drummer, and the whole tour was a lot of fun. I got on particularly well with David and oh joy he enjoyed playing practical jokes as did Terry Jones our Tour Manager. Although it was a UK based theatre tour, some nights we had to stay over in a hotel depending on distance and location.

One night I climbed wearily into my hotel bed and wondered what the hell was going on as I slithered onto a load of slime. David had filled my bed with shampoo and bubble bath and conditioner and such like! This was followed by a little knock on the door, "Nicky are you coming out to play?" to which I grumpily snapped back, "No I'm not...!"

We all got on really well though and Terry our Tour Manager came up to me a couple of nights later and said that if I wanted to get David back for doing my bed. He knew his room number and happened to know that David was at that very minute eating in the hotel restaurant, so the coast was clear.

He went on to say that if I went to reception and gave them the room number, they would let me have his key and I could do something in his room to pay him back. Well I didn't need any encouragement whatsoever and made my way immediately to reception and asked for the key to this room. The receptionist gave me a withering 'look' and said, "No, we don't want your kind in this hotel."

"Excuse me?" I replied, the hackles beginning to rise.

"We don't like your kind in this hotel and we won't have your kind in this hotel!" she answered back pursing her lips and fixing me with an even more steely glare.

"We know you are a prostitute and we would like you to leave now."

I just went ballistic at her, and let loose in a full welsh diva strop, "Do you know who I am? I am one of Brotherhood of Man," I yelled in my most indignant voice. "I'm not a prostitute."

As the words came out I looked to my left and there in the corner was Terry Jones killing himself with laughter. Unbeknown to me he had only gone to the receptionist and warned her that a Welsh girl with black hair would arrive soon and try to get into David Soul's room. She's prostituting herself he told the receptionist and went on to say I'd been hanging around the tour bus and they'd had to get rid of me once already! I ask you!

Terry then had the good grace to come up to the receptionist and confess. The poor girl then instead of laughing was absolutely mortified that she had been so rude to me and I ended up consoling her and telling her it was ok and not to worry! I then managed to get the key and sneak to David's 'suite' firmly encouraged by Terry. The suite comprised of bedroom, bathroom and lounge areas.

I couldn't really find much to shove in his bed so had to resort to the shampoo, conditioner and shaving foam. I was just in the middle of doing it all when suddenly the door opened and in the doorway was a sea of flash cubes going off. Terry had this time run into the restaurant and shouted to everybody to come quickly cos Nicky was doing David's room up! Of course they were all up like a shot including David himself and all armed with cameras. I'm sure somewhere out there must be pictures of me in mid flight across this room trying to find somewhere to hide!

David grabbed me by the scruff of my neck and marched me around the room and in his American accent drawled, "Ok, let's see what we've got here ... mmm anything in the bed I wonder? Oh yes here we go..." as he started pulling back the covers "not very original is it Nicky, shampoo, a bit of conditioner...?"

And so it went on relentlessly. In the corridor of this hotel there was a big ice machine where anyone could get ice for their drinks. David then proceeded to get a load of ice from this machine, laid me on the floor and packed as much ice as he could get down my front and my back. I think that was my come uppance for 'doing' David Soul's room!! Believe it or not it was great fun!

A good friend of mine Charlene, who just happened to be in the C.I.D. in the Met, came to watch the last but one show of that tour in Reigate. Earlier in the day I had told her all about Terry and his practical jokes and how he was always catching me out etc. She then asked if I wanted to get one up on him for a change. Did I?? She mentioned that she just so happened to have her warrant card on her and her friend who she had brought with her to the show was a PC from the Met who also had her card on her. We were due to go along to the theatre early that day for a sound check. When we got there we went for a cup of tea first until everyone else began to arrive. I was under instruction to go up to Terry and say hi to him nonchalantly so she would know who he was.

I did as I was told and a little while later she went up to him and said, "Excuse me are you Terry Jones?" which of course he confirmed. She then showed her card and continued, "C.I.D, we believe you have drugs on board this coach and there has been some use of an illegal substance. We would like to search the coach."

Well Terry went a deathly shade of white and was rendered completely speechless. My friend did really well; they had the seats out of this coach, the lot with Terry looking on in a state of shock. Of course I had to tell David about this so he was in on the gag. He was the star of the show after all and I didn't want him put off thinking that the old bill are doing a drugs raid on his Tour Manager. Well, he stepped up to the mark and straight into acting mode. He wanted my friend to handcuff Terry, take him to the police station, the full works. He was running away with it and absolutely loving it! It was quite unbelievable seeing the actor in him take charge.

My friend had pre-warned me that if things got heavy and he got in touch with the local police in Reigate then we would have to own up and tell him quickly that the whole thing was a wind up. The place was in uproar now. Everyone in the theatre was being searched for drugs. The police were threatening to arrest David. It was absolutely perfect and couldn't have been planned or written better.

Suddenly Terry came into our dressing room. He was in a hell of a state and muttering how he couldn't believe this was happening and how dreadful it all was. He then went on to say that something was bugging him and why was the Met on this patch which was surely out of their area? He just didn't understand it and announced he was going to ring the local police station. The others looked at me with a 'you're going to have to tell him' expression and I had to come clean.

"You've been had my old son. It's a wind up. Those two from the old bill are from the Met but one of them is my best mate."

There was a brief pause whilst he digested this nugget of information before he shook my hand. "Absolutely fantastic Nicky. I've got to hand it to you that was absolutely bloody fantastic".

Well I was a star! Now everybody on the show was coming up and shaking my hand, telling me how great that was and that no-one has ever got one over on Terry Jones like that before. The following night which was the final night of the tour I was watching him like a hawk. Everywhere he went now my eyes were following. I was really worrying about what was going to happen after my stunt and combined with the fact this was the last night. Nothing happened and when I mentioned it to him his reply was, "Nicky how could I have topped that?!"

He really was a great guy and so much fun. I had never ever met him before and funnily enough have never come across him since. We did bump into David some months later when he was doing a seaside show from Blackpool with Sally James from Tiswas and we got together and did a song but have never seen him since then either. David's band were such a great bunch too and we did the whole thing where we ripped up pound notes in half between us and each kept a piece so if ever we met up again we'd have a quid to spend on a drink! That whole tour in 1983 was so memorable but mainly for me getting one over on Terry Jones.

While Barry was still with us we also completed a short tour of the Middle East in around 1984. We got up to some terrible things on that tour, Martin and I would unscrew numbers off the hotel doors and change them all around. We created absolute havoc in our wake! Another Barry, Barry Tomes was our Tour Manager and looked after us on this tour.

Shortly afterwards Barry left the act. It was quite sad really because Martin, Sandra and he didn't really gel together and we decided it was best to call it a day. Consequently there was this period of time when we weren't doing anything at all.

Meeting HRH Princess Margaret in 1984

Brotherhood and backing band, Dukan Fields, Middle East, Christmas 1986

Chapter 31: Which Way Next

By this point I decided to venture out of the comfort of the group to see what else was available. I thought perhaps a solo career was the way forward and Barry Tomes who had accompanied us on the short Middle Eastern tour asked if he could manage me. Together we embarked on forming a solo act for myself and I also went into the studio and recorded four songs which although were covers I thought I could send to people to give them an idea of what Nicky Stevens sounded like on her own.

I did a few gigs but it never really came to anything unfortunately which just goes to show that no matter how good you are if you are part of a successful group and sold as that group, there is no guarantee you can have the same success as a solo artiste. The two girls from Abba tried making it on their own at one point and didn't succeed. In some cases it works with people like Phil Collins and Paul McCartney but they are in an entirely different bracket altogether and have achieved mega status. Having said that you can't get more mega than Abba, can you? The whole experience left me feeling a bit despondent, having thought I would easily achieve more success. It's a funny old business.

I decided to try my hand at some session singing. I would travel to studios in Worcester owned by a well known jingle writer called Muff Murfin for regular recording sessions which would often run on to the early hours of the morning.

I was living in Buckingham at the time and on the night when we had those terrible gales in the 80s when Sevenoaks in Kent lost one of their big oak trees, as usual I had been working in the studios until about 3.00 a.m recording lots of jingles for Capital Radio.

Where we were was quite sheltered so when I was driving home I remember thinking how much debris there was all over the place but my Ford Escort at the time had excellent aerodynamics so wasn't responding too much to the violent gusts of wind. It was only when I got home and pulled my car onto the driveway of my house and opened the door that it nearly wrenched my arm off. I had no idea that the winds were so high.

I had a lot of fun doing those jingles. Brotherhood was going through a bit of a dry period, we weren't having the hit records any more and work was sparse.

Lee was still song-writing and I would visit his recording studio in his house and make demos of his songs for him. I also joined a gig band which was majorly doing all the London hotels. Now I was getting a chance to sing songs that I would never normally have a chance to sing. Songs from musicals, waltzes, fox trots, pop numbers, it was great I wasn't restricted to our own material now and I could sing anything!

Brotherhood may have been down but was definitely not out and one day Lee who at this point was still not in the group received a phone call from a television company asking if we wanted to appear on this programme with Little and Large which was being presented by Noel Edmonds. Lee met up with us for a chat and decided he would like to come back to us if we wanted to start up again. We had nothing to lose and everything to gain. You didn't have to ask any of us twice, that's for sure. The others had thought about diversifying and had bandied a few ideas around but like me nothing had come to fruition. Now we were all back together but sadly the work still wasn't plentiful.

At the time the girl singer in Alan's group, Patricia, was very friendly with the late Linda Bagainni of the Vernons Girls. She heard they were looking for another singer and recommended me. Subsequently I received a phone call one night from Linda who explained that their then trio comprising Sheila Bruce, Linda herself and another girl who had just left the group very suddenly to live abroad. They now found themselves minus a singer with a tour lined up and she wondered if I would be interested in filling the gap? I did a bit of research and found out that the act performed all sixties material. I did vaguely remember them from the late 50s and 60's even though I was still in school and my memories were of a bunch of girls who wore shorts and tee shirts singing a song called 'Who Wears Short Shorts'.

I quizzed Linda further about the material and stage outfits eager to know if they were still singing all the great sixties stuff and wearing all the sticky out frocks with the big petticoats underneath which she confirmed they were. I was now excited and it worked out that I could do this tour because we didn't have any Brotherhood work in.

I went along to Sheila Bruce's house in Watford to meet up with them all. Sheila was married to Tommy Bruce a well known pop-star of the 50s and 60s who had a great hit with 'Ain't Misbehavin' amongst others. We rehearsed our material with a band at a local recording studio. Sixties songs are very easy to harmonise with: Sheila was the tune, Linda was the third underneath, so all I had to do was plonk a third on top which was very easy for me as a musician, no problem at all. They were suitably impressed and I hit the ground running.

I did a few tours with them where I ended up performing on stage with stars of the 60s that I used to watch in complete awe when I was a little girl such as the Dallas Boys. My parents had only ever allowed me to stay up to watch Sunday Night At The London Palladium, which was usually way past my bedtime, if the Dallas Boys were on. Also on the bill was Eden Kane a tall good looking singer who had many hits in the early 60s, Jet Harris and Heinz who I used to wind up mercilessly, god rest his soul.

When Heinz was preparing to return to the hotel after the show I'd tell him quite seriously that the girls and I would be waiting on the bed for him in suspenders and stockings. He'd be absolutely terrified and we ended up having to reassure him that it was ok, we wouldn't be there in stockings waiting to have rampant sex with him and he could relax. Poor man, we were wicked!!

There was a lovely chap called Hal Carter who had been Billy Fury's Manager as well as Liverpool Express, and basically Hal would get us all this work and put us out on tour. Again like anybody touring will tell you there is always fun and games. On the final night of one of the tours we finished off in Jersey after having travelled all around the country having a whale of a time.

The Dallas Boys came into our dressing room in their underpants all except one of them who shall remain nameless to preserve his modesty, and who had put his watch around his tackle. They stood there and sang this most beautiful song that I'd never heard before in my life with the most wonderful harmonies and then turned around and walked out again as if nothing had happened!

Where our dressing room was situated, they would have to have been very careful of the route they took and would have taken the risk of the audience seeing them especially the least dressed member so to speak! Anybody reading this book who actually knows the Dallas Boys will know exactly who I'm talking about!

Another night we were backing Eden Kane who was singing this lovely song and suddenly I saw a figure at the side of Sheila and I just out of sight in the wings. It was our Mr Dallas Boy again! I then saw this zip slowly coming down and his trousers dropping to the knees and one by one Sheila and Linda disappeared.

I resolutely refused to look. I had a fair idea of what I would have seen if I had looked but I was determined to be a pro to the end and I was the only one left standing backing Eden Kane! When we told Eden afterwards what had happened he remarked on how he thought the singing sounded weird and how it seemed off key at one point. The result of trying to sing whilst stifling hysterics! One of the worst things in the business to happen to you and can happen at any time!

Even just the other night we were singing a song that we have been performing now for at least ten years where Lee takes the solo. For some reason though, Lee could not remember the words and was making up lyrics as he went along. The three of us kept to the front joining in with our harmonies in the chorus and didn't dare look at him or we would have gone!

Prior to joining the Vernon Girls I had taken up knitting. What was very much in vogue at the time was 'Knit a Sweater in a Day'. These huge knitting needles came out that were about an inch thick and you could get all this fabulous sparkly wool. The sweater was knitted in plain stitching but because the needles were so big, it formed this great pattern. Sheila was also into knitting prior to me joining and we will both vouch for the fact that when we met up neither of us ever took up a knitting needle again. We became soul mates, best friends call it what you will but to this day she is my dearest and closest friend.

Inevitably we were getting offered gigs that I couldn't do because of my Brotherhood of Man commitments so we had a few girls lined up who acted as deps for me. It wasn't an ideal situation though and I told Sheila she needed two girls who could commit full time to this act as there was still a lot of mileage left in it. She did exactly that and got Penny Lister who was a great session singer and one of the Ladybirds popular on television at the time and Maggie Stredder who was also a Ladybird and one of the original Vernons Girls.

Out of the fourteen Vernon Girls that you would see on the television, one stood out for wearing big glasses, a bit Dame Edna Everage style. That was Maggie, she was known as The Girl With The Glasses. Out of interest Maggie was also the original singer on the Fairy Liquid advert. They were professional singers and knew their jobs so it worked out really well. The Vernon Girls themselves continued working without me and doing all these fabulous solid gold rock and roll tours with the likes of Marty Wilde, Joe Brown, Eden Kane and John Leyton which I would go and see when I could. As I said though, Sheila and I had struck up a friendship never to be severed.

Me as one of the Vernon Girls 1984
Top: Sheila Parker
Bottom: the late Linda Bagaini

Chapter 32: Keep Straight On

Bill Thompson who bless his heart is dead now, was an agent from the North East of England who I also used to work for right at the beginning of my career. He offered us a tour of the Middle East and Far East in 1986 which was a tremendous opportunity and meant we were to be away for six weeks altogether. Again our musicians came with us, Mike Holmwood on drums, Nigel Hart on keyboards, Robin Hames on bass guitar. Alan didn't accompany us on this tour as by now he had left our backing band and had joined another.

We were such a jovial crowd and the fun seemed to start from the moment we got on the plane. I beckoned the stewardess and told everyone else that they must not say a word whilst I was talking to her. I then explained to her that we had been booked first class but there had been a problem with our ticket and the ground staff had informed us that were was no time to sort it out and that we must get on the plane and explain to a stewardess that our booking had been mucked up and see if anything can be done. She then went off to investigate the situation further.

With that Martin turned round and said if I pulled this off I would get ten gold stars. So there we were four of us in the band, four musicians, a road manager and a comedian all silently agog as to what would happen. The next minute the stewardess approached us and asked us to follow her. We all got up trying not to look surprised and were upgraded to business class flying all the way to the Middle East in first class comfort with all the goodies that entailed. Again we were back to being children as if we were ten years old and had never seen anything like this before in our lives.

That was a marvellous tour, the first part of it was in the 'dry states' and we were working some of the clubs of the oil fields, for instance there was the Norwegian Sector and the British Sector all of which are right out in the desert. People are allowed to drink on the premises in the clubs but not outside them. We had many a narrow escape such as when our drummer was walking along the road with a bottle of gin not realising that he wasn't supposed to be carrying it.

One venue I can always remember is 'Dukanfields'. We travelled there in two big luxurious type land rover vehicles across this desert and hit a sand storm. You hear about these sand storms but it was quite spectacular to actually be there and witness it up close.

We arrived there on the Saturday but weren't due to actually perform until the Sunday. The living quarters were absolutely full of sand. It was everywhere. No matter what you touched, every surface you ran your hand over was covered in sand. Only to be expected I suppose when you are slap bang in the middle of the desert. Martin, Sandra and Lee managed to get themselves changed into an apartment block which was a lot better but me being one of the lads wanted to stay with the lads and have more fun which I did.

The comedian on the bill with us was Tony Jo who was very funny. On our last night at this place the manager of the club had brought us a load of booze so we could party. As we were about to leave, me being Mrs Tidy collected all the bottles and put them in the corridor, stacking them neatly in boxes. The next morning as we were about to leave to move on to the next venue we were working, the police screeched up to a halt and ran into the building where we were staying.

The next thing I remember was Bill Thompson running out shouting, "What bloody idiot has stacked these bloody bottles in the bloody corridor. Move it now, go, go...."

And with that we all shot off in various directions! One jeep went one way, and one went the other and we met up about an hour later at this roundabout before carrying on along the same road. We learned later that apparently we shouldn't have had the booze in the first place! Bill was hysterical; he would always be so irate and end up shouting at everyone all the time.

When we did a spell in Bahrain the hotel had provided a minibus for us to travel to our venue. We obviously had a local driver and I remember Bill asking him if he knew where the British Club was to which this poor chap replied in his broken English but with Arabic accent.

"Yes I am knowing where the British Club is," but then just sat there and didn't really expand upon it, so Bill in frustration had him by the throat screaming, "Well bloody well drive us there then, don't just say you know where it is!!"

He practically burst a blood vessel on many an occasion and we would be on the floor in hysterics.

Another place we worked at was Oman and it really was fantastic. The show itself was on the beach and when we arrived at night to do the show it was all lit up with what seemed like a million candle flames which was absolutely breathtaking. Tony Jo got out of the minibus looked around at this wondrous sight and at the top of his voice started singing Barry Manilow's 'One Voice'. He got as far as the first line when yet again Bill Thompson started screaming at him, "Are you f..... mad, have you lost your f...... mind?? Shut uuuuup!!" Well by this time we were all shaking with laughter literally.

We were allowed the use of some guy's flat to get ourselves changed and ready, and he kindly supplied us with loads of booze. As we left to get on the minibus, we all had a stash of booze with us and Bill who was on the bus with us quick as anything said, "You will have to take all that booze back immediately because if we are stopped by the police there will be trouble." With that every single one of us got up and sheepishly filed back into the flat taking care not to spill the already opened bottles of beer!!

I, however with Martin's encouragement managed to keep two bottles of champagne in my bag and was petrified that these bottles would clink and Bill would find me out or worse that we would get stopped by the police. I'm glad to say we didn't and we all enjoyed the champagne when we got back to the hotel.

Tony Jo quite made the tour for us. He was so funny and used to do a wonderful impression of a dog barking. So much so that we would be in a restaurant in the hotel, he would do the impersonation then the waiters would come running in looking underneath the tablecloths for this non existent dog. It is the most unbelievable and realistic impersonation of a dog barking that I have ever heard.

In all the hotels that we were staying in, we were having a heck of a lot of fun with this as you can imagine. There was one hotel where we were also performing and the stage was out around the pool area. On this one occasion Tony was on stage doing his own stand up act which was somehow made funnier by the fact that nobody really understood what the hell he was on about, due to the language barrier. His room was adjoining mine and while he was on stage we went into his room and totally cleared it of everything and then made it up as if it had been serviced.

I was then able to lock the door from my side so he couldn't get into my room. When he came off stage and into his room, it looked like he was in the wrong room although he knew that he wasn't. Whilst we were on stage ourselves we suddenly heard echoing around the pool area, this voice from about the twentieth floor of this hotel block, "BASTARDS, where's my f......... gear??!!" How we didn't collapse with laughter on that stage I do not know.

Of course he got us back because every time one of us spoke he was hanging out of his window doing the dog impression whilst we were trying to hold it all together. It was absolutely hysterical.

We were out there over the Christmas period and Tony taught us all the most filthy version of the 'Twelve Days of Christmas'. We were going back to the hotel one night and about half a mile before we got there, Tony just started singing his version of this song which we had never heard before. Each day of Christmas just got dirtier and dirtier and by the time we reached the hotel we were screaming with laughter.

We couldn't get out of the minibus because Tony hadn't finished the whole twelve days and as we continued to laugh all these local Arab men in their traditional costume gathered around us inquisitively, just staring at us through these windows whilst the van was rocking with laughter. We pulled open the door and spilled out onto the pavement like British lunatics in total hysteria.

Tony finished the tour with us in Bahrain and didn't come on to Hong Kong and Kuala Lumpur which was a shame. We missed him dreadfully, he was such good fun.

New Years Eve that year was spent in Kuala Lumpur and we stayed in the wonderful Shangri La Hotel. Anyone familiar with the Far East will know the Shangri La group is very prestigious and out of this world. Basically it is everything you want a hotel to be. We did the show which was in the hotel, and when it came to midnight all the staff paraded around the hotel banging anything that made a noise mainly saucepans and spoons with all different rhythms and the band would follow them with any instruments they could play whilst walking along. It was the most fascinating experience and very exciting.

What I loved about those hotels was the attention to detail. In the lift there was a fitted mat which would be changed daily according to what day of the week it was, Monday, Tuesday etc. We thoroughly appreciated those kinds of touches.

The tour was very intense and we spent a lot of time in each others company.

So much so when I came back home and fell asleep on the settee in my lounge, I would wake up worried that I had lost my piece of paper and didn't know what rooms the boys were in. I was completely disorientated and thought I was still on tour.

Towards the end of the 80s we went out to Ireland. When we arrived we were split into two cars. We were in one car with the promoter and his son, and the boys in the band went in another car with a very nice chap from Thailand who had only been in the country for a couple of weeks and didn't speak any English, which was no help to the boys at all because the driver was supposed to be following us and unfortunately lost us.

There were no mobile phones then so the driver did not know where to take the boys and the boys didn't know where we were working. All they knew was that it was somewhere in Ireland with a vague idea of area but certainly no name or address. They found out by going into a local newsagent and getting hold of a newspaper.

The whole trip was a complete disaster really. The promoter had booked us into all these out of the way venues where people didn't really go to for a night out. They were more like places where you might stop off overnight en route to somewhere else in order to break up a journey. Don't get me wrong I absolutely loved the Irish people but everything that could go wrong did go wrong. In fact, so much so that I began to keep a diary of all the shenanigans. I kept that diary for many years but eventually threw it away more's the pity. It would have made a great book on its own!

To begin with the tour itself wasn't very well promoted and on our very first night and first show, not one solitary person turned up to see us. I kid you not. There we were all dressed up waiting to go on and wait we did because we never did go on. It was an empty hall! However there just so happened to be a bar in this place so I went in and began talking to people and I must say received the most wonderful Irish hospitality. I was in my absolute element drinking draught Guinness and consoled myself with a good few pints of the stuff so I was well happy. Sod the audience or lack of!!

Another time the venue was so bad that we didn't even bother putting stage clothes on. It was out in the countryside playing to a load of farmers who really didn't care if we were there or not. We just sat outside in the car with the window down and when we heard our name being announced we legged it in through the fire exit, closed the door behind us, went on stage, did the show, came off, straight through the fire doors, back into the car and drove away back to the hotel! I don't think they even noticed us!

We were staying in a hotel across the road from one of the clubs we were playing and the boys went across first to switch on the equipment as we had previously done a sound check in the afternoon. About half an hour later we went over to join them already dressed in our stage gear. The doorman wouldn't let us in and when we explained who we were, he looked at us in disbelief and just said in his broad Irish voice that 'they' had already arrived about thirty minutes ago. He was absolutely adamant and we were there for about five minutes trying to convince this doorman we weren't imposters. Eventually he relented but I still don't think he was convinced.

It was just one thing after another; even the hotel we stayed at had its own peculiarities. For example if the room was number 103 then for some bizarre reason the phone number of that room would be 104. Also as in most hotel rooms we had the complimentary tea and coffee along with a kettle provided. This sounds straightforward but in Martin and Sandra's room, in order to boil the kettle Martin had to stand with the kettle in mid air because the plug socket was high up on the wall. He would have needed a three foot long lead for it to have reached properly. I laugh just thinking about Martin with that blessed kettle.

We had a keyboard player with us who we hadn't worked with before and therefore wasn't used to our childlike pranks! Of course we couldn't resist this temptation and while he and his partner, who he had brought along on the trip, were fast asleep in their room, our sound engineer Paul Stratford and yours truly changed the numbers on the door with our 'magic screwdriver' which we seemed to be going round the world making a habit of doing!

The next morning at breakfast we were told by said keyboard player that they had woken in the night to find this irate drunken Irishman screaming at them to get out of his bed. He had apparently come in late and upon realising he couldn't get in the room went downstairs to the night porter who obligingly came up with the pass key. As far as this Irishman was concerned he was in the right room and started screaming and swearing at them to get out of his bed. Needless to say it was all sorted in the end!

This was a bit of light relief in what really was a soul destroying time. Eventually after abysmal attendances we got a call from the Promoter one morning to tell us that he had just received a phone call to say that if we went on stage that evening we would be shot! By now we were wising up to all these shenanigans and realised this was just a cop out to get us to go home and give up especially after finding that the sound guys had taken all the equipment away already! I mean weren't they going to wait to find out if we wanted to be shot? It was a complete farce and we returned home immediately after only a couple of weeks. It's a shame because we met some lovely people it was just that the venues were all wrong for us!

Little did we know then that this was to be our last major tour. Of course we have kept working constantly and have done plenty of one nighters and television appearances since but no more touring. We were lucky in as much as "Kisses" was a big hit in 33 different countries and as a result we were regularly invited to those countries to perform and do television appearances.

And of course each year when Eurovision comes around we will quite often be invited to various countries to appear on Song for Europe and provide the cabaret in the interim period whilst the votes are being cast. We went to Ireland in 2012 for that very reason. It was held in a television studio in Dublin and there were five songs altogether. Jedward were entered for the second time and again won. They are lovely shows to do and a great source of work for us.

Without going into much detail Alan and I grew apart and at the end of the 80s decided to call it a day due to irreconcilable differences as they say. We both went our separate ways and I have only seen him twice since in the early part of the 90s. We are still civil to each other however and diplomatically exchange Christmas cards each year with the odd bit of important news thrown in every so often.

Now luckily Eurovision and the 70s is a winning combination as far as working in the business is concerned! If its not one it's the other. One show we recorded for television was Songs of the Seventies which included artistes from the 70s but also artistes of the day singing seventies songs. Donny Osmond who fits into both these categories was presenting the show, with acts such as Steps and Hearsay and it was great to be part of it.

There is no doubt that other countries take Eurovision a lot more seriously than we do. It is an enormous occasion for them and they really love it. One year we appeared on television in Rome. I had previously holidayed there but the others had never been there before. As we walked on to the set we received a spontaneous round of applause which happens quite often in other countries and is not only a mark of respect for the song which won all those years ago and people still know now, but also the fact it's the four of us walking on set, still the same original line up and now pensioner's! The best one was a few years ago when we were working in Paris and again Eurovision time had come round and there was a programme on all about it. We were due to sing live and there was a thirty two piece orchestra waiting on set. As we made our entrance the whole orchestra applauded us. That was really really lovely and we were quite touched. True appreciation for a song that has given us our livelihood and our longevity in the business!

Rainer Haas who is a big agent in Germany loved having all the seventies bands over to perform in the big stadiums of the country and throughout the nineties we went over a few times to perform to around 10 to 12 thousand people along with other well known British bands or acts of the seventies. The show was called Olde Nacht which translated means Oldies Night which sounds quite insulting but it wasn't at all. One of the things they would do is leave a CD in the dressing rooms of all the artistes and songs featured in the show

We had the most fantastic audiences and wonderful times and so much fun. Bands such as Smokie, The Tremeloes, The Rubettes, The Swinging Blue Jeans and Leo Sayer all together on one bill was fantastic. Being the party animal that I was, I was totally in my element after each show and was never in bed before 3 or 4 am. The backstage catering in these places was always fantastic with plenty of alcohol and food available. You could have a party every night if you wanted too. I loved it and had an absolute ball with all these wonderful acts.

One night where we were working was quite a distance from the hotel as there wasn't a hotel available nearer that could accommodate us all. This meant we all travelled to the venue and back on a coach and consequently all had to leave together and come back together. This also meant you had to stay for the duration of the show whether you liked it or not. We would get back to the hotel at about 4.00 am because after the show we stopped off at a restaurant out in the sticks that had put on a buffet for us.

As we were all on this coach we had no choice in the matter and by the time we got back to our hotel one of the guys from Smokie declared that it was a bit pointless going to bed as we had a wake up call 6.30 am for breakfast as we were booked on an early flight to Heathrow. Of course I pipe up as the lone voice of Brotherhood that this is a great idea. Everyone else in the band would always sensibly go to bed even if only for a couple of hours but no, not Nicky. I would always readily agree to a couple more hours of partying!

Ray from the Swinging Blue Jeans had noticed that the bar next door was open all night so we went along. I was with the Blue Jeans and Smokie. I remember Lee was very concerned about how late it was and there was I full of gusto and the only female with all these blokes going into an all night bar. I loved being one of the boys! One of the guys in Smokie must have overheard Lee voicing his concerns and he came over to him and told him not to worry and that if I was with them I wouldn't come to any harm. They would look after me which of course they did.

Sandra loves to retell the story of how I walked into breakfast that morning and she couldn't quite believe how fabulous I looked. She didn't realise at the time that I hadn't actually been to bed and still had all my make up on from the previous night and the same outfit! I came straight in to the hotel, put my vodka and tonic down on the bar then walked into the restaurant and sat down for breakfast.

I was absolutely fine until we got to the airport where I basically just passed out. Not because I was drunk, I was just exhausted coupled with the few drinks I'd had! Every single moment or opportunity I could sit down on that journey home I would just promptly fall asleep. Knowing I had a barbecue planned for when I got back and had invited quite a few people round didn't help!

I think that was the most unreal I had ever felt and I swore after that, no matter how many hours it would be, even if it was only one or two hours, I would go to bed and snatch that little bit of sleep. I learnt my lesson well and truly that day that I couldn't stay awake all night and carry on the next day as if nothing had happened! Not any more!

Lo and behold that day actually came. The usual thing happened, we were out there doing a gig with a party lined up afterwards, and I declined saying it wasn't for me and I was going to bed! I can't tell you how many mouths just dropped open and froze as if they had lock jaw. Nicky had hung up her party hat! I still to this day have the odd relapse like a few months ago when we were doing a fabulous show in Gateshead. I wasn't exactly late to bed but I could have been in bed a good two to three hours earlier. I'd had a few wines and got on the karaoke and of course suffered for it the next day but these days I know the cure is loads of water!!

Nowadays as far as partying is concerned I've been there, done that, got all the tee shirts, all the hats and most certainly all the hangovers!

And boy when you are older the hangovers are so much worse. It's funny now when we travel round and I bump into my ex party animal mates, they are all exactly the same as me and keen to get their beauty sleep!

After Alan and I split, I moved to Colchester and it was there that I became a voluntary worker at Severalls Psychiatric Hospital working two days a week in the day unit with elderly clients at various stages of Alzheimer's disease. Some people were also there to have a break from coping at home with their disabilities. I worked with the occupational therapists Leslie and Melanie and I enjoyed my work so much and got very fond of a lot of the patients. I used to entertain them by sometimes playing the piano and once gave a talk on my life in the entertainment industry.

I was there for many years and Melanie and her husband LeRoy became wonderful friends of mine and in turn introduced me to their many friends at The Dog and Pheasant (you all know who you are!). Many a great night was spent at that pub, as I lived in Colchester for 11 years. Mel's Mum Renee was a great joker and when one of our friends Patrick was having a party, she informed me that it was fancy dress and as I had the slim legs, I should go as "Rose" from the programme Keeping Up Appearances. I readily agreed and went all out dressing up as a tart only to arrive at this rather lovely garden party which was definitely not fancy dress and people there who did not know me (and believe me there were plenty of them) who thought that was my normal dress. I could see the looks and hear the whispers. Renee even introduced me to the vicar. His face was a picture, great memories of great people.

I have a very close relationship with my niece and have had ever since she was born. Not having had children myself I like to think that I am close to all three of my nieces and nephews, Mark who is Elvyn's son and Sadie and Dean, are Dorrien's children. When Mark was born I was still in school but being born that much later I always maintained Sadie and Dean were like the children I never had. Sadie would love dressing up in my stage clothes and we used to have such fun together doing that whilst she sang along pretending to be me. She always used to say that she didn't want to get married until she was 26 as she wanted to travel the world first and be a famous singer like me.

It is an extremely difficult business particularly nowadays. It is not easy to get known and it is certainly not easy to get work. The business has changed considerably now and is totally different to the one I made it in. The reality shows are all very entertaining and undeniably produce a lot of good singers. They're a great chance for somebody unknown to be known, but my personal take on it is that they are big money making machines. A lot of the singers are told what to do, become very manufactured and hence lose their own direction. They become 'stars' first then go out and learn the trade.

The likes of me and many others from the same era had a big advantage. We were able to learn our trade thoroughly. We could work in a club every night, seven nights a week and go on to a night club as well, effectively doing 14 gigs a week if we wanted to plus a Sunday lunch time.

All four of us had careers before we formed as Brotherhood. Martin, Lee and Sandra were in big bands and I was doing my cabaret so we had plenty of experience and consequently when we hit the big time and had our hit records, we could walk out on any stage as professionals and we could handle whatever the business threw at us.

I really do pity the acts who are put together for one situation. You cannot gain professionalism over night and you cannot be told how to do it. It has to be learnt. You have to learn to be a 'pro'. I know the X Factor produced Leona Lewis who totally blew me away, but you don't really hear that much of her now and I find myself wondering what she is doing. It seems to be nearly a year after winning the show that they bring out an album and again I often wonder why? Is it because they are perhaps not up to the mark?

When Pop Idol first came on our screens, I absolutely loved it and thoroughly enjoyed watching as it was a novelty but if I'm honest find them all a bit tedious now. I actually know people who have gone to audition for X Factor who can really sing but haven't even made it past the preliminary stages to see the judges! They put a lot of the bad ones through initially or the ones with a good sob story because it makes good television and entertainment. Anybody in the business knows that and even the general public have wised up to it now. It's the same with Britain's Got Talent. A good friend of mine who's a great singer auditioned for that show and didn't even get a look in with the judges.

That said, these shows have been good for a lot of artistes, Ray Quinn for example has got a great career going along now doing all sorts of things. He didn't win but you usually find the ones that don't actually win seem to do better than the winners themselves. Will Young is perhaps the most consistent of all the winners and is now doing musical theatre which is a genre I have never tried. If I am being totally honest I'm not sure if I could manage such a gruelling and punishing schedule of work at my age!! But I still harbour a hope that there is a musical theatre role out there for me somewhere!

I suppose I first heard Sadie sing properly when she was about nine or ten. I was staying with them in Wales at the time and I was upstairs when I suddenly heard this voice belting out 'Ride on Time' by 'Black Box'. I just could not believe it was her! I have always actively encouraged and supported her whilst at the same time trying to be realistic. I explained to her how many people are out there trying to do the same thing but she was insistent so I did try to help her follow in my shoes for a while.

She attended Performing Arts College and at one point we both agreed that she needed singing lessons. She couldn't find a good vocal coach in her area and no-one knew of anybody to recommend.

On a whim I contacted my old singing teacher John Hywel Williams to see if he was still giving lessons, not even knowing how old he was by now! I worked out I was only 14 when he taught me and he was only a young man at the time, even though anyone over 20 is old when you are 14, so it had to be worth a shot. Anyway I phoned him and lo and behold, yes he was still alive and still teaching! Sadie attended lessons with him for quite a few months and he has helped her tremendously with breathing and vocal techniques that she needed to brush up on. I found it incredible that I was taught by John back in 1964 and here we were in 2011 at the time and he was now teaching my niece.

Unfortunately though, Sadie hasn't followed through with her singing for various reasons. She has a family now, two boys, and a job which takes up a lot of her time. There is no denying she has talent and a fantastic voice. Whenever I go back home to Wales nowadays, many a night we go out together and wind up somewhere where they have a karaoke as she is so keen to get up and sing. I just wish I lived nearer, as I know I could help her such a lot. For now though unfortunately it remains a hobby for her.

When I was home with her just recently, a male singer she knows rang her up and asked her if she would be interested in forming a Brotherhood of Man tribute band. Apparently he told her he had worked with us and knew us really well. Of course he had no idea that Sadie was my niece so she went along with it and said that she would be interested as long as she could be Nicky Stevens and explained why. She hasn't heard from him since!! At the time she showed me his photograph on Facebook and if he does know me I certainly don't know him!

After my marriage break up I had a series of boyfriends none of which lasted for any length of time but they certainly helped me get over my marriage, before then embarking on a lovely relationship with a young English lad I met called Nick who at the time was living in Spain. I quickly became very close to him and his family. He was fourteen years my junior so I suppose nowadays I would be called a Cougar. The fact is everybody commented on the fact we looked good together so I never gave any thought to the age difference. We enjoyed quite a few years together, living in Colchester, as his family, who I got on tremendously well with, were all Essex based. We would all go on trips to Spain together to visit Nick's parents who lived there, and had a wonderful time but sadly the relationship ran its course and ended in 1992.

What I needed then was a dust myself down, pick myself up, type of holiday, so I headed straight out to America to visit my friends Raleigh, an ex-commander with NATO and Lee, his wife, in Virginia Beach, Virginia. We first met when they used to live in the house opposite to us in Watford when we were at the height of our success which was rented out to NATO at the time by the couple who owned it, who themselves had gone to work abroad for a while.

We became very friendly with them when they were over here and socialised a lot with them going to many a NATO do in London with them including a NATO Ball. Their sons were teenagers at the time and the family were only here for a limited period of time on business before they returned home to America. However, we kept in touch over the years and this was now my ideal chance after thinking about it for so many years to actually go out there myself. I rang them up and they asked when I would like to go.

"Next week?" I asked. They were delighted and I in turn was very excited about the prospect. There is something about America for me. Every time I get on a plane bound for the States I always get incredibly excited. This is something I don't experience going anywhere else in the world. I just love the country.

Raleigh and Lee had the most stunning property on a lake in Virginia which was very colonial. Their sons had now grown up and promptly bestowed on me the title Miss Nicky and would often ask me to accompany them to night clubs. This worked really well for me as I'd go out with Lee and Raleigh for the first part of the evening till about 10.00 pm as they liked to go to bed reasonably early, then off I would go out with the sons, meeting all their friends and not getting home till about 3.00 or 4.00 in the morning, and absolutely having the time of my life in Virginia Beach, Virginia, oh yeah!

At one of these parties I met a particular friend Brett, and it didn't take long before we embarked on a torrid affair. When recalling this time in my life I always describe it as 'my brain going out to lunch'. A very long lunch at that!

Following the same pattern as Nick before him, Brett was fourteen years younger than me. We decided after a very short but passionate dalliance, so to speak, that we were very much in love with each other but I had to now return home, madly in love with Brett and totally consumed by my feelings for him.

My whole life was then spent writing letters and on phone calls to America and within a few months he came over in the November of 1992 and we got married the following May. Looking back this was so ridiculous because neither of us really knew each other. It was totally the wrong thing to do and a big mistake and needless to say the marriage didn't last and we didn't even see our first wedding anniversary. I finally divorced him for mental cruelty.

I always used to think that mental cruelty was perhaps a lot of arguing or being shouted at a lot. In fact it is extremely complex and can wear you down. By the end of the relationship I had nothing left, no self esteem and certainly no fight in me. Not wishing to dwell on it further, that was the end of my second brief but incredibly intense marriage.

Me riding an elephant

Releasing a baby turtle
into the sea

Bathing an elephant in the river

Me sampling tea

Chapter 33: Putting On The Brakes

Animals have and always will play an extremely important part in my life. As a girl our next door but one neighbours Mr and Mrs Thomas had a wonderful budgie called Peter who could talk for England. When they used to go away, Peter used to come and stay with us. I was fascinated by this budgie as it would talk to me and tell me in the third person how Peter wanted to come out of the cage and then how Peter wanted to go back in the cage. He would also play football with a little ball along the table. He was quite a remarkable little bird and would take off Mr Thomas laughing perfectly. I was so young but thought Peter the budgie was just the best!

Anyone who knows me will tell you I have a bit of a soft spot for Yorkshire Terriers, ever since Billy from The Fourmost had bought me one on my return from South Africa. Apart from a cat who was my very first pet as a young child, if you can call it that as it lived mainly next door, this dog was my first real pet and we named him Taffy. I loved having a dog but unfortunately it was totally impractical as I was on the road so much and it wasn't fair on Taffy. Subsequently my Mam and Dad ended up looking after him.

Eventually years later I acquired another Yorkie. Her kennel name was Cariad of Kimmeridge. Cariad being Welsh for darling, which I myself shortened to Carrie. I got her in 1981 when I was still married to Alan and when we split the dog stayed with me. When Brett came over in 1992 we went down to Wales for Christmas, stayed at my brother's and spent Christmas day at a friend's house with his children.

We had finished lunch and were on the cheese and biscuits and suddenly this jolt went through me and I felt as if I had been shot. That is the only way I can describe it. I slammed my hand on the table immediately and said, "Where's my dog?"

The door was wide open and no-one could see any sign of Carrie's whereabouts. Apparently my friend's children had gone out to play and kids being kids didn't think twice that the dog was with them but not on a lead. They had no perception of the idea that she could run onto the road and get run over. It wouldn't have entered their heads. Very sadly that is what in fact happened. My little Carrie had been knocked over. Whoever was responsible had picked her up and laid her on the grass verge. Happy Christmas Nicky!

I can categorically say that losing her, and in such a brutal way absolutely destroyed me. My last words to her were basically telling her off. I was in the kitchen helping with the dinner, handling hot roasting tins and she had been pestering me. Tempers were frayed and I'd snapped at her and told her to clear off into another room.

I'd always felt that since Brett had arrived from America I had neglected her somewhat and pushed her to one side. Of course I fed her and went through the motions of daily care but it wasn't quite the same and I suffered so much guilt over that. We buried her in my friend's garden and I was absolutely heartbroken at losing her. Things weren't particularly good between Brett and myself, I could already see the relationship was beginning to crumble and I knew it wasn't going to work as we were totally different people, so I found myself on a very downward spiral and began to suffer badly with depression. I was haunted by this little dog's death; it was just tearing me up.

I felt that I had just dumped her in a garden miles away from home and it got so bad my Doctor actually said that if anyone could face exhuming her little body, bringing her back to Colchester for me to then put her in the pet cemetery there, it would give me closure.

Brett and our keyboard player Tim did offer to do this for me even though they were warned it would not be a pleasant sight as her body would be partly decomposed by now. However I decided I could not go through with it and disturb her. I think it was the mixture of everything that was happening at the time. The unhappiness of my marriage and losing my dog, combined together put me in a very bad place indeed.

This came to a head when one day I had to nip into town to go to the post office. I parked the car in a multi storey car park, went to the post office and joined the queue when suddenly an overwhelming panic took over me and I just felt I could not go through with it and had to make my escape. I rushed back to the car as fast as I could, went home, locked the door, drew the curtains, got into bed underneath the duvet and finally felt safe. I went through a very bad patch which altogether lasted eight years.

I tried all kinds of ways to get back on track, including telling myself tomorrow is another day and things will change. I read countless books on positive thinking, positive feelings, don't let the situation control you, you control the situation and suchlike. They are all very spiritual and come from within and all helped in a way I suppose.

The one thing that really seemed to help though was being part of Brotherhood of Man and singing on stage. That was my saving grace during this period. It was like a kind of therapy and was my life blood, constantly reminding me who I really was. I remember during this time bumping into a police officer I knew in Colchester who was an ex-neighbour and when I saw him again much later on he told me how relieved he was that I was looking better as he thought I had looked absolutely awful. Something I certainly didn't realise. We can't always see ourselves in the mirror as others see us.

First of all I was put on medication but I discovered some side effects that I didn't really like and didn't suit me although at first I didn't make the connection between what was happening to me and the medicine. I was staying in Swansea with my brother and when I confided in him about this he confirmed it was the effects of the drugs, at which point I decided to take myself off them and try to heal myself.

Dorrien then told me that he was regularly attending the Spiritual Awareness Centre in Swansea and invited me to go along. He wasn't sure if it would be any good for me but it had been an enormous help to him and there was no harm in trying. At that point in our lives we seemed to be travelling along the same road and had a lot in common. His wife had left him and my second marriage had finally collapsed.

I felt I had nothing to lose by going along so Dorrien took me with him on his next visit. I walked into this room and I immediately felt such a great powerful surge of energy, love and comfort which I have never ever forgotten. The service started with a hymn 'How Great Thou Art'. I was wearing a sweater with a big roll neck and the tears just started seemingly from nowhere and just streamed down my face. I silently cried through the whole of that service. By the end the front of my jumper was saturated. I had found a starting point for my healing process right there in that room. I also embarked upon my spiritual path that day.

They were wonderful people who gave me the strength and healing I needed at the time and it is a place I will always hold dear in my heart. My recovery didn't happen overnight, it was a long slow process of about eight years, but whenever I was down in Swansea I would visit the Centre and each time it helped a little bit more. I also learned a great deal about myself along the way. I became aware of my attitude towards other people and how I treated them, and from then onwards have always tried to show acts of kindness and compassion which would not have occurred to me before. It certainly altered me and my way of thinking and has made me a far more emotional human being as well.

If I had to give myself a label I suppose I'd call myself a Spiritual Christian. I believe in Jesus and I believe in God. I haven't read the bible even though recently I have been given one as a present. It is a vast book to read and so I have been told a great manual on how to live your life. I believe God is the creator and the Great Spirit. I believe in life after death and that when you die you go to a spiritual place and that is where my parents are. I feel their presence around me at times. This contradicts the Bible as communicating with people who have 'passed over', through Mediums, is regarded as the 'devil's work' and is where I struggle with a bit of inner conflict, as I have been to a couple of excellent mediums who wouldn't be able to do what they do unless they truly were in touch with the other side.

All I know is I haven't harmed anybody, I believe in God, I believe in Jesus and I'm quite happy with that! If the Devil is making me believe that through a Medium I am hearing from my Mother and Father, then it certainly hasn't stopped me believing in God.

My recovery hasn't been easy and I still have my ups and downs. I've even thought occasionally about going back to the Doctor's for help. Another thing that has become very apparent these days is if I've had a heavy drinking session, then the following day I will feel absolutely lousy. I'm ok with a glass or two of wine but unfortunately can't party like I used to!

Photo taken by a fan

Signing autographs

Chapter 34: Slowing Down

We have worked with a variety of talented musicians during our career, one of them, a bass player by the name of Alan Evans would periodically play in our backing band and one night he brought his wife Julie to watch the show. We became friends and she invited me down to their home in Sturminster Marshall, Dorset to stay one weekend. Julie introduced me to friends of hers Gary and David who at the time owned a local hairdressing salon with treatment rooms attached.

We became friendly and some time later they asked me if I would be interested in going to work for them as Front of House Hostess. The idea was that I would welcome clients and show them to their treatment room or make them comfortable whilst waiting for the stylist. Basically a glorified receptionist! They also said I could live in the flat above the salon which was situated in Parkstone, Dorset.

You have probably gathered by now that I never waste opportunities and I absolutely grabbed this one with both hands. I had wanted to leave Colchester for years and I couldn't figure out how, purely because of the location and how long it took me to get home after a gig. The others would be home and tucked up in bed whilst I was still on the M25!! I still maintain that if Colchester was in Dorset I'd live there.

Anyway it wasn't just a case of selling up and moving. It was moving to where? That was the question. That place, wherever it was, would need to have people there that I knew and this seemed the ideal solution. Every time I had ever worked in Dorset I fell in love with the place even more, so in January 2000 I made the move.

Realistically I knew Gary and David were reaching too far with the business but I could also see where they were coming from. Of course they hoped I would get them a load of publicity which I did. The local Echo did a four page spread in the weekend magazine and I was interviewed on all the local radio stations, so they gained their publicity and I gained my stepping stone to a new life. I wasn't there for much longer than three months which didn't surprise me as they weren't doing any business at all, but while I was there the entire episode was a win win situation.

By now I had found somewhere to rent so when the business fell through I was fairly settled in the area and more than happy to stay put. I eventually bought a property and have stayed in this part of the country ever since. I feel like it was meant to be.

Not long after all this happened I received a telephone call from Keith Bartlett, a drummer I had met years ago at Ronnie Scott's nightclub. Keith told me he was in a three piece band in Weymouth at The Riviera which was previously one of Pontin's holiday camps. He also said the trio needed a girl singer and would I be interested? He had tried to get my number a few times from Alan Evans who apparently had refused to give it to him. In Alan's words, "There's no chance you'll get Nicky Stevens to join your band!"

In actual fact when Keith spoke to me about it adding he wasn't sure how much work they could offer me, perhaps one or two nights a week, I absolutely jumped at it because here I was now being given the chance, similar to back in the 80s, to sing material outside of the group. Of course I stressed that I was still working with Brotherhood of Man and doing gigs with them to which Keith responded, "We've managed before and we'll just get by so that's no problem."

I went down there on my first night, met the other guys in the band, bass player Steve Reynolds and on keyboard Paul Stewart, and we all hit it off straight away. We did the first set which seemed to go ok, and I was enjoying a coffee whilst the cabaret was on. Keith meanwhile was speaking to the Manager who thought I was absolutely unbelievable and offered me six nights a week there and then!

The idea horrified me at first! I mean six nights!! I hadn't worked that kind of schedule in many years! I spoke to Dorrien about it and suggested maybe I'd tell them I could only work five nights, to which my brother turned round and asked me what on earth was so important that I was going to do on that sixth night?

I had to admit he had a point so somewhat reluctantly and with a great deal of trepidation I once more found myself as a band singer somewhat older, maybe wiser but hey I was only doing six nights instead of seven and at least I wasn't touring around! I ended up staying there for two years and thoroughly enjoyed the whole time there.

My animal companion at that time was Aslan my beautiful cat. When I had lost my little Yorkie, Carrie in the Christmas of 1992, the following May some neighbours moved and took their cats with them. However, there was one particular cat, a huge male tabby called Aslan who kept managing to find his way back to the area which was approximately three miles away from his new home and which he clearly did not like!

Each time his owners would duly come and get him to take him back and Aslan would promptly make his way back to his old home again. This happened on several occasions each taking various lengths of time as he explored different routes. I even took him back a couple of times as I knew where they had moved to!

I had met Aslan before when his family still lived nearby and as soon as I sat down he would make a bee line for me, lay himself on my chest with both his front paws around my neck and proceed to rub his face on mine. I remember thinking how amazing this cat was. He was more like a dog! Eventually I suggested to Aslan's owners that he come live with me as it was clear he was not going to settle with them in their new home. They agreed this was the best thing as he was at risk of living wild if he continued the way he was.

That was all very well but the next thing was trying to find him. He could be anywhere between the two areas in any garden or up any tree! I was in an apartment complex in Colchester surrounded by quite a few apartment buildings separated by huge lawns and gardens. This was going to be like searching for a needle in a haystack so I just stood in the middle of the car park and called out his name. Suddenly I heard meowing and out of nowhere Aslan appeared. I swear to God all I said quietly was, "Come on, you've got a new home."

I didn't encourage him, I just walked across the car park, up the path, in through the security doors, up two flights of stairs, into my apartment and he followed me in, sat on the settee and purred louder than the television, as happy as anything. I firmly believe he had chosen me.

However this now set me on a guilt trip as I hadn't long lost Carrie and I remember saying to him, "Right there's your food, there's your water, there's your bed but don't expect much else!"

Well he had other ideas didn't he? If I got up, the cat got up, if I went into one room, the cat followed. If I came out of the room, the cat followed, if I sat down the cat sat on top of me, if I got up he was right behind me again. It was just like he was saying, "You will love me. I will make you love me!"

He was a bit of a naughty boy and used to go out a lot, always picking fights. He was like the Darth Vader of cats! I would watch him as he thundered across to his next victim then I would see all this fur flying. It was after one hell of a cat fight that he developed an abscess on his neck which was huge and bigger than a golf ball. He had to be operated on and the night before the operation I had taken him to the vets where I received my instructions for the following day.

Aslan was such a unique, funny cat. He would let you nurse him like a baby and would be in his element. As I held him that evening I prayed that this lump would not get any bigger during the night as I had been told there was a risk of this. I just looked at him and burst into tears and told him how much I loved him and that he couldn't die! That was my turning point and I lost all guilt about giving another animal a little love.

I have to hand it to Brett at this time as I remember him saying to me that nothing would ever ruin the love I had for Carrie and I should mentally wrap it up and place it on the shelf where nothing at all could touch it. Then I should open up my heart for a new love. I'd never thought about it like that before and I've since given that advice to so many people who have also appreciated it

I loved that cat with a passion and because my last words to Carrie involved shouting and telling her off I swore I would never ever ever shout at Aslan in case anything should happen to him.

Another day he came home covered in blood. It was obvious he had been hit by a car and somehow managed to find his way home. I rushed him to the vets absolutely distraught and was transported back to that Christmas Day when I had lost Carrie. I was hysterical whilst driving the car, screaming and begging him not to die on me. Luckily he wasn't ready to die yet but had stitches all the way up his leg and on his face. He fully recovered and was fine.

After that incident if ever I was outside near the road and picked him up to give him a love, he would struggle to get free if a car was approaching. I'd asked the vet at the time if he thought Aslan had learned his lesson and he said probably not, he'd no doubt go back out and use up another life, but I believe he definitely had.

What eventually took him from me was cancer of the nostrils. It was awful; he was in such terrible pain. I was petrified at the prospect of having him put to sleep. My brother was brilliant. He reassured me by saying that Aslan absolutely adored me and had the utmost respect for me and that the greatest most unselfish gift I could give to him was to put him out of his misery and that only I could do it for him. His trust was in me to help him and of course he was right.

So the decision was made while I was working at the Riviera in Weymouth and I came off stage one night knowing it was only a matter of time before I would have to have him put to sleep and just burst into tears. The rest of the band shut the door wondering what on earth was wrong as by now I was sobbing my heart out. I had totally lost it and was terrified. I explained to them I had never taken an animal to a vet before to have them put down and I really didn't know how I was going to cope. Our bass player Steve Reynolds was so kind and understanding. His words meant so much and he helped convince me I was doing the right thing.

The night before I was due to take him in, I went home and filled the place with calming spiritual music and lit lots of candles. Aslan just laid on my chest looking into my eyes as I explained to him that he was going on a journey without me as I couldn't join him and he had to be a very brave boy and that I would see him again one day but not quite yet. We stayed like that for a couple of hours, he then slept with me on the bed and in the morning I took him to the vet.

The whole time that the vet was preparing him for the injection, that cat was transfixed on my face, looking directly into my eyes as if he knew something was happening but he wasn't sure what. He didn't take his eyes off me and I just kept telling him what a good boy he was. It broke my bloody heart. I couldn't go into work that night nor the following night but that is me. I love my animals and that is the price we pay for that love.

Not long after I left The Riviera, a guy called John Dutton got in touch; he had seen Brotherhood working and liked our four individual talents. He also liked my comedy style and thought I was a natural comedienne and consequently he wrote a show about the decade of the 70s with us very much in mind.

We loved this idea as it contained narration combined with music. When we first performed it on stage, it was far too long. Some things worked and others didn't and in the end we edited it right down. As anyone will tell you, you have to try new ideas or songs on stage first to see if they work. If not you go to Plan B, always assuming there is a Plan B!! It's the only way. We kept all the songs and theme tunes from movies and television shows and we chopped the narration practically in half as it was a little bit tedious.

Then we started taking certain songs from this show and putting them into our 70's Express Show which was one hour of non stop 70's songs and worked perfectly for the many 70's revival shows we had started doing. So much so that we have basically kept this format for our act today and it has opened the door for other ideas to develop around it. For instance you may remember Mike Batt and The Wombles were very big in the 70s and we have a core group of fans who started to give us 'Wombles' as presents to keep.

There is one very large one in particular called Orinoco who was given to us and Martin uses it as a puppet on stage. Obviously it is a silent puppet as Martin is not a ventriloquist but Martin speaks and his timing with this Womble is absolutely fantastic and it goes down a storm. He puts his hand up the back of Orinoco's waistcoat to move his head and body around and has such a great connection with the movements and co-ordination of this Womble, it really is very realistic! So much so that I have ended up screaming with laughter on stage because he literally brings life to this puppet!

One night Martin with this silent Orinoco instigated a pretend punch up at a club where it was a 70's night and there was a Smurf in the audience. This Smurf came to the front of the stage and they had this mock fight, it was absolutely hysterical! If Martin could learn how to do the voice, I reckon he would be a brilliant ventriloquist and have a whole new career!

Tragically Orinoco was nearly left behind in a dressing room one night. We have a saying in the band, "Last one out look around." Martin and Sandra left, I then went to leave and looked around, couldn't see anything and Lee was last to leave. Luckily he also looked around and found Orinoco very nearly abandoned in a carrier bag in a dark corner of the room. Of course I couldn't let this pass and I emailed the others on behalf of Orinoco to say how disappointed he was and how he had looked upon Martin as a mentor and had learnt such a lot in the business from working with him and how he had really thought he was of greater value than just something to be left behind in a carrier bag in a cold dank dressing room all on his own.

Orinoco went on to say how frightened he was and had even wondered what was to become of him if his glittering show business career were to end abruptly! However he was extremely grateful to Lee for coming to his rescue and taking him back to his house and looking after him so well, and to warn Martin that if this ever happened again he would bugger off and join Bucks Fizz!! To this day I am glad to report that Orinoco is safe and well, makes regular appearances on stage and has never been left behind again!

We have been so lucky to have kept working as a band, perhaps not as much as before but certainly on a regular basis doing some really lovely concerts. Television work still comes in occasionally as well and recently travelled down to Devon to appear on Dick and Doms's mad children's television programme. I had heard guests get gunged and all sorts of horrid things happen but there was none of that with us!

The revival and popularity of the 70s has ensured plenty of lucrative work for us on the back of it, including many Butlins 70s weekends. Butlins was and still is a marvellous place for entertainment and these weekends are totally dedicated to it. We are usually booked to do one spot but the guests will arrive on a Friday, leave on the Monday and the whole of the weekend is packed with different bands and singers in two big rooms. Sadly not all the acts are the original line up like us and there are countless tribute bands that do the rounds. I think at last count there were fifty million Abba tributes out there! I don't know of any Brotherhood tribute bands although there nearly was courtesy of my niece! I don't think any one wants to do us!

Mind you all the places such a band would work we already work there anyway!

And it's not just the 70s; they put on all types of themed weekends such as 80s and Soul which is a great source of work for artistes of that genre. Whatever the theme these weekends are absolutely fantastic and great value for money. Audiences are always encouraged to attend in fancy dress and I believe you can hire the costumes on site. It really is amazing as the curtains open on a couple of thousand people where over half of them are in seventies gear and some in particular have gone to such huge effort.

It's fabulous because looking out you actually feel as if you have gone back in time. They are our favourite gigs to do and we have such a ball. In fact when we sing our own hits we actually get drowned out!! The amazing thing is there are some people in the audience who weren't even born when we won Eurovision but have grown up with their parents knowing our songs.

The beauty of our career now is we are being offered a high calibre of work and are able to pick and choose what we do. We don't find the work itself tiring but the journeys can be draining. Another lovely source of work for us is the Warners Leisure Hotels which are adult only breaks. We still get to travel around the country and pop up when least expected. Most importantly we are still enjoying what we do.

My beautiful cat Aslan

My beautiful Yorkshire terrier Carrie

My Mum

My dear American friends Lee and Raleigh Smith, 1992

Me with some of the lovely clients at Severalls Hospital in the 1990s

Chapter 35: Emergency Stop

Recently I've been to a very good Medium called Tom Smith who is well known locally. I've met with him twice and my Father came through both times for me and I firmly believed that my Mother had joined him in Spirit. I was told by a very close psychic friend of mine that my Mother was very weak when she passed over and she just about had enough strength to take my Father's hand. In her last few days on earth my Mother who was barely conscious told me she thought it was best that she should 'go' as anything had got to be better than the pain she was in.

With tears streaming down my face and trying to control my voice and gain some sort of composure I told her not to be afraid and that where she was going would be fine, she would be safe and that my Father was waiting to meet her and she would see Granny and Granddad and all her sisters who had passed before and would all be waiting too. I got no reply to this because she was in and out of consciousness. I reminded her of all the good times we had shared together to which she managed a nod and a smile. I gave her permission to 'go' and not to worry about me, or my brothers and that we would all be fine and would be coming behind her. And so twenty one months after her initial diagnosis of cancer my dear Mam passed away.

Cancer is a terrible disease and a total disrespecter of the human body. When you witness what the body has to endure because of it, it really is a dreadful thing for both the person suffering and their loved one watching. It had taken a year before Mam was even diagnosed because it was a tricky and unusual form of cancerous tumour that was growing high up in her bowel area. They never did find out where it actually originated. We had to accept that nothing could be done to treat it and they could only offer palliative care. She did have two small bursts of radiotherapy which almost killed her but I was there for her each step of the way and went for every test with her.

Towards the end I cancelled a gig and explained to the others that she could go at any minute and she was certainly not going without me being there. The group were very understanding and phoned up the theatre manager who had not long lost his own Mother and quite understood. The show was cancelled and people had their money refunded and we were booked for later in the year. I also cancelled a gig with The Vernon Girls and they went ahead without me. I didn't care about anything or anyone else, Mam was my absolute priority.

I was adamant about being there. It was almost like I had to make sure everything was alright. Mam and I shared a special closeness, perhaps because we were two females I don't know. My brother Dorrien however could not face that prospect. He did not want to see her go.

It's very strange though as Idris always tells me from his experiences in hospitals. Many a story he can tell where death is lurking, but kept at bay by the person who is dying until they have seen somebody, somebody who perhaps they are not right with leaving yet and need to say goodbye to. He's told me some fascinating stories on the subject of people who just refuse to go until they have seen a certain person.

I saw this for myself because by now Mum was in a wonderful hospice called Ty Bryn Gwyn Hospice in the grounds of Llanelli Hospital South Wales. I was sleeping on the chair on and off alongside my Mother's bed and put my hand underneath the sheet to hold hands with her all night. One of the nurses told me that a few times in the night they nearly had to wake me as they thought she was going but then came round again. I must have been spark out as I don't recall any of this.

In the morning the staff swapped shifts and another lovely male nurse came on duty. I told him what had happened and we had nearly lost her in the night. By now I wanted her to go anyway, and for her suffering to end. It was just a matter of time anyway and what this damn illness had done to her I just wanted Mam to go to a better place then this bloody cancer would die with her. She was in excruciating pain and was on a syringe driver to control it. Even though she appeared unconscious it was as if she was aware of her surroundings and what was going on. The nurse then matter of factly explained that she was probably waiting for Dorrien to come. He was due to visit that teatime. The moment he walked out of the room after his visit her body began to shut down.

I knew that she'd gone to where I told her she was going and nothing would make me believe otherwise. However I still went to see Tom Smith for that extra reassurance and my Father cropped up again as in the previous reading. Eventually my Mother came through. I was desperately waiting for something to be said to convince me that this was definitely her. Lots of Mediums will say general things like, yes she was pleased she had a good send off and the flowers were lovely. I needed something concrete from Tom. I never told him I was testing him so apologies Tom if you are reading this!!

All of a sudden Tom asked the question, "Who told her about passing over and what would happen?" I confirmed that I had and he then told me I had made it easy for her. I thought that was ok but again that was fairly general and I still didn't have that vital reassurance I so needed then. We continued and then all of a sudden he said "Who is Idris?"

Idris of course, not only my lifelong and dearest friend, but also a vicar, had spoken to my Mother a lot latterly and he would phone her regularly at the hospice from Lanzarote. He has such a wonderful way with words. He had also sent her a card with a passage from the Bible "Your Weakness is my Strength", meaning when you are weak this is where my strength comes to hold you and carry you through. I remember teasing my Mam about taking all her get well cards down but leaving the one from Idris. I told her it was favouritism to which she replied the words gave her comfort and strength. Idris couldn't have chosen a better card for Mam.

Tom then went on to tell me all about Idris himself and I just silently thanked God. Tom didn't know Idris at all and here he had just confirmed and proved everything I needed to know. He also went on to talk about Mam's friends and mention names of people she had met up with in spirit. I am a spiritual person, it is what I believe in and sometimes I feel that Mam is with me and speaking to me. A voice or thought will just pop into my head which I just know is her.

Many's the time I've had a couple of psychic friends who whilst visiting me here will suddenly feel a presence and tell me that my Mam is here with me. As friends they have got no reason to lie to me. After my Mam died I had her wedding picture, scanned by a friend of mine then cleaned, enlarged and was recommended a place to have it framed. It is a beautiful picture and hanging proudly on my wall. Mam was 19 and Dad about 23. During my visit to Tom he also mentioned this wedding photograph to me. He told me that they stand in front of it looking at it. He ended by saying that when I pass over the first face I will see will be my Mother's. As far as I am concerned I have had my fair share of confirmation of what I believe in and I haven't felt a need to return to Tom for another reading. I know she and my Father are around now.

However I did take my cousin Elizabeth to see him not long after she had been widowed and Tom told me that my Mam and Dad had appeared to him in his garden one day. Now Tom always refers to his wife as the old lady and he said it was her who had seen them first then they glided past him arm in arm and thanked him for all he had done before disappearing again.

When Mam died I stayed in Wales for a while and cleared her house out on my own. Although it wasn't a council built house and used to be privately owned, the landlord had sold it some years ago to the council. Even though the council were very good and told me there was no need to rush and no time restrictions were put upon me, I didn't want to dilly dally. I just wanted to get it all done and sorted. Consequently I managed to get it all done within a couple of weeks and was on the go the whole time. I had so much to do and cope with that I couldn't let myself go or I just wouldn't have been able to do all the things I had to. I was almost dreading coming back here as I knew that the full force of bereavement would hit me like a tonne of bricks.

Travelling back home I couldn't fit another thing into the boot of my car. A boot incidentally that everyone always remarks upon as being massive. The inside of the car was also full to the ceiling. I just had a small gap that I could peer through to allow me to drive safely and enough room for me to sit and actually drive the thing. Other than that it was chocka block full.

My lovely friend Julie told me that because it was winter time, no way was I going back to a dark house and she insisted I was to go to hers in Sturminster Marshall. When I got there she had all my wonderful girlfriends there waiting and we all had a meal together.

Julie's husband Steve subsequently arranged to take the day off work for Mum's funeral, hire a big people carrier and bring all my friends to Wales to attend the funeral. On the day itself the weather was atrocious and people were advised by the Met Office not to travel unless they absolutely had to. There was debris on motorways, trees were down, it was really appalling weather so sadly they didn't come. However because they couldn't make it, they all went to Julie's for lunch and

Steve took a photo of them all together and made it into a card which everyone signed and which is now a very treasured possession and an indication of how special these friends are to me.

As far as I was concerned everything had to be dead right for Mam's funeral. This wasn't about me and my grief now, it was all about her. I had plenty of time to grieve and cry in the days to follow. One of the lovely male nurses had said to me that I must be sure to eat well as I had some dark days to come. I knew what he meant.

I wrote the eulogy for Mum's funeral and I gave it to our Minister Mr Davies to read out because I knew there was no way in this world that I would have been able to do that. When it came to the service, Mr Davies took out the piece of paper and explained to the congregation what it was about and suddenly out of the blue I interrupted him and asked him if it was alright with him I would like to read it myself. I still don't know to this day where that came from and cannot believe I did it. I sang my heart out during that ceremony with no hint of a tear, and felt a tremendous strength.

I was the total opposite of how I always thought I would be. I used to tell people how I dreaded my Mother dying and I would have to be dragged or carried into church for the service as I wouldn't be able to cope. I swear on that day and also on the day that I held my Mother as she took her last breath I wasn't alone.

At the end of the day I went back to the house and there I sat for a while looking around my Mum's home, all on my own in total shock. I cannot even begin to describe the feeling that came over me. I then went out with my old school friends, Sharon, Leslie and Mary to a pub just around the corner that in all the years I'd lived in Carmarthen I had never visited, and got absolutely sloshed. I often feel ashamed and guilty that I got drunk on the day of my own Mam's funeral but then I reason with myself and think if anyone had the right to get drunk then I did. I was in unchartered territory and didn't know what to do with myself, or what to eat and drink. I even bought some fags thinking they might help and by then I'd given up smoking.

When everything had calmed and I did return home on my own, it was like a massive fist slamming down into my face. Reality kicked in big time as I knew it would. It was finally all done and dusted. My Mam had gone. My home that I had known all my life had gone and the keys had been handed in to the council. Everything in it had either gone to charity or thrown away.

This was when I cried like I'd never cried before. One night I was in bed and crying so badly that I knew I was starting to hyperventilate. I knew what it felt like because I'd had an accident not all that long before and had badly bruised all my ribs and couldn't breathe with the pain and had started to hyperventilate then. It is quite a terrifying feeling I was totally alone and shouted out, "For God's sake if anyone can hear me please help me!"

Suddenly in the depths of my despair this voice that I didn't recognise or powerful thought came into my mind telling me to go into the spare bedroom and get the box of pictures that I had brought back from the house then to go downstairs and look through them.

I duly did this even though there were a hell of a lot of pictures to look at, made myself a stack of toast and a cup of tea and started to go through them. It was then I came across one of my Mother where she had a hat on with all the corks hanging from it like an Australian hat. It was taken on a night when she had been here to visit me here in Dorset and we had gone round to my next door neighbours at the time and Mam had consumed one too many glasses of wine!

Not being a drinker it had gone straight to her head and it had made her very very giggly and this picture had been taken when she was killing herself laughing. Her eyes were looking straight down the camera lens and when I saw this picture, the tears that were streaming down my face continued into tears of laughter. I was then able to return to bed and sleep. I have never forgotten that moment.

Anyone who has gone through bereavement will understand what I am talking about. It is the cruellest most heartbreaking thing I have ever had to endure and a dreadful rollercoaster of emotions. Nobody else knows how you feel apart from yourself. Somehow I managed to put on a cheerful face whenever I spoke to someone else and consequently everyone thought I was doing fine but I wasn't doing fine at all.

You begin to realise that you can't keep telling people how you feel. You feel guilty about burdening them with your misery all the time and that they don't want to hear how bad you feel. You feel totally alone with your bereavement, it is a very isolating experience.

This is where I count myself so lucky to have Idris as a friend. He has been a source of utmost strength for me in my bereavement. In his role as Hospital Chaplain he has worked so much with the dead and dying in his life that he always knew what I was going through and has always even to this day has made a point of finding out how I am. "How are YOU?" he will always ask. He genuinely wants to know so that he can help. He is such a wonderful man and marvellous friend.

I'm not saying it is a fault but some people don't understand what you are going through, other people are not good at dealing with the whole process of bereavement or with anyone going through it and so shy away from it. They don't know what to say and feel awkward. They will always try and change the subject to something jolly to try and cheer the bereaved person up which speaking from experience left me feeling as if my emotions were being stamped on which in turn made me feel worse and the offending person would not realise. It's a dreadful process with no time limit placed on it. No book has ever been written about it. Yes, plenty have been written about the stages of bereavement and the emotions you can expect to feel but nothing on how to actually deal with it because every person has their own journey to travel and it is one hell of a nightmare journey.

When I lost my Father the journey was different. Possibly because I was younger, and had so much going on in my life. Plus I still had a lot of life to live myself.

However, losing my Mother in my late 50s has marked me considerably and probably changed me forever. I miss her dreadfully, I really really do. I still cry several times every week. I find I have become a very emotional person generally and can cry at the drop of a hat at things that wouldn't have affected me before. For instance I can see something on television, even something really happy like a reunion perhaps of soldiers returning from Afghanistan and picking up their little children and it sets me off.

I like to think that after eight years I am now over the worst of it. That first initial rawness is tremendously painful. I honestly thought I was going to die from it and did not know how to carry on with the dreadful pain. The human body is an amazing thing though and although we might not think so at the time is conditioned to withstand this type of pain, just like it is conditioned for childbirth and so many other things in life, both painful and joyous. Fate or life whichever way you look at it will only dish out to you what you are able to take and let's face it some of the things you can take are pretty horrible.

I remember the pain I felt when losing my little dog and in later years my cat. Those were bereavements too but in shorter terms. I have never forgotten my Father, he has always been in my life, I've often felt him talking to me and whenever I've had a problem I will sit down and say out loud, "Dad what would you have done?" and the answer comes through loud and clear. I've never let him be far away from me nor have I forgotten the anniversary of his passing. Not a year goes by when I don't remember that day and I always put flowers in the house in his honour. I do the same for my Mam and also do flowers for her birthday.

Emotions can also strike at odd times. For instance when I was recently sitting at my computer finishing off writing my one woman show. I was describing how the piano used to be in the parlour and how as a family we would all go into the parlour in the evening and gather round the piano to sing. Most people would call this room the lounge but Mam always called it the parlour because we lived in the kitchen and that is where the television was. It was quite a large room with the kitchen units at one end and the dining table, a couple of arm chairs and a settee at the other end.

This got me thinking and wallowing in many memories about how the parlour was kept for 'best' and Mam would shout at me not to make a mess if I dared to venture in there. I had to stop writing and cried for about half an hour. Deep inside after losing my Mother I don't think I will ever be the same again. The emotional scar will never heal and there will always be a great void there. That is not to say however that I won't carry on living my life the best I can.

Chapter 36: A New Journey

Brotherhood of Man have been together for over forty years now and we intend to keep working as long as we can. I do realise however that I am the youngest member of the group which begs the question just how much longer can we all keep going in this vein? I live on my own and I am driven by the need to keep working and busy. Mentally I have to keep active. I find it incredibly boring just to be at home pursuing a hobby whether it's a game of golf or going shopping or meeting a friend for lunch, it's just not me. I simply cannot do that day after day.

I feel now that I am ready and would like to step outside the comfort zone of Brotherhood Of Man and start looking to do other things. Not for one minute do I wish to leave the group. Brotherhood of Man will always be my major concern and priority both for work and enjoyment. It has been my life for so many years now. But I do need to prepare myself for when the time comes when the others feel that they perhaps have had enough and would like to slow down, not work so much and maybe just do a few gigs a year.

There are still plenty of things left that I would like to do and have just finished writing a one woman show for myself about my journey to Eurovision and beyond, combining a PowerPoint presentation with a few songs to remind people of the hits we had. It's a whole new direction for me and one which ten years ago I would never have dreamed of doing. I can't wait for the next phase in my life and what it has to offer. I'm always looking to see what doors are available to knock on and if I feel they suit me I shall knock on them. If they open that will be a bonus.

I don't kid myself. Nicky Stevens on her own isn't a draw and I can't see myself in theatres or clubs, but to start with I'd love to go round Women's Institutes, Universities of the Third Age, all those sorts of venues to talk about my life and try to make it an interesting experience for the audience which I would anticipate appealing mostly to women.

I would like to broaden my horizons a bit talent wise and my first step towards that goal was appearing in Cinderella at the Tivoli, Wimborne in 2012 and the following year at the Pavilion, Weymouth which was a huge personal achievement for me. It enabled me to be a team player in a theatrical production, something I hadn't had a chance to do since Aladdin in Swansea, and I hope to capitalise on that. My part was rewritten especially for me as a comedy role enabling me to use my exaggerated Welsh accent which never fails to make an audience laugh! You only have to think of the likes of Billy Connolly or Frank Carson when some of the things they say aren't necessarily that funny but combined with their strong accents make it very funny indeed! As Frank himself said, "It's the way I tell 'em!"

Something else I would love to do is be a Loose Woman panellist. When we appeared on the programme I practically begged one of the producers, Emma to let me be on the show. Unfortunately there were no spare seats at the time but they said they would remember me in the future. Emma if you are reading this, remember me? Oh how I'd love that!

Another thing I would dearly dearly loved to have done is to appear in a musical, but I don't think my voice is strong enough or could stand up to it now, purely because it isn't used to that level of work. However, never say never and with the right role I would no doubt relish the opportunity if it was given to me.

On a personal level I am open to meeting that special someone but it would be a difficult transition now as I have lived on my own for twenty years and as anyone who lives on their own will tell you, it is quite wonderful in a way! You can have the heating on when you want it. You can turn it up as high as you want it! The television is yours along with the remote control with no one else dominating it. You can eat what you want and when you want. Basically anything in your life bar work which has its own restrictions you can do literally in your own time.

I will be honest here and say that yes I have lonely days. I do have wonderful friends but you can't be with your friends 24/7. They too have lives to lead. I do regret being quite a distance from any of my family and worry about growing old alone. I have to remind myself though that dwelling on it too much will spoil the here and now. I sometimes wish I could take a dose of my own medicine because it's ridiculous to worry about something that hasn't happened and indeed may not ever happen.

My Mother had a marvellous saying: "Helen," she'd say, "Don't go down the lane to meet the lion." You wouldn't believe the number of people I have told that to and who have used it and found it incredibly helpful. Try it, it really helps.

Somebody else many years ago also said to me, "You're letting the situation control you, turn it around and you control the situation," which is another good one and funnily enough popped up in an episode of Emmerdale recently! The moral of my story is that it's pointless worrying about what may or may not happen and I don't want to spoil my happiness now. Deal with it when it comes and not before.

I'd like to think I could remain independent and live on my own quite happily. My ideal would be to stay in the home I have now and end my days here. The thought of going into a care home mortifies me but as friends rightly tell me, I don't know how I'll feel years down the line. I might have had enough by then and be glad to go in a home to be looked after. I'm thinking of it in terms of my perspective now. I can drive, I can do my gardening, I can do my own decorating, I can walk and basically do everything for myself.

The antidotes to my loneliness are my two little Yorkshire Terrier dogs who I love to pieces. They don't fill the gap of a human being but they do fill a massive hole as any dog or indeed animal owner will understand. Wherever I go in the house they are there with me as my little shadows. If I sit in my office they have their own bed in there, and if I am exercising they join in!

My life has been tremendously successful career wise. I've been lucky to earn a living using a talent I was born with, a gift I was given. I have been fortunate to travel the world while working and singing which is the greatest love of my life. I have been blessed and I don't think many people are lucky enough to say they have been able to work and earn good money doing something they love the most in the world. Yes plenty have, but many have not.

However, I put my success to being in the right place at the right time. I wouldn't specifically put it down to the fact I had any greater talent than any of the people I competed in the Eisteddfods with in the early days. I was lucky; I never intended to go into show business. I was very happy working as a telephone operator. If my sister in law hadn't intervened I had every intention carrying on with a normal job and normal life. I suppose I would have always had singing in my life doing the odd local concert perhaps but I never ever dreamed of being successful in the pop industry.

The very strange thing is and it is something I have often looked back on since becoming famous with Brotherhood. I remember walking up the street one day with my Father. I was still in grammar school at the time and he said,

"Have you got any idea Helen what you would like to be when you grow up?" I remember my response as plain as day and still find this statement amazing.

"I don't know what I want to do," I said, "but I do know I am going to be somebody. I'm not going to be like a lot of people who leave school, get married, have children at a very young age and push prams around. I'm going to be somebody but I don't know at what!"

It was like I had a premonition that came from within me that I would make something of my life and not follow the usual path. I'm not decrying that lifestyle in any way but I just knew it wasn't for me. I've never ever forgotten that. I had a deep feeling of conviction within that I was going to be famous. I was predicting my future but never in a million years put it down to music. And that's the honest truth.

The experiences I have had, the beautiful places I have seen on this lovely planet of ours, seeing and performing to such different cultures has been priceless. To work with the same three people for over forty years enjoying their friendship, talent and the gifts they all have in their own rights along the way has been absolutely tremendous. I have been blessed to have made people I love who are close to me, extremely proud of me, especially my Mother and Father, which is the best feeling in the world. My success meant I was able to be a daughter that they could be proud of. Of course all parents are proud of their children in different ways whatever they do, but to be part of a group that quite literally has been world famous gave my Mother a new lease of life after losing my Father and as I've said before that was the greatest gift I could have given to my Mother and therefore my greatest achievement in life.

Privately I would say my life has been OK. I have been married twice. Both failed. I always tell people I can pick my nose better than I can pick a man. In fact I would like on my tombstone 'She is still picking her nose'!! I wish I'd looked after my money well in the 70s when we acquired our fame. I was a bit silly but I'm not the first and certainly won't be the last. My one personal wish and ultimate dream in life is that I had a huge sum of money to buy a decent sized plot of land, to build a myself a modest little house and use the remainder of the land to house an animal sanctuary where I could hire fully qualified veterinary staff and spend the rest of my days looking after the animals. I would be in my element.

I don't have regrets. My way of looking at things is that every experience in life is a lesson. Even the bad times and relationships, however hurtful they were and whatever the outcome, I have grown within myself spiritually and come out of it at the end, a much better person than when I went in. I know it sounds clichéd but life is a lesson and we don't always like the lessons but we always learn from them. Some well, some not so well. Learning is knowledge which in turn makes you a wiser person. That's how I live my life. I am always looking for the next lesson.

Brotherhood of Man c. 1990

Special thanks to .....

Martin, Sandra and Lee

How do I start to thank you? I think you are wonderful, you have shared forty two years of my career with me. That is a lot of life in anyone's book. How great that we are still performing.

Back all those years ago when I met you all in Tin Pan Alley (Denmark Street) I would have never thought even about the year 2014, let alone that we would be still singing together when that year arrived!

As Brotherhood of Man we have been so lucky to have lived, laughed and loved together through so many tremendous experiences which have all been so incredibly special. I laugh with you like I laugh with no other.

You are three exceptional individuals. I have always looked to you as my friends as well as colleagues and my affection for you and admiration for your professionalism and talent goes beyond any words that can compliment you adequately. I love you all dearly.

Still performing after 42 years and still the original line up

Special thanks to .....

My friends

For my most special friend The Rev. Idris Vaughan. Our friendship is one of my most treasured possessions. When I have had my dark times you have given me light and when I have had my brighter times you have given me sunshine. You have always understood me and never criticised or judged me and with your invaluable friendship you have always been a constant source of strength and comfort. I have said many a time that if you have Idris as a friend, then count yourself as being very blessed. I love you dearly.

Charlene, Sheila and Clive

Thank you so much for being my friends. I have known you for so many years and as we have all grown older our friendship has remained strong. I thank you for all your love, support and care throughout the years. May we have many more good times. Love you all.

I am very blessed in the fact that I have many good friends in my life. How lucky am I, some people don't have any. You all know who you are and I thank you all from the bottom of my heart for wanting to have me as your friend.

And family

For Mark and all my family. I love you all dearly and will always be here for you.

Nicky currently lives in Dorset with her two adorable Yorkshire Terriers Ossie and
Amber as her faithful and loving companions